The Heretic

Michael Deeze

INDIES UNITED PUBLISHING HOUSE, LLC

ISBN: 978-1-64456-144-7

Library of Congress Control Number: 2020938676

INDIES UNITED PUBLISHING HOUSE, LLC
P.O. BOX 3071
QUINCY, IL 62305-3071
www.indiesunited.net

Prologue

It had been almost six months to the day since I had left upstate New York in early July without much of a plan for the future. The only thing that I knew at the time was that I couldn't or shouldn't stay where I was any longer. At that time, sitting across a dining room table from my friend, David Dean, something had clicked in my consciousness. David had the unique ability to see beyond current situations and visualize possibilities hidden in even the darkest of places.

Without expressing it openly, he had laid out my circumstances at the time and teased my thoughts into action. In the space of a thirty-minute conversation, I realized somewhere inside of me that I did actually want to move on.

I had returned from Vietnam almost four years previously and although my wounds had healed, my thoughts had not. I returned to a different world than the one I had left, into a world and a society that did not want to acknowledge the war or those returned from it. I returned an outcast. Instead of leaving the violent experiences of war behind me, I brought them with me. My consciousness and sense of self believed that society's shame for the Vietnam war translated to shame for me, and my response had been to accept it. I had become someone that I personally hated and embraced the darkest activities that I could find. I had become someone that no one would want as a friend, because I believed that I deserved it, and my life had begun to resemble the nightmares of my sleep.

Since returning from the army, I had met many people that I feared and more that I disliked. Anyone that had demonstrated one iota of integrity had been taken away from me.

Through his strength of character and his words, David was possibly the first person that I respected in a very long time. David Dean had shown me that I might have the potential to be someone else. He awakened in me the germ of an idea that I might not be the unscrupulous character I had been trying to become, that I might actually be a good man that had been trying very hard to become the opposite. He had teased my thinking into the possibility that I could move beyond my negative beliefs.

What's more, I needed to, and although I was still unclear about what I would discover over the horizon, I no longer feared it. With that realization, it seemed that a door had opened just as another closed, and I was going to step through it and take my chances.

I left New York and took the long way to wherever I was going. A long time ago—a lifetime ago it seemed—Chrissy, another and a much prettier friend, had stared into the sunset on a California beach and told me that if you didn't know where you were going, then just about any road would get you there. I pointed the truck west and took the time to see Niagara Falls and the Rainbow Bridge. I had crossed the broad flat expanse of southern Ontario, only angling south and crossing the border when I arrived in Sault St. Marie and the Soo Locks at the eastern end of Lake Superior. Once again back in the States, I crossed the extreme northern edges of Michigan, Wisconsin, and finally into Minnesota. Crossing all three states but still traveling along the southern shoreline of the immense lake. In Minnesota I left the lake behind and continued into the deep native forests of the north woods. I had spent the last days of summer in the Superior National Forest, fishing, hiking—and thinking. In those two months, I didn't speak to more than a handful of people and no more than a handful of sentences. It had taken that long to work through who I wanted to become next, and if not why at least how.

As the nights began to cool and color touched the edges of the maple leaves, I packed my tent, camp stove and gear into the old truck and turned south. I had spent the time to be sure that any decision I made was going to be my decision and not directed by anyone else. In the quiet solitude of the deep woods, there was no David Dean to offer deep insight, or Jaimie Claire, the woman I had left behind to take these last steps to get here, to tell me that it would be all right no matter what. The parade of people could no longer speak for themselves, yet haunted me, admonishing me to make something of myself. And most of all, in every dark corner hidden out of the light was the memory of Dutch. Of her light, and unreasonable belief that I could be more than what I believed I was. I began to sense a call to purpose. Perhaps for the first time in my life, I had wanted to take responsibility for what was going to happen next instead of allowing circumstances to dictate my choices and direction and having something or someone else to blame for bad outcomes. I had taken stock of the tools and talents I possessed and resolved that this time, it was up to me to accomplish whatever that purpose might be. The days had been spent in an epiphany of reflection, the nights in a tug-of-war of self-doubt versus new-found optimism.

When I can look Life in the eyes, Grown calm and very coldly wise, Life will have given me the Truth, And taken in exchange—my youth.

~Sara Teasdale

Foreword

I swear to fulfill, to the best of my ability and judgment, this covenant:

I will respect the hard-won scientific gains of those physicians in whose steps I walk, and gladly share such knowledge as is mine with those who are to follow.

I will apply, for the benefit of the sick, all measures which are required, avoiding those twin traps of overtreatment and therapeutic nihilism.

I will remember that there is art to medicine as well as science, and that warmth, sympathy, and understanding may outweigh the surgeon's knife or the chemist's drug.

I will not be ashamed to say "I know not," nor will I fail to call in my colleagues when the skills of another are needed for a patient's recovery.

I will respect the privacy of my patients, for their problems are not disclosed to me that the world may know. Most especially must I tread with care in matters of life and death. Above all, I must not play at God.

I will remember that I do not treat a fever chart, a cancerous growth, but a sick human being, whose illness may affect the person's family and economic stability. My responsibility includes these related problems, if I am to care adequately for the sick.

I will prevent disease whenever I can, for prevention is preferable to cure.

I will remember that I remain a member of society, with special obligations to all my fellow human beings, those sound of mind and body as well as the infirm.

If I do not violate this oath, may I enjoy life and art, respected while I live and remembered with affection thereafter. May I always act so as to preserve the finest traditions of my calling and may I long experience the joy of healing those who seek my help.
Hippocratic Oath

Introduction

My name is Robert Emmett Casey. In my life I have been called many things and many names. Each one had a meaning and each one at those times had meaning for me. For a long time during my life I attempted to live up to those names, or live them down. I no longer care what people call me anymore. Because at last—I am my own man.

Old Bill Travers was lying on the gurney between the two of us. He was not blinking, staring hard at the hanging overhead light and trying not to listen to our conversation. Bill was a 'good old boy' who ran the local auto salvage yard on the outskirts of town. He had lost his footing while cutting up sheet metal, fallen and had laid open the front of his right thigh on a sharp piece of steel. He had been chosen as my Guinee pig.

"Here, now watch and learn." Tom Dunbar was all business. "The suture is very strong so you can't really break it. But you can pull it out of the skin if you pull it too hard or too tight. You're supposed to be gentle anyway but I know how ham-fisted you can be at times, so be gentle but firm."

When I had arrived in rural Wisconsin, I was fresh out

of university and full of the impassioned zeal of a converted heathen. With my diploma clutched in my sweaty hands. I couldn't wait to heal the sick, help the lame to walk again, and the blind to see. But reality had come quickly. There were multitudes of patients that definitely benefited from my chiropractic ministrations, but there were the others too. For every five patients, one of those I couldn't help. They were beyond my skill set. They still needed help but were just in the wrong office. What they needed was medical intervention, but who they trusted was me.

Tom Dunbar was a physician's assistant who had undertaken to teach me some simple Army field hospital first-aid procedures. Today we were both dressed in scrubs and masks standing at a gurney in the Emergency Room. The poor guy on the table was not upset, other than wanting to get back to work, but the wound was fairly deep and widening with every flex of his leg muscles.

Tom, along with some of the other medical doctors in the group had repeatedly encouraged me to learn how to stitch open wounds. This was partly due to them wanting to reduce their own workloads but mostly due to the sometime need for expediency. I frequently encountered serious injuries far from the hospitals while doing house calls, and sometimes minutes mattered.

Tom deftly looped the first stitch around the fingers of his right hand, making a cross.

"Now around the middle finger and pull. Cinch it tight and then cut it behind the knot."

He pulled the finished with a flourish and held out his hand, palm up.

"Your turn."

Picking up the needle, I clumsily tried to emulate the motions I'd just seen Tom perform.

"This kinda goes against all that zealous chiropractic

dogma doesn't it?"

"What d'ya mean?"

"You know, chiropractors…no medications….natural healing. With hands only crap. It's like a religion with you guys."

"Well I'm learning to practice the 'water-ever-it-takes' technique. Just because my philosophy says one thing, doesn't mean the patient doesn't need something more."

The thread slipped out of my fingers just as I tried to pull it through the loop. With a sigh from Tom, I started over again.

"So then…you're some kind of chiropractic heretic."

This time I pulled the silk through and cinched it down across the open wound.

"I guess so. I looked up at his eyes above his surgical mask. "So be it."

The Heretic

The light is slow to come on these winter mornings. The biting cold presses in from the outside, causing the old house to groan and crack as the cold seeks to compress it into a smaller colder space. Standing at the kitchen sink, I wait for the coffee pot to boil and feel winter's frigid touch pressing against window glass, frosting its way onto the inside without asking permission, making beautiful snowflake landscapes in thick Jack Frost patterns.

Even in my woolen socks and slippers, I feel the chill of the wooden floor under my feet, causing them and my calves to itch. The cold makes my knees ache more than usual. I shift my weight from one foot to the other patiently waiting for the little percolator to sputter and drip my coffee, filling the small chilly kitchen with the aroma of fresh coffee and candle wax.

The electricity is off again. The storm that blew in Sunday and stayed through most of Monday and into Tuesday took care of that. It is not uncommon for us living so far out in the country, even in summer, to lose power once or twice a month. Winter outages are more frequent and for my old bones, more inconvenient. Thankfully I still have gas in the LP tank in back of the house, so the stove still works. Taking a cup down from the cupboard, I pour coffee. The dogs follow me as I shuffle to the front room. In the fireplace, a fire crackles cheerfully, filling the room with welcome warmth and the pleasant, faint smell of wood smoke. The darkness of the early winter morning creates a sense of coziness in the comfortable little room. With the electricity off, the fireplace is the only source of heat in the house, unless you count the dogs, both of which throw themselves down on the hearth with a thump and a sigh. I pull an afghan off the back of the recliner, wrap it around my shoulders and ease my aching knees down into the high-backed wing chair close to the fireplace, careful not to spill the coffee. Cradling the cup between my hands, I lean forward and stare into the fire.

I am an old man now. Aged by the mileage of experience and the erosion that years bring. The frenetic energy that fueled my life has finally burned itself out. My body, the vehicle that I have used all these years, has arrived at this point broken and patched. Only now, at the far end of my life, appreciated for its former abilities and accomplishments. The end is much closer than the beginning. I marvel at the dependability this body provided and wish, as all old men do, that I had taken better care of it. The doctors smile and tell me that I am doing just fine, but the look in their eyes tells a different story, and I understand.

We are alone now, the dogs and I, all of us too old and worn for any more adventure; hopefully, too smart as well. My children, grown and gone to lives of their own, call on Father's Day. She too has been gone many years now. The passing of time has softened my memory of the hard years together and brightened memories of the good ones. I stare into the fire and reflect, turning back through the chapters of memory. I recall the different lives that I have lived, and the lives that I have touched all in this one lifetime. The memories arrive unbidden, random and not in sequence.

Instead, each one is connected to the next by the emotion it stirs, triggering the progression. They are not distinguished by time or date. Yet they are not random but related at a deeper level. I try to recount these lessons and victories that came with a cost. I recognize that every person's journey is storied with tragedy, love, sorrow, pain, and joy. Mine has been no different in that regard. I think about the people that have passed through my life and the impression they have left on me. I consciously give thanks—for all of them, the good and the bad.

I take a mouthful of my too hot coffee. Setting the cup down, I lean toward the fire and rest my elbows on my aching knees. The dancing flame, hypnotic in its ability to conjure past experiences and their lessons. I remember those more vital times, sorry and glad at the same time that they are no more.

Maggie O'Donnell

"Go fish."

I looked up at her face. Her lips frowned but her eyes smiled. She had an unusual way of cocking her head to the side, lidding her eyes and smiling in a way that only touched the corners of her mouth. Unless you had seen it a hundred times, you wouldn't know that it was a good look. It was a secret private look that she shared only when we were alone, and I would have crawled through broken glass to get it—it felt that special. I looked forward to these days where she and I spent the afternoon alone in the old house. During those times, I was treated to a different, secret side of her. A larger than life figure—the unquestioned ruler of the Casey clan— she was stalwart and strong-willed; unwaveringly honest. She could be humorous and clever, both wise and street-smart. I had known her to occasionally display a ruthless nature when one of the family was threatened. When we were alone, she didn't need to be anything other than herself, and that person was fun to be around.

I reached and took another card from the scattered deck on the small folding table in front of us. She was not about to let me win if she could help it.

"Have you been practicing?" She asked as she

rearranged the cards in her hand. "Yes, grandmother."

"How's it going?" She held my gaze over her cards, "Do you have any fours?"

"It's hard." As I pulled out the two fours that I'd been hoarding and handed them to her. "Da almost surprised me the other day."

"Your father never had a talent for it; didn't like it." She put the new cards into her hand and sighed, her gaze drifted toward the window. "Always his father's son he was."

She favored me with a sly one-eyed wink, "You're more after my side of the family, the O'Donnell's. So is your sister Kate."

"I can do it more often than I used to."

It was midsummer, even with the windows open, there was little breeze to cool the room. The air was heavy, humid and hot, full of the smell of floor wax, old varnish and dark wood. The card game had digressed into a desultory exercise that made the room seem hotter and the air more stifling. Tapping her chin with a knobby finger, she set her cards down and started to rearrange her housedress, "Help me outside Em. I need fresh air."

I moved the small card table away from in front of her and stepped in close so that she could grasp my arm. I braced my feet, and she heaved herself up out of the rocking chair that was her daytime perch. Once on her feet, she wobbled for a moment, catching her breath from the pain that shot through her hips and knees while she gripped my arm and shoulder.

"Okay Em, slow at first. Out the back door. It's shadier on that porch this time of day."

We shuffled down the hall, her slippers scuffing along the shiny hardwood floor in the quiet house. By the time we reached the kitchen, Maggie was almost in full stride, only lightly touching my shoulder as she made her way out through the screen door and onto the back porch where another rocking chair waited. Easing herself into the chair, she took a deep breath and closed her eyes. Outside, the hot air smelled of dust and mowed grass. Cicadas were in full throat. Somewhere close, a house wren rejoiced in the heat and sun of mid-afternoon July. A smile spread across her face.

"Tea." It was a demand and a request all at the same time.

I went back into the kitchen and set the kettle on the stove. Opening the cupboard, I reached down her favorite cup and saucer. Snapping open the little tea ball, I spooned in loose tea leaves, getting it ready for when the water would be hot enough. No tea bags for Maggie O'Donnell Casey, that was not the way *the good people* took their tea. The whistle of the kettle would alert me when it was ready, so I returned to her on the porch.

"Do you know where the smokes are?"

"Yes Grandma, the red flower pot."

"Well they're not going to walk over here on their own, now are they?"

"No Grandma." I lifted down the pot from its place, high up on the shelf near the back door and pulled out the pack of Lucky Strike cigarettes and the small box of wooden matches that were hidden there. Shaking one out, I noted that there were only a few remaining in the pack. I would have to write another note so that I could buy them at the Sunshine Market. It was a tribute to the dutiful nuns at Our Lady of Grace that my penmanship looked grown up enough to buy cigarettes and beer when I needed to. She nodded to me and pointed at the pack; I took out another.

Taking out a kitchen match, I snapped it with my thumb to ignite it. I lit her cigarette first, then my own.

"I started smoking when I was thirteen. Of course, I'd tried chewing tobacco before that but never liked it much." She took a long pull on the cigarette and then regarding the smoking end of it. "How old are you now Em?"

"Twelve."

"Always precocious." She took a long pull off of the cigarette, staring out over the railing into the back yard, "I'll give you some money, we're going to need another pack of cigarettes."

She punctuated the sentence with a racking cough, which went on for a full half minute. She leaned back in her chair and spit a wad of phlegm over the railing and far out into the yard. Once she'd settled back into the rocking chair, she took a deep breath and let it out with a sigh.

"Alright…show me."

"Here?"

"Yes, here. Use the maple tree," pointing to her right where a ten-inch thick maple stood shading the back of the house and the porch. "The knot just below those first two limbs."

I pulled the knife from my back pocket and unsheathed it. It was one of our shared secrets. The knife had once been hers. I only hazarded carrying it on these private days that we spent together. The handle had always seemed warm to my touch and a perfect fit; the blade dull grey carbon steel and double-edged, honed sharp enough to cut dry leather. I set my feet and brought my arm back while I judged the distance.

"No! Too long, too long. Think long, think wrong Emmett. You need to just do it, not think about it."

"I have trouble when I do it that way."

"Give it to me."

She held out her impossibly huge red knuckles and crooked fingers. Taking the knife, she turned it in her hands regarding it as one would a loved one.

"This is not a toy Emmett. It is a weapon, and you must never give up a weapon unless you have another—or if you are sure you won't need it again." She balanced the knife by the handle on her middle finger. "Be sure of your target; be sure of your goal. Don't think about how to get it there; concentrate on the result you want. The way to get it there will become clear then, but do not hesitate. Always be sure and whole-hearted or things will not go well for you."

Then with a sideways flick of her arm and wrist, almost too quick to see, it was gone. A solid chunk from the maple tree fifteen feet away revealed the knife protruding three inches to the right and five inches below the target knot.

"Hmpff, I'm getting rusty." She said around the cigarette dangling from the corner of her mouth.

Early Morning Today

Standing at the kitchen sink, I take my morning medications. It's become quite a handful, and I resent every one of them. The melted snow I'm using to take them with is so cold that my throat closes and the capsules catch, making me gag. I quickly switch to hot coffee and slug down enough to get them past my gag reflex, but the effort triggers a coughing spasm that doesn't stop until I have to grip the sink and stars swim in my vision.

After my vision clears, I take my new cup of coffee and wander. The morning light outside is coming up as I visit the grey-lit rooms of the darkened house, only stopping long enough to take in the snow-covered fields beyond the windows from a different angle. The rooms have lost their vibrancy; the life that filled them at one time has gone. Gone to sunshine and to other rooms—in other homes.

Back at the fireplace, I stand before the flames and warm my hands that have gotten cold after the tour of the icy house. Idly scanning the numerous photos that crowd each other along the entire mantle in the dim light, my gaze stops at one in particular, a study in black-and-white. There are three people in the photograph. In the center and in mid-laugh stands a young Maggie Casey, my grandmother, tall and straight holding a small rifle in one hand and a brace of rabbits in the other. On her right, is a young boy, his hair is dark and shaggy and his scowl is noteworthy and familiar. On her left is a man, a glimpse of the man that the boy would become. Inches shorter than Maggie, he is darkly handsome, reed-thin and also in mid-laugh, he leans toward her—a shared secret, a special moment.

"You're more after the O'Donnell's than the Casey's," she had said. Again, I wondered as I had many times before, if that were true, why had I yearned so much to be that scowling boy in the photograph, my father.

The Woods, the Snow and Da

"Where are we now?"

Da had stopped walking. We stood at the edge of a large clearing filled with cattails and waist-high grasses blanketed in snow. Normally he would reach into his coat pocket and bring out his pipe and start packing it. Instead he hitched his backpack higher on his shoulders, staring across the fen. There was no smoking allowed when we were in the woods.

I hitched my smaller backpack up and slung the .22 rifle I'd been carrying over my shoulder and scanned the surroundings. Behind us and to both sides, the deep woods spread up and away until the undergrowth and bracken obscured the distance. The boles of the trees, black against the background of the white snow, created a three-dimensional view that spoke of vast depth and distance—unbroken calm. The forest was asleep, content to wait for the warmer sun, still months away.

This was one of my father's favorite games. On Friday night, after he arrived home from work, we would pack the car and he would drive into the night for hours until we were far into northern Wisconsin or the far western parts of the Michigan Upper Peninsula. I would sleep during the ride, fitfully waking when he stopped for fuel, or at a tavern for something to drink. If Kate or Andy were with us, we would all sleep on in the car piled on top of each other until he returned to resume the drive. In the morning we would enter the unbroken forests, driving down long curving fire lanes, the dirt and grass lanes cut deep into the heart of the wild woods, cleared to allow fire-fighting equipment into the deep recess of the forest if there were to be a forest fire. We'd drive the lanes until they ended in a wide turn-around, marking the beginning of the trackless wild. Once there, we would load up our backpacks with bagged lunches and a small rifle for me, a shotgun or large-bore rifle for him, and leave the car far behind as we struck off into the trackless reaches of the forest.

Each season brought a different reason to be there, grouse or snowshoe rabbit hunting in the fall, blackberry picking in the summer, and sometimes, no reason at all. For the next few hours we would hike into the woods. The trees grew thick and tall, cathedral-like above us. We skirted marshes and peat bogs filled with ducks, geese, mosquitoes and heinous deerflies in summer. When the sun was at its highest point, we would pause and sit on ancient tree stumps cut during the great lumber days of old, the stumps fully five or six feet in diameter; a testament to the greed that desecrated these gentle rolling hills at the turn of the century. We would eat our lunch, respectful to not break the silence of the trees with the trite conversations of humans. Hours would often pass without a spoken word.

After a suitable period during our stroll, he would stop and ask his question, this time it was, "Where are we?" Although it could be, "Which way back to the car?" or "How many yards to the dead tree at the far side of this clearing?"

Obviously, there was only one right answer to these questions: his. The wrong answer would draw a snort and another hour of silent walking. The right answer would earn a nod and another question. This is what passed for conversation with him, and right answers guaranteed an extended one. Today I knew the answer to question number one.

"We just passed Bell's Mound on our left. Twenty minutes' walk straight ahead of us will get us to Seamus' deer stand, the big stump at the foot of Mable's Ridge."

I got a nod for that one.

"So, the car is which direction?"

I pointed to my left. With a snort, he flicked his thumb back over his right shoulder. "Close."

He immediately struck off, heading toward Seamus' stand. These were his woods. He knew them like the back of his hand and could never be lost here amid the silence of the trees. When he was in these woods, the constant hunch of his shoulders would disappear and he often displayed a rare smile, or a flash of humor as he pointed out landmarks, or watched a mother doe nurse their spring fawns, careful not to disturb them.

Now it is winter, deep winter and the snow is deep—undisturbed. We are snowshoeing across it, staying under the tall trees when we can to avoid the deepest of it. We're not sightseeing today, we're here on family business, here to retrieve something left behind when my father and his brothers left their deer camp. A treasure hunt of sorts, twenty minutes ahead of us, a long slog through the snow —a longer one going the other way. Already the unfamiliar but necessary gait of the snowshoes has made the front of my thighs ache. I would never think of complaining about it, however. Instead I fix my gaze on the back of his shoes and focus on keeping up. At twelve years old, I already weigh more than my father, so I sink deeper into the snow than he does. He, on the other hand, seems to glide along without any noticeable effort, as comfortable on snowshoes as he would be in his boots.

This is the first time I have been invited on this trip. It is exciting—a manhood thing. I get to carry a gun, and I will do *man's work* before the end of this day. I often have fantasized this adventure as I've watched the men of my family in their red plaid hunting clothes disappear into the trackless wilderness of the north woods. They reappeared a week later, beards scruffy, smelling of wood-smoked flannel, whiskey, and pine resin, their deer carcasses strapped to the fenders of their cars, the car trunks filled with rabbits, grouse and the occasional porcupine.

Each deer carcass was hung heads up from the crossbeams of my grandfather, Thomas Quinn's, shed at the back of his yard. Carcasses hung in rows until the space was crowded by their population. My mother's father lived directly across the street from the Casey home. The two families were so integrated, by proximity and childhood, and deer season was a fraternal event for both. Each of the hung deer represented tale to be shared with the younger Quinn's and Casey's and embellished to a point that stretched beyond belief. We were satisfied only to imagine the heroics necessary to accomplish such an intrepid adventure and never questioned the veracity of the account. It filled our minds with pictures of vast snowfields and deep dark woods, inhabited by the clever and elusive deer, wolves and danger. The survival of the men was always in peril; the dangers ever-present. We thrilled with the thought of it and counted the years until we could go with them and learn the closely guarded secrets of the wild ways.

Today was my day, my first adventure, accompanying the stalwart hero figure that was my father. Striding through the deep snow, skirting the marshes and staying within the cover of the deeper forest we made our way through the watchful silence of the trees, accompanied only by the scolding chickadees. As the exuberance of the event waned with the accumulation of sweat inside my clothes, I focused only on the snowshoes breaking trail ahead of me and keeping up. I was resolved to not disappoint him and to justify my presence.

Twenty minutes later we skirted the base of what the men call Mabel's Ridge and approached the edge of a vast peat bog. The open expanse of the treacherous swamp is dotted here and there with scrub jack pine and volunteer juniper, but otherwise empty in every direction. At the edge sits a lone white pine stump that has been sawed at two levels, one side higher than the other resembling a large chair. It is the perfect place to be if you have to sit for hours, which is what you need to do if you are hunting. This chair is where my Uncle Seamus takes his stand during the long hours of deer season, and it is a good spot.

Farther on, beyond the stump, we catch a flash of bright red against the stark white of the snow and deep green of the pines. Another fifty yards ahead, along the edge of the clearing, there are two red rags, twenty feet apart tied to low-hanging branches of the pine trees that encroach upon the bog. They move in the breeze that blows across the open space. My father does not pause at the stump but continues until we approach the two markers.

Arriving, we shuck our backpacks and stand our rifles against a nearby tree. Immediately, my father begins to sidestep back and forth in the snow in front of the closest rag, packing the snow. Over and over, back and forth he deftly dances at the edge of the tree. With a wave and a point, he directs me to the second flag and points at my snowshoes. I get the message and wade to the next marker and mimic his dance, pushing the fluffy powder down with each step until it crunches as it begins to pack down. I watch as my father loosens and kicks off his snowshoes. He stands on top of the now solidly packed snow. I do the same. Without hesitation he uses one of the snowshoes as a shovel to dig into the drifted snow at the base of the hanging branches. I do the same.

Slowly as I dig, a deer carcass begins to appear—frozen solid, buried deep in the snow. A buck, his antlers the first thing I see as I continue to excavate the rest of him. The body is encased in a solid layer of ice, a testament to being covered while it still retained some body heat. Several revolutions of baling twine bind its front legs tightly against its body. The hind legs are stretched out directly behind its rump so that it can be dragged without the legs catching on passing brush or low hanging branches. We are here to retrieve it.

With each deer-hunting license, the Department of Natural Resources issues a corresponding deer tag. Each deer taken during the hunt must be tagged, inspected and registered with a designated representative. It is illegal to take a deer without a license. The Quinn/Casey clans rely on deer season for the majority of their meat supply for the upcoming year. Even with as many hunters as they field, they cannot take enough deer. The Casey's have hunted these woods long before deer licenses were required and regard the rules as for everyone else but them. Today we are poachers.

Finished with his deer, Da, his snowshoes back on his feet, approaches my deer, hacksaw in hand. Kneeling he begins to saw off the buck's antlers just above the brow tines so that they too won't snag on branches or brush. While he works, I open my pack and pull out a looped bundle of sturdy rope. Making a noose at one end, Da drapes it over the shortened horns and secures it stretching the remaining length out eight or ten feet. Then he makes three large loops and ties it off to the extended length.

I put on my snowshoes and shoulder my backpack, Da drapes the rope ends across one of my shoulders and I pass my other arm through the loop. Nodding to me, he returns to his deer and does the same. Once he is ready, he looks at me and nods once more. This time he breaks the silence.

"We'll stop and rest as soon as we make the hardwood. Use your whistle if you need to stop before that."

I reach in my pocket to make sure I still have the whistle. Squeezing it in my gloved hand, I'm reassured. It's not really a whistle; it's a spent 30/40 rifle cartridge. The men, deeply respectful of the peace of the forest, only communicate with each other with coded whistles by blowing across the open end of the cartridge. The high-pitched sound it produces travels a surprising distance in the otherwise silent woods. I hope I won't need to use it.

Without another word, Da turns back onto the track we created when we arrived and steps off, throwing his weight into the rope harness to break the deer carcass from its frozen crypt. We start our trek back to the distant car. As soon as we start, snowflakes begin to drift down. Within minutes, snow is falling fast and thick. Visibility drops, masking everything in the distance. The silhouette of the man in front of me whitens as it accumulates on him. The blinding snow hisses as it falls, accompanying the soft crunch and shuffle of our snowshoes, the only sound, making my labored breathing seem loud and intrusive. I silently give thanks that there is no wind.

The deer carcass, even after being field dressed, still weighs almost one hundred and fifty pounds of solid frozen dead weight. The car is more than a mile distant, closer to two. I am winded within a hundred yards of the start. I start to lag behind.

Additional deer, if shot illegally, must be retrieved when no one is watching. Hence, someone must re-enter the woods to locate and retrieve the deer a week or two after the season closes and the forest is empty. The trip must be timed to arrive back at the vehicle after darkness has fallen to further avoid observation. Therefore, we'll travel the last half-mile in total darkness.

I pat my coat pocket to make sure I still have my whistle.

It is a hard slog. Because of the weight behind me, my snowshoes sink into the snow much more deeply as I lean forward against the weight. With each step, I must be up on my toes to keep them from sliding backward. I pray to God that the bindings do not break. Soon, I stop watching Da in front of me. Instead I concentrate on my breathing and watch the toes of my snowshoes, panting hard as I focus only on the next step. The rope digs into my rib cage, complicating my already labored breathing. I'm committed to being up to the task as the walk takes on an endless quality and daylight begins to fade. The range of my vision closes in around me.

The ensuing darkness is soon almost total. Even with the white snow in the background, I can only dimly see the contrasting dark of my snowshoe tips as they chug back and forth ahead of me. I can only tell when I step out of the broken trail by how far I sink into the softer fresh powder. I am walking by feel, not sight. Da has disappeared into the darkness ahead, occasionally the sound of a broken branch, or a rustle as he scrapes through some of the brush tells me how far ahead of me he is, and that he is still there. Otherwise, I am alone, encased in a shroud of darkness. My vision does not extend beyond the length of my arm. The only sounds are the *shoosh* of the snowshoes, the hiss of falling snow and the scrape of the deer that follows relentlessly behind me.

I can't tell how long I've been walking. Time doesn't mean anything because only the end of the walk is important. It seems like forever already. With the effort required there is no room in my head for my thoughts to wander. My only thought is on my next step and the next panting breath. Slogging down a slow incline, I step directly onto bare ground. A couple more steps confirm it.

There must be a canopy above me that prevents the snow from falling here. There is nothing to contrast the darkness. I can see nothing, in front of me, behind me or in any direction. I know that I've reached what Da calls *the hardwood.* I pull up my earflaps and listen—hard. But there is no sound. Neither the hiss of the falling snow nor any sound ahead of me where I'd hoped to hear my father. I realize that I've not heard anything of him for some time, long after I was unable to see him in the falling snow. I had no reckoning of how long he has been separated from me. In the oppressive silence, I am suddenly aware of how isolated I am, in the dark forest, unaware of which direction I have been walking or which one I need to go to get out.

As I wait for some sound, the fear of my situation presses down on me. The longer and harder I listen, the more I imagine hearing things that weren't there. The sound of creatures— some real and some the subject of a nightmare. Wolves perhaps, hunting me now after first following the scent of the deer carcass, hidden behind the blanket of snow and darkness creeping ever closer.

I remember my whistle. Should I use it, was I overreacting? I don't want to be weak and considered a child, too young for such an important task, but I don't want to be eaten by ravening wolves either. I ponder, each second ticking by as the hungry creatures begin to surround me in the darkness. My little .22 rifle will only hold them off for a little while; the end would be inevitable.

Pulling off my glove, I pull out the bullet casing and lick cracked lips, not sure that I'll be able to make it work. I'd practiced before, there were always plenty of spent shells, it had taken me a bit to get the angle of the opening just right, but I'd gotten it, producing a very satisfying man-sized shriek. I blew across the opening. The accompanying piercing whistle, insulting the darkness, echoing away under the trees.

"Jesus, Mary and Joseph!" My dad didn't even try to muffle his voice. "That just scared the living shit out of me!"

I was practically standing on top of his deer. Also under the canopy of trees, he had stopped to rest. I had caught up to him. He couldn't have been more than fifteen feet in front of me, but I couldn't see him anymore than he could see me. With a flush of warmth that had nothing to do with the soaking sweat of my inside clothes, I took a shuddering breath. The wolves wouldn't get me after all. I would pass the test; I had done a man's job for my father.

Today

with more burnt coffee

I reheated the cold pot of coffee, but in my daydreaming, I had let it boil and now it was burnt and bitter. It would have to do. There was no telling when I would go to town for more, so I'd make do with what I had.

It was only in these later stages of my life that I'd come to understand my father's approach to life. He was an excellent provider but ill equipped to be a good father. He would make spasmodic attempts from time to time to befriend one or the other of us, but always on his terms. Kate had been the only exception to this rule. He visibly softened in her presence and modulated his tone and bearing. It is only now that I realize how lonely he had been his whole life; now that it is too late to become his friend.

With coffee in one hand, I put a couple more logs into the fireplace and find my seat again in the wing chair. The seat already grown cold from my brief absence. The full morning light has arrived unnoticed, dull steel gray with the promise of more snow soon. I take a drink and ponder on the enigma who had been my father. A relationship dotted with moments of shared intimacy and comradery followed by long periods of estrangement. Estrangements probably caused by our mutual fear of revealing too much of ourselves to the other.

Camping Out Fun

It was not the first time it had happened. The tent had collapsed again during the night under the weight of a fresh snowfall. I hadn't been inside when it happened; I worked nights these days. I sat at the wooden picnic table, just in front of the mess, the ice-cold seat slowly freezing my ass. With my back to the tent, I stared at nothing, a zombie after a long night shift. The darkened trunks of the trees lent contrast to the stark white landscape in my field of vision. The woods were muffled, silent with their blanket of snow, the only sound the occasional *plop* as a branch let go of accumulated snow and let it fall to the ground.

It was too early for any human activity in the area. Not that there would be a lot of activity anyway, campgrounds aren't very busy in January. With only one glaring exception, the campground was completely empty. I was the exception.

I had been camping here for more than five months. In that time my prospects for a housing upgrade had not significantly improved. Now it was January. Winter already felt like it had lasted forever, but there was almost as much of it left as had gone by. The snow was an occasional visitor, but the cold had been relentless.

The coffee cup in my hands had cooled almost

immediately. Leaning to my left I raised the lid off of the old percolator on the burner of my beat-up little two-burner camp stove and poured the cold coffee back into it. Swirling the cold with the hot, I poured another cup and resumed staring at nothing. Tired and sleepy are two separate things. I was bone tired but it was too early to sleep. My body was exhausted but my brain was spinning out random thoughts at high speed.

Today would be my last day at this campsite. Every fourteen days, as regular as the sunrise, the park ranger would arrive after he finished his own hot breakfast—and hotter shower—to inform me that I needed to change my campsite. Even without another soul as far as the eye could see, protocol apparently needed to be maintained. Campers were only allotted fourteen days at any one site. I would need to break down my tent, pack it up and move forty or fifty feet to the next fireplace ring, the next ass-freezing picnic table, reassemble the tent, set up the stove on the table and get used to a new view of nothing special. I'd pay the ranger fourteen dollars for fourteen days camping and he would tip his hat, climb back into his dark green park ranger truck and drive slowly away. I wouldn't see him again for two weeks. There would be no sense in reassembling the collapsed tent this morning.

Once I got the most recent campsite situated, I would need to go back into town. I'd bitten the bullet and purchased a month-to-month membership at the YMCA. It was a necessary expense. I needed a place to shower, shave and change into my *going to school clothes*. School was tough enough for me without also having hygiene issues to apologize for. I was a college boy now.

I was fortunate that I had engaged in several occupations that allowed me to move quickly from one job to the next at the local temp agency as soon as the previous one ended. The most recent, a night watchman at the local television and radio station. It had several advantages in exchange for severe sleep deprivation. It freed my daytime hours so that I could attend the local junior college. I had plenty of time to crack my textbooks and develop study habits in between walking my rounds, which was something I had never had to bother with before.

I had a lot of catching up to do academically. Never having to study in high school had not taught me how it should be done. I had no interest in rote memorization and no talent for the lesson regurgitation that written examinations required. My younger fellow students were at ease with the requirements and gymnastics required to succeed and I simply could not progress on my wits alone. I had little academic ammunition to work with. I soon learned that for the time being, I would have to be satisfied with average work and average grades, instead focusing on progressing to the next benchmark. I was twenty-six years old and so far, my greatest accomplishment of note was narrowly avoiding a long-term prison sentence—twice.

Out of the corner of my eye, movement caught my attention. The new snow had covered the sound of the approaching vehicle until it appeared in my vision. It was not the park ranger's forest-green truck with the county emblem displayed on the cab doors, but I recognized it immediately. He had been driving the dark green Ford station wagon for more than ten years. Its appearance was not just unexpected; it did not bode well.

Never in a hurry, my father slowly eased the old Ford through the snow, sliding to a stop inches short of the rear bumper of my old pickup truck. I took a drink of already cold coffee and waited. This would be no ordinary friendly visit. He had something on his mind or he wouldn't be here. I could only imagine what time he'd had to leave the house this morning to arrive here just after daylight.

He packed his pipe and lit it, puffing it up while he

regarded me through the windshield. Once his face started to disappear into the cloud of smoke, the door opened and he set a foot on the ground. Almost immediately, the familiar scent of his Amphora pipe tobacco wafted to my nose. He had smoked that brand as long as I could remember, and just like now, it awakened all sorts of memories—good and bad. Reaching back into the car, he pulled out his coffee mug and approached the table. He picked up the coffee pot, gave it a swirl and poured about half the contents into his cup. He took a sip, sat down on the other end of the bench on the same side as me and aimed his attention in the same direction as mine.

Without changing his gaze, "Cold."

"That it is."

He took another drink and then twisted around and looked back at the collapsed tent. "Canvas tent wouldn't do that."

I didn't change my focus of where I was looking into the distance. "I know."

"Side ropes would keep it up."

"I know."

"Pretty dinky, this one."

"Easier to move."

We both went back to our coffee, looking forward at the nothing in front of us. We hadn't spoken in over a year. That was after he'd told me to stay away from both him and the rest of the family in no uncertain terms. That made his arrival something of an event. I didn't have to wonder at how he knew how to find me. My sister Kate would have supplied that information. Kate always knew where I was and what I was up to. She insisted, and I knew better than to deny her authority. In a way, I was glad he had come and sorry all at the same time. Kate's arrival would have been a different story.

"Your mother's well."

"That's good."

"Kids too."

"Glad to hear that."

He looked up at the sky and cocked his head to the side a little, "Gonna snow again; pretty soon I'd guess."

"That would figure, but it's cold enough so at least it won't be a wet one."

He took another drink of coffee and made a face.

"Thomas had a stroke; doctors say it's any time now."

That explained the visit. Thomas Quinn was my mother's father, my grandfather. In my world he was second only to my Grandmother Casey in my hierarchy of love and respect. In my life he had always seemed ancient and wise. It had never occurred to me that he might be mortal. I took a drink of coffee, still looking into the woods. He took a drink of coffee and poured the rest on the ground. Standing up, he made ready to leave. He'd accomplished what he came to do.

"I guess I'd better get to Madison then."

"Might be good." He fished out a kitchen match and struck it on the side of the picnic table. Relighting his pipe while he looked at the green station wagon. "You can ride up with me if you like."

Today

9:30am

I took a long drink of the cold burnt coffee in my cup. The room had begun to cool as the light had slowly grown outside and the fire had burned itself down. Together we had broken down my little campsite and moved it one campsite south, then I'd packed enough clothes for a couple of days, making sure I also had an outfit suitable for a funeral should it come to that.

Stopping at the ranger's residence I interrupted his hot breakfast and paid the fourteen-dollar fee for my next fourteen days, two fives, three ones and four quarters.

We headed north towards Wisconsin in the old green Ford. The snow had begun almost immediately.

That had been one of the longest rides of my life, but not because of the weather. The snow had begun falling thick and fast. The wind blowing it straight across in front of us no matter which direction we were heading. There was little traffic, with most people satisfied to wait out the storm in a safer and warmer location than on the roads. We needed to hurry, but couldn't as we white knuckled through the one-hundred-seventy odd miles of twisting country roads. It was the worry of what awaited us at the end of the trip that made the drive excruciatingly slow.

As we had both strained our eyes out through the

windshield, my thoughts had been filled with memories of Thomas Quinn. Thomas had been more than my grandfather; he had been my mentor and my ally. He had been a voice of wisdom and the foundation of my sense of humor. I had expected him to live forever and now he too was going to leave me.

The drive had taken hours longer than it would normally have required. I trusted my father at the wheel completely, and if the situation had been reversed, I knew he would have trusted me. We had never relied on conversation between us and hadn't tried to fill the quiet spaces with useless small talk. The swirling storm around us instead created a cocoon of quiet. we were both alone with our thoughts. We didn't need to make small talk. We weren't built that way.

Rising, I set the cup on the mantle and stoked the fire, surprised at the emotions these memories brought up. I punished the burning logs sending sparks shooting up the chimney flue. Time and distance had not softened the feelings.

Thomas Quinn

The hospital ward featured the universal aroma of all hospitals. The pervasive smell of antiseptic cleaning agents, alcohol and at the very edge of my sensory spectrum—diarrhea. The hospital room was small and cramped. Made too hot by the sheer number of family members crammed into it and an overly exuberant radiator pinging along under the window. In order for Da and I to enter the room, two others had to exit. And once in, there was a general good-natured jostling of positions to allow us to approach the bed.

My mother sat in a chair next to the bed, her eyes puffy and her face tear streaked as she petted the hand of the person in the bed. Next to her sat Grandma Casey, straight backed and waving her hands for emphasis. She was in the middle of a humorous story about porcupines and shotguns. There was general laughter, and some good-natured ribbing taking place elsewhere in the room. Several people expressed pleasure in seeing me. There were pats on the back as well as the offer of a flask that was making the rounds.

In the bed Thomas lay on his side, his once expressive blue eyes staring into my mother's. His lips trembled under a full oxygen mask covering the lower half of his face but his chest barely rose and fell in spite of the appliance. His thin and bony legs had been uncovered against the intense heat in the room. I had never seen his legs bare and he appeared shockingly fragile. In the crowded room of big men and bundled women, his normally robust form had been minimized, a baby bird lying in a nest before it has fledged.

Grandma finished her story and took a pull off the flask that Thomas Jr. handed her. She looked at us both, and the acknowledged matriarch of both families gave us the current update.

"The doctor said he is stable, but for how long he couldn't say. He is conscious but has lost the ability to move or speak. We're telling him old stories and having a laugh because that is what he'd do if he were in my seat. It's good that you made it Em." She handed me the flask, "He'll be going home soon."

With that pronouncement, Ma began to sob. She was joined by her sisters, and not just a few of the men looked away and reached for their handkerchiefs.

Today

mid-morning

As the fire burned down, the room had once again cooled. I surface from my reflections to the chill. I may have dozed off, but my dreams will have to wait. The room seems unusually quiet, only the occasional slight rumble of logs in the fireplace as they settled into grey ash. It is several moments before I realize that the schoolhouse clock on the wall has stopped. The familiar tick-tock is missing. I've forgotten to wind it. Standing up I confront it and consider doing it now but don't really care enough to start the process. Instead I replenish the wood on the fire.

My coffee has gone cold again. The fire in the fireplace having burned down to coals and ash, the red glow of heat dancing back and forth across them in the winter-darkened room. It will take some time for it to reheat the tiny radius near my seat. It is still morning. It surprises me somewhat that the narrative of my memory can travel so far and yet real time drags its way through the early hours. With a yawn, I stretch and shrug off the afghan. It takes some strength of will to embrace activity, but I recognize the need to accomplish something, anything.

The dogs, comfortable on their throw rugs, follow me with only their eyes as I limp to the front closet, each step a little easier than the last as my aching knees adapt to the new effort. I open the door, pull off my robe and hang it on a hook on the back of the door. I reach in to pull out the well-used hooded parka and shrug into it. Shuffling to the front door, I slide off my fleece-lined slippers and step my stockinged feet into a pair of black rubber barn boots that stand just inside the door on their rubber mat.

As soon as it is clear that I intend to go outside, the dogs push themselves to their feet and stretch, their faces pulled back into long grins. Shaking themselves off in a storm of floating dog hair, their nails clack across the wooden floor to the door where they stand at a respectful distance expectantly waving their tails. They stay well back of the doorway though. They both know better than to bolt out the door as soon as I open it. They've made that mistake before. It can be unpleasant because as soon as the door opens more than a few inches, two tabby cats, puffed up from the cold squeeze themselves through the crack and into the house where they turn and complain to me about nothing in general. The dogs have learned to wait until the cats clear the doorway before they take their turn to exit. It is the morning changing of the guard. The two species nose each other briefly, the cats on their way to the fireplace, the dogs off to outside adventure.

Once open, the dogs rush out the door and leap into the deep snow beyond the porch, snow-plowing their way with their heads down, their tails wagging above the snow, marking their progress and unaffected by the cold. In no time at all they will reduce the pristine snow around the house and garage to a trampled and thoroughly sniffed mess of footprints. Eventually they will return to the porch where they will spend the rest of the day napping and watching for visitors.

Stepping outside onto the porch, I pause and breathe in the frigid fresh air. Beyond the woods below the house, there is nothing to stop the driving wind and snow. The gale of last night has blown the snow into waist-high drifts surrounding the house and garage, obliterating the walkway and covering any sign of yesterday's outside activities. And most of all, effectively sealing me off from the outside world.

The snow still falls lightly, silently in the quiet windless air of the day after a storm.

On both sides of the door, waist high and running the length of the house, firewood is stacked. It is covered with a light dusting of snow that has snuck in under the roof. Chickadees, unconcerned with our presence, sing "chicka-dee-dee-dee" in the spruce trees near the porch as they flit to and from the bird feeders lining the porch railings. A lone cardinal, his red plumage standing out against the white of the snow and the blue green of the spruce trees, eyes us suspiciously.

Pulling off the lid of the steel trashcan that sits in the far corner of the porch, I reach in and scoop birdseed into the bucket that was upended next to it and methodically refill the feeders. I watch a single Nuthatch land on the nearest feeder and inspect my work. Apparently judging my efforts to be sufficient. He selects a single sunflower seed and flaps off with it across the yard toward the woods below the house, dipping and bobbing in his characteristic nuthatchy flight. He will store the seed for a later leaner time by finding a crack in the bark of a tree and hammering the seed into it using his woodpecker-like bill. How he finds them later is a mystery to me.

I reach into my parka pocket to rustle out a crushed pack of cigarettes and a lighter. I sit down on the woodpile and shake one cigarette out and light it. I take a deep drag. The smoke triggers a coughing spell and for a moment I am light-headed. I bend over at the waist to catch my breath. The cough goes on spasmodically for half a minute before I bring up some phlegm that I spit onto the snow-covered porch floor and note that it is brighter red than usual.

Once the cough ceases, I lean back and take another drag of the cigarette, noting with some amusement what my children would say about this activity. They would shake their heads and tsk-tsk before beginning yet another lecture. The lecture is far too late. The damage was done long ago. It is much too late to worry about such a trivial thing.

Once I complete my outside chores, I carry in a few armloads of firewood and pile it on both sides of the fireplace. I fill the now empty seed bucket with snow and make a few trips to empty it into the kitchen sink. I set a final bucketful near the hearth to melt for drinking water and more coffee. Back in the kitchen I stand in front of the open refrigerator door. Even without the inside light, I can see that there was nothing inside that remotely interests me or my stomach. Instead, I reheat coffee and retreat to my chair near the fire.

After sharpening her claws on the armrest of the chair, the smaller of the two tabby cats curls in a ball in the crook of my noncoffee-cup arm and goes to sleep. The chores hadn't taken long enough, the day was still young, and the time passed too slowly.

Still preoccupied with my previous thoughts of Thomas Quinn, I rearrange the afghan on my shoulders and with a sip of the hot burnt coffee, I stroke the cat and lose myself to the flickering flame.

Six Handles

Like hospitals, funeral parlors have their own unique and universal essence. The lighting is indirect, aimed mostly at the off-white walls and draperies. The subdued lighting reinforces the somber feel of the event it hosts and softens the effects of overly enthusiastic, but sometimes necessary make-up of the deceased. The floors are thickly carpeted to muffle intrusive heel strikes. The air is thick with the cloying smell of lilies, roses, and embalming fluid.

For Thomas Quinn, only the largest viewing room would do. He had touched many lives, and he had gotten smiles at every turn. The immediate family comforted each other quietly in the time before the wake was scheduled to begin. A last few moments of private time. A lengthy line had already formed outside of the front door in the bitter wind and snow. Once inside, each shook off the snow and began the joyful process of saying hello to everyone in sight. Coats were hung, piled and draped over chairs, tables or arms of husbands. A few of the men began to unpack fiddles and mandolins. The women gathered to assess the flower arrangements and estimate the cost of each. The men circled near the far corner where the bar would have been located if this were a wedding. Almost all of them had brought a pocket flask. Willy Donovan, quite possibly the most well-known man in the room and proprietor of Willy's Tavern, stood ready with a few bottles of Jameson's whiskey for those that might have forgotten to prepare properly.

Willy, his face flushed with the heat in the room, and an early start on the Jameson's, wiped his eyes and blew his nose on a handkerchief. Despondent over the loss of his best friend, and favorite customer, he did his best to keep up with the lively conversations and friendly laughter. He and Father Dempsey, the venerated pastor of St. Patrick's, stood shoulder to shoulder weaving in tipsy unison.

The front rows in the room were filled with more serious mourners. Thomas Quinn had sired four beautiful black haired, blue-eyed daughters. He had one son, and all sat silent while they accepted the heartfelt condolences of each passerby. Their spouses sat in the row directly behind their mates. At the front of the room, in a brightly draped alcove, lay the late Thomas Danby Quinn. Laid out in a solid oak casket of his own design and fashioned by his own hand. He was attired in his only suit and probably only tie with his rosary clasped in folded hands, a single gold band on his left ring finger. A Beloved Father and Grandfather bouquet of stunning proportion draped across the foot of the box easily outdistanced the nearest floral competitor.

Many years ago, Thomas had laid down his written instructions on how his funeral and wake was to be conducted. Amazingly, none of his children had produced a single Quinn heir. The number of girl grandchildren was legion, however. I could never be certain which one went with which aunt or uncle or which name went with which cousin. There always seemed to be new ones every year at Christmas. All looked exactly the same—long black hair, a slightly turned up nose and the bluest of blue eyes— making it hard to distinguish one from the other.

Thomas had selected the hymns to be sung and the Epistles to be read and who would read them. He had designated who his pallbearers were to be. He had chosen from his second family, his second set of sons. He had designed his casket with six handles and had chosen six tall men of stature—he thought. My uncles; Seamus, Arthur, Andrew, and Daniel. My brother Andrew—and me.

I sat next to Grandma while she held my hand. I didn't want to join the men back in the corner, or sit with my father behind Ma. I already missed Thomas and suddenly for no reason, all I could think about was another funeral. It had been more than two years since Dutch, my Dutch, had been taken from me. A cruel twist of fate, and a stunning reminder of the inevitability of karma, had combined to end her life in a plane crash, just as ours had been beginning. It was two years that I'd spent running. Trying to outrun the feelings and the loss. Two years of denying the pain of not having her in my life, waking up next to her, not having her wisdom or her smile. Suddenly she was no longer the shadow in the corner and the weight of that burden I'd been dragging behind me became real. I didn't care and I couldn't help it, something let loose inside of me, and the pain of it was incredible. It hurt; I hurt—I began to cry, my body shaking from the force of the release.

After a bit Grandma turned to me, "I'm glad to see you can still do that. I was beginning to worry."

Ashamed, I turned my face away and wiped my eyes with the back of my hand.

"We should spend some time together again Em. There are things we need to talk about—you need to talk about. Come home with me for a few days Em. It's time we had a little talk."

Wisdom of the Aged

Buttoned up into in a long winter coat and wrapped in a thick quilt, Maggie Casey sat in the old rocker on the front porch of the old house. Gone were the zephyrs of summer, or the noisy wrens celebrating the day's heat from the shady trees. The gusty winds of winter blew eddies of snow around the corners of the house, piling it under the eaves and into the empty flowerpots that lined the shelves below the porch railings.

Oblivious to the cold or wind, she clutched a small briar pipe in her gloved hand, casually smoking and watching quietly as the swirling cyclones of snow danced across the yard and out into the street. The Quinn house across the street was a beehive of activity. Light from the windows on all three floors spilled out into the early darkness. Figures hurried back and forth behind them. The driveway and street in front of the house and down the block were bumper to bumper, filled with cars, trunk lids open to the weather, engines running as families carrying suitcases and pillows prepared to leave for their far away homes and lives. Thomas Quinn had been laid to rest. The chapters of his life would be written by his children now.

The Casey men and their families were gathered on the sidewalk outside of the Quinn home, saying their goodbyes, shaking hands, patting the men on the shoulder, but most of all keeping their distance from where I stood.

I stood uncomfortably against the outside wall, to the left of Maggie and watched the activity from a distance. I sipped my tea, holding it in both hands to keep my fingers from freezing. Maggie sat next to me content to rock and smoke.

"Can you still do it?"

"What?"

From under the quilt, her hand produced an old friend. The knife still in its sheath, large in her gloved hand.

"Show me. The limb on the oak, the one on the right."

I took the knife from her and pulled it. I had returned it to her in my teens, thinking it wasn't shiny enough, or that it was too clumsy. I hadn't touched it in years. In spite of the cold, the handle still felt warm in my hands.

"I can still do it."

"Can you repeat that whenever you want to?"

"Seven times out of ten, probably."

"I don't hear any satisfaction in your voice."

"It's just a circus trick Grandma."

"When you were young, you didn't think so."

"When I was *young* there were a lot of things that I thought were more important than they turned out to be."

"Growing up will do that to you."

I looked out across the street. I was physically and mentally tired. The events of the past week had brought the events of the past years back into sharp focus and worn me out emotionally. I was spent; felt hollow. I didn't think I could have summoned a single give-a-shit if my life had depended on it. I was tired of growing-up exercises, and I didn't have the energy to look ahead. What was behind me haunted my every decision, and if growing up meant losing more of the people that were important in my life, I didn't want to grow up anymore.

"You're pretty young to have had so many lives pass through your hands." Grandma broke through my musings. "Thomas told me about the army time and the war. I had expected something like it after you came home with those burns on your face. You left something over there when you came home, you left your smile."

She rearranged her quilt, and tucked it up under her chin.

"Seamus told me about that business in Chicago. No, don't get excited, I made him tell me. The whole clan was involved on some level, and we all had a part in it. Seamus needed to let us know that it was for a good reason. You did what you needed to do, and from what I can see, you handled it like I would expect you too." She took a pull on the cold pipe and then looked into it, seemingly surprised that it was empty. "But it was a lot, and it was a lot for a long time."

She sat silently for a full minute as the doors of the few final cars across the street were slammed and final goodbyes were shouted at the closed windows.

"And then she happened."

"Some go through an entire lifetime without that responsibility. They can't imagine the tragedy of such a loss. You've kept going, but you haven't faced it yet. You're trying to outrun it—and you can't. That's got to be exhausting."

Two years since Dutch, my Dutch. It had not been until I could no longer tell her that I had realized how much I had loved her. Instead, I ran from one side of the country to the other. I tried to substitute physical pain and deprivation for the emotional pain that I was seemingly unable to accept.

I hadn't smoked a cigarette in over a year, but suddenly I really wanted one.

"She was something special, wasn't she?"

The pain that shot through my chest was real.

"She got to you, and you refused to admit it, didn't you."

"Grandma, I'm sorry I broke down at the wake. I don't know what that was all about."

"Admit it!"

"Yes Grandma." I looked out at the house across the street, the hugs being passed around, the handshakes, the warmth being shared in the cold winter evening. "Yes, she did."

"Did you ever tell her?" She tapped her pipe out on the armrest of the rocking chair, letting the dark ashes fall into the drifted snow around her feet. She began packing the pipe again. "No, you wouldn't have."

Dutch and I had been roommates for over a year. Along with our friend Angie we had been a happy threesome. It had been a year of joy. I had rediscovered my smile. Dutch was going to have our baby, and then suddenly merciless karma had caught up with me and I was alone again.

"I'm so sorry Grandma, I'm just so sorry about it. If I had told her, or if I had just said something it would have been so different. I thought I was doing her a favor. She was too good for me."

"Ha! You can't bullshit a bullshitter. I think it might have been one of the healthiest things you've done in years, those tears I mean. They were a long time coming. Now stop and relax. I wanted to talk to you because you have two directions to go, and for a change, you can decide which one. It sounds as if you've started on the right track for a change, going back to school and pointing yourself away from all of that business, but I wonder if it's for the right reasons."

"Thomas always worried about you, you know. He thought you had more trouble pulling yourself up from the sadness and destruction than some do. He said you were too good to be bad, but you were somehow drawn to it, the darkness that you somehow felt you deserved it. He prayed that you would find your way to something better."

"I told Thomas that there couldn't be forgiveness for some things. I could go to confession for the rest of my life, but forgiveness is something that the priest doesn't just give you. You have to accept it."

"Forgiveness is by God's grace Emmett; it's not yours to accept or deny."

I took a deep breath and let it out. Pushing myself away from the wall I walked to the porch railing. "Well, I'm just waiting for the retribution. Sooner or later, it will come. If there is any justice in the world, it will come. I hate how it comes in little pieces, a little bit here, a lot there."

"So, you've walked on the wrong side of the law, you've taken lives, you've lost your one true love, and…?" She let that hang in the cold air for a full minute. "You can't go looking for your retribution or hasten its arrival by getting into trouble. That just creates more time in the confessional."

She waved at one of the cars as it pulled away from the curb. The back seat was crammed with cousins, all waving back.

"I can't get past the belief that somehow killing Dutch was punishment to me. She was a good person. She deserved her life, but in some way, by taking her away from me, she paid the price. How can you believe that God would do that to her."

"Your road, whatever you decide what road that is, is in front of you Emmett. You've turned around, but you're still looking back over your shoulder. Start taking bigger steps."

"I think I'm looking for a way to atone."

She sat quietly for so long that I thought the conversation was over.

"That's a good word. But how much atonement would

be enough? Don't sins accrue interest over time?" She waved as another of the cars pushed its way by heading up the snowy street. "If you imagine them to be bad, heinous, will you be able to accept that you've done enough penance, or do you beat yourself with the shame stick until the trumpets sound?"

"I don't know," I said that because I didn't actually know the answer. Until she had asked, I hadn't thought about it in those terms. "But I think I have to try and find out."

Today

The cup of coffee in my hand has gone cold again without me taking even a sip. Putting the full cup on the side table. I check the schoolhouse clock out of habit and see that it is still stopped. It didn't wind itself and I hadn't rewound it when I'd had the opportunity. Now I couldn't reset it because I didn't know what time it actually was. I toss a couple of larger logs on the fire; the clock will have to wait until I start to care about what time it is again.

Pole Dancers and College

"So why should I hire you instead of somebody else?" The nameplate on the desk in front of me just read, Cecil.

"I don't know, maybe you shouldn't." You didn't have to be very worldly to recognize that the nameplate should have said, Son-of-a-bitch, or maybe just Dirtbag.

There had been an economic downturn in the Quad Cities. Formerly healthy industrial manufacturers, John Deere, Farmall, International Harvester, White, and all the companies that supported them had fallen on hard times all at once. A couple of them had already declared bankruptcy, and at least one was for sale. The area depended on a healthy farm and agricultural equipment industry. Within a few months, the unemployment rate had rocketed to the high 20 percentiles. I hadn't been able to find steady work since then, and things were beginning to look bleak for R. E. Casey.

Cecil hadn't even tried to be cordial. The nice guy approach hadn't worked at some of the other interviews lately, so I had decided that I'd match his attitude with my best *Hole* persona and see if it worked. I wasn't too sure about the job myself, but a job was a job and I still liked eating regularly. "Seems like a job I can do."

"Well, you ain't as big a guy as some others I've had.

This ain't some candy-ass job.

There's real assholes we get in here all the time."

"Then I guess I'm qualified, cuz' I'm already an asshole."

"Bein' an asshole don't mean shit. You could be just as much trouble as all the other assholes. That's why I got so much fuckin' turnover."

"You hire a lot of assholes?"

"They end up bein' assholes." His beat-up office chair gave a small shriek of protest as he leaned back and scratched the wad of hair sticking out of the gap in his shirt, near where his bellybutton had to be hiding. He swiveled toward the two huge velvet pictures of Elvis and Marilyn Monroe hanging on the wall of his crappy little office while he relit the chewed cigar stub hanging in the corner of his mouth. Marilyn was scantily dressed and Elvis was wearing a Speedo.

"You like tits?" He was looking at the Marilyn picture but I was pretty sure he was talking to me.

"I'm a big fan." An easy question for me if there ever was one. "Yes."

"Well we're in the tits business here. You get enough tits waved in your face and *bam* you're an asshole in no time flat."

"So? I like girls. Sue me. But if you want someone to do your bouncin' then I can do it.

But if you want to split hairs, hire somebody else."

"Like I said, you're a sorta big guy, and you talk tough enough, but sometimes shit gits kinda nuts around here. I need ta know if you can handle it."

"There's the size of the dog in the fight and then there's the size of the fight in the dog." Cecil seriously needed to be introduced to my father. "You hiring or not?"

"R. E.? Can you help me?"

"Maybe, what's up Shelby?"

"I got a sliver and I can't get it out. It's killin' me."

"Okay, let's have a look."

"It's right here." She cupped her left breast and lifted it. A small bloody spot highlighted the hefty splinter that barely protruded but could be seen under the skin for at least a half-an- inch. Even in the low light of the bar, it would have been hard to miss.

"How the hell d'you get a splinter there?"

"I dropped my Chapstick and it rolled behind the make-up table. When I tried to reach down behind to get it, that piece of shit table stabbed me."

"I don't have my knife on me, do you have a pair of tweezers."

"Yeah, right here in my pocket." She laughed. She didn't, in fact, have any pockets or pants or socks. Maybe a bobby pin but not anything else. With the exception of a sequined g- string, she was naked.

"Funny." It would have been too if I hadn't been so tired. "I'll go out and get one from my truck. Can I finish my coffee first?"

"I got tweezers. Once I get this shit off my hands, I'll get it for ya." Tracy was seated farther down the bar from us. "My tips are getting pretty shitty. I gotta try something different, maybe a new outfit or somethin'."

All the girls that danced started out in an outfit of some sort, but it was an exceedingly temporary thing.

Tracy was not exactly statuesque. She was relatively short, blessed with ample hips, a tiny waist and a colossal set of breasts. I was no expert on breast size but they were the biggest ones I'd ever seen—or heard of. Right now, she was slathering oil all over them. It was quite an operation. Pouring the oil into her hand, she would put the bottle down, then lift one, (no small feat), and spread the oil over it, her chest and almost nonexistent collar bones. Once she finished with the petroleum prep, she snapped open a different small bottle.

"I got this at my niece's birthday party last week. Sugar sprinkles. They use 'em for cupcakes and shit."

She doused the bright red and sparkling sprinkles over her chest, breasts, shoulders, the bar, and the floor.

Looking down at her work, "Shit, it's all uneven!"

"Cecil's going to shit green if he sees that stuff all over the place."

"Cecil probably shits green on any fuckin' day."

Tracy stood up and did a couple of hops up and down, trying to shake some of the clumpy sprinkles loose. It took several seconds for the two mega-hooters to stop reverberating. For those few moments, I was mesmerized. If she did it more than a few more times, her breasts were likely to trigger a seismic event.

"Gimme those tweezers Tracy, and go wash that shit off." Shelby apparently wasn't as impressed as I was.

After digging around in her little make-up bag, Tracy produced a pair of tweezers and jiggled off toward the back room. Taking the tweezers, I bent down while Shelby held her left breast up.

"Cecil says that you got your balls shot off in the war." Shelby had been sitting at the bar alternating between grinding the heels of her hands into her eyeballs and drinking the horrible coffee. Now she was an objective observer into the ongoing surgical operation and looking for a distraction.

"Cecil says a lot of shit." I also had been sitting at the bar drinking horrible coffee, but now I leaned over and examined the splinter close up. It was four o'clock in the morning, the bar was closed, and all of the clients had been escorted to the parking lot. The girls were finishing up their night, sitting at the bar and counting the prodigious stacks of one-dollar bills from their night's efforts.

"So, you've still got 'em?"

"Such as they are."

"But you don't like us girls?" She was trying to look anywhere but where I was working. "You queer?"

"Hold still Shelby." I reached out and pinched her right nipple. "Ouch! Son-of-a-bitch!"

I held up the tweezers with the bloody splinter in them.

"Oh, you bastard," she rubbed her nipple, then smiled, "Thanks."

"No sweat Shel, no I'm not queer. I just try not to let my balls get me in any more trouble. Go get some Mercurochrome on that before it festers," I raised one eyebrow and smiled at her, "or maybe some sugar sprinkles."

I had been bouncing at Pole Cats for almost two months. The winter had passed and the spring was almost half over. I'd found a little apartment in town and thrown the well-used tent in the dumpster. I was beginning to look ahead, and school had immediately become easier because of those two things.

The pay was good and the job consisted mostly of standing around and watching the customers become increasingly stupid over the course of too many drinks and the crescendo of testosterone brought on by the girls. To an objective observer, there was an atmosphere of melancholy as customers clutched their dollars bills hoping that it might buy them a few moments of eye contact. Occasionally I would have to escort one or another out to the car when they acted out a scenario that was only playing in their own head. When that happened, they were usually apologetic and embarrassed as soon as they hit the outside air.

The girls, for the most part were college students trying to pay their tuition, just like I was, or single mothers trying not need social services so much, and older women at the far end of their chance for love in all the wrong places. All of them, the men and the women, were good people mostly, which made spotting the bad ones easier.

The bad ones weren't as much fun and they weren't much for conversation either. What they lacked in social skills they made up for in bluff, bluster, and bullshit. Too often they were not alone, accompanied by friends and hangers on, so that they didn't back down easily either. Tonight had been one of the kinds of nights when I should have checked to see if there had been a full moon. I'd been busy. There had been more than one escort to the parking lot, and there had been what the police call an *incident.*

"Let me see your hand?"

"It's alright Shel, it's no big deal."

"Give it." She wasn't a very big girl, petite in fact, cute instead of pretty. But I'd seen her deck a full-grown man with one punch when he'd climbed on stage with her, so I gave her my hand.

"Needs stitches, but it's all swelled up now." To the bartender, she said, "Billy, give me some ice in a bar rag."

Once she had the rag, she gently pressed it onto the cut on my hand.

"They won't be able to sew it up anymore, it's too late now. Did you do this on his teeth?"

"His belt buckle, I think. I used my knee on his teeth."

"Jeezus R. E.!"

"He had a knife." The cold felt good, but the ice cubes hurt the way she was pressing on them. The hand was going to be sore for weeks. "I was just keepin' it a fair fight."

"The cops said that one of his friends had a pretty bad head injury."

"Hard to tell. The parking lot was dark."

"Yeah, it's dark for a reason dipshit and now those cops are gonna be cruisin' through more often than they already do."

Cecil, chewing on an unlit cigar, had walked up behind

us. He was struggling to get his belly stuffed back into pants while he tried to look taller. The reason it was dark was because some of the girls engaged in another form of commerce out behind the dumpster, and Cecil took a cut of that business as well.

"Goddammit Casey! You're supposed to just take them out to their cars and send them on their merry way, not almost beat them to fuckin' death—in my god-damned parking lot!"

He ran an index finger through the sugar dust on the bar and squinted at it in the dim light, then stuck the finger in his mouth and scowled.

"Dammit Casey, now I gotta fire you. If those fuckers come back here lookin' for you it's gonna be a shitstorm. I'll give you a week's pay and the rest of this week, but you are out of here. And that means N. O. W., now!"

I took the bar rag full of ice off of the back of my hand and shook the ice out of it and onto the floor, and his shoes. "No good deed goes unpunished, eh Cecil?"

"Cecil you are such a prick." Shelby swiveled out on the barstool. "C'mon R.E., I'll get dressed and we'll go get your hand fixed up. And then, **by God,** some breakfast!"

Today

That had been one of the best breakfasts that I'd ever had, and it had lasted eighteen months. She had called it a little marriage, all the benefits none of the entanglements. I looked down at my right hand, tracing the scar that ran down my index finger and across the back of my hand.

We had both been going to college, pursuing the American dream of bettering ourselves. She was a rabid student, spending every spare minute she had to study. For her, there had been only one goal, and there was no obstacle large enough to deter her from it. She was going to be a Wall Street broker. "I'm gonna be fuckin' rich and I'm gonna own my own fuckin' house and I'm gonna own my own fuckin' car, and I'm never gonna eat Ramen Noodles again—ever."

As far as I knew that was exactly what she had done. The day she graduated, her suitcase was already packed, and I drove her to the airport. She bought a one-way ticket to New York City smiled, and waved to me just before she disappeared up the jetway.

I had smiled, too. That was when I knew for sure that I was going to be okay—but there still were times when it was going to be a near thing and the next one was right around the corner.

The Integrity Exam

I had worked hard, and thanks to Shelby, I had maintained my focus. As a result, I had finished my prerequisites and been accepted at the college. It was not medical school, like my Uncle Seamus had hoped, and it was not veterinary school as many other family members had hoped. It was chiropractic school, and it did not have a waiting list or an entrance exam like the others had.

I didn't know anything about the chiropractic profession. I had never been treated by one, and I didn't have an appreciation for the fervent philosophy that most chiropractors embraced. I did know a few chiropractors, like my previous mentor David Dean, who personified upstanding citizens and exuded integrity from every pore. They believed in service to others, and they expressed honest caring and empathy. If I could realize even a fraction of that character, I wanted to be a chiropractor too. I figured I'd work out what they did for a living as I went along.

Compared to the classes that I'd taken to get accepted, the studies at the college were several degrees higher in difficulty. At our first day orientation, the president of the college greeted us and spoke on what the next four years would be like. Two of the statements he made left a lasting impression on me and both proved to be true.

"You will find that there is so much information being pumped into you that it will seem like you've put your mouth over a fire hydrant that someone opened up."

And…

"Please look to your left and greet the person on that side sitting next to you. Do the same to the person on your right. Take a very good look at each of them because in less than six months, one of the three of you will be gone from this institution."

I was sure that he had said other things as well, but those two statements were plenty for me, and they set the stage for what was to come. He wasn't exaggerating, and his prediction more than came true for me personally.

The classes were mesmerizing. I found it difficult to take notes because I was so fascinated by the subject matter. The journey became increasingly more important than the end of the quest. I basically just sat and listened, enthralled. The anatomy and physiology alone transfixed me with the tremendous wonder and wisdom of how human beings are built and maintained. I was constantly amazed at how nature had considered even the smallest thing in the creation of every living thing on our planet. I felt privileged to be able to appreciate the information, even if there was too much of it to absorb.

Appreciating the information and absorbing the knowledge is one thing. Being able to regurgitate it on an examination was another thing altogether. Oral examinations were easy. I loved the classes so much that I could discuss them with at least some understanding of the overview that was part of the intent. It also allowed for some slight leeway in the interpretation.

Written examinations were tough and confusing for me. Multiple-choice questions often had four or five choices for an answer, all of them in some way the correct answer. But one was more correct than the others, and subsequently my downfall. As a result, I was making my way through the curriculum with a solid C average, but loving all of it. Then came PNS.

PNS, or peripheral nervous system, was basically an hour every day of memorizing the name, location and function of every nerve in the body outside of the brain and spinal cord. It would have been difficult enough, but the class was taught in an airless classroom in the heat of summer. The professor had been teaching it since the close of the Civil War, and subsequently lost the ability to add any timber to the pitch of his voice or animation to his delivery. In retrospect, it was entirely possible that any display of emotion may have pushed him into a serious cardiac crisis.

The class was a mandatory hurdle halfway through the program and a true soul-crusher and quite possibly the last opportunity for the college to weed out those unfit to graduate. As such it presented a daunting hurdle and not surprisingly, almost half of the entire class did not have a passing grade at the end of the term.

There was little satisfaction in the knowledge that I was not alone. Where the more well- funded students were stressed, I was in full-on panic. My eating regularly depended on two primary sources of income. The first was any crap job I could find to do when I wasn't sleeping in class, and the second was my G.I. Bill stipend. The jobs came and went, some were better than others. All of them stole sleep and study time, and some more than others. The G.I. Bill stipend came as regular as clockwork; it wasn't much but bought groceries and books. The only requirement to keep this anemic cash cow producing was that I show steady progress in school. If I stumbled, the money would stop and I would have to reapply once I fixed the problem.

Fixing the problem might take a week, fixing a government entitlement payment option might take months. I didn't care that I didn't earn top grades like my more gifted fellow students, but to fail a class would be tough to overcome. On my level of economic survival, it might prove impossible.

For three days I had studied my brains out. Several classmates took pity on me and quizzed me, showing me different memorization techniques, and buying me coffee. I gave up sleeping anywhere but in my classes, and gave all my time to pass this one test. If I passed it, I passed the class. If I didn't pass it, all the aluminum cans in the county that I could find to recycle weren't going to help. It didn't help my retention skills any that I was a walking anxiety attack.

The test would be given the first hour of the school day on the last day of the term. In my sweat infused, sleep deprived state, I arrived early, stopping only long enough to visit the restroom to wash my face, empty my bladder and give myself a pep talk in the mirror over the sink. The guy looking back at me seemed less than optimistic. He also needed some make-up tips and a haircut. I had coached myself that all I needed to pass was seventy-eight percent, but the harder I had tried to memorize names and function, the harder it seemed to retain any of it.

Standing at the mirror with my face still wet, a fellow student entered behind me and stepped up next to me. I regarded him in the mirror. He was clean and fresh. His clothes were neat and his hair was combed. I hated him immediately.

"You takin' the PNS exam?"

Not liking him seemed a poor excuse for being rude. "Yeah, it's gonna be a bitch."

"Here man, got somethin' for ya'."

He reached into his back pocket and pulled out a folded

postcard-sized piece of paper and laid it on the sink next to me.

"What's this?"

"It's the answer key for the exam." He combed his hair, watching me, then turned to leave and with his hand on the door, looked back at me one more time in the mirror, "Good luck."

I picked up the paper and unfolded it. Sure enough, running down the left side of the page was a numbered column. After each number was a letter A through E seemingly random as they descended down the page. It looked exactly like an answer key, and it looked legit, but was it? It could be my downfall if I used it and it was a scam. It could be my salvation if it was correct.

I looked back at the exhausted face in the mirror. I looked past the tired eyes. I needed this; I needed it badly. I folded up the paper and shoved it into my pants pocket and left the restroom. The testing room was a left turn, but for me there wasn't any doubt. I turned right.

"Is this the answer key for the PNS exam?"

I handed the sheet of paper across the desk of my PNS professor. His office smelled like what you would imagine a full ashtray might taste like if you licked it, and smoke hung in the air from the ceiling to just above my head. He unfolded the paper and looked down at it for a long time, long enough for his cigarette ash to lengthen and then fall onto the stack of papers on his desk. Finally raising his gaze to me.

"Congratulations Mr. Casey, you've just flunked PNS."

Later, I sat on the tailgate of my beat-up old Ford pickup truck and stared out at the mighty Mississippi River from the bluffs above the city. I knew in my heart of hearts that I had done the right thing. I had also found a way to make my situation worse. I had to live with myself, and I was okay with my decision, but now it was going to be a tough climb no matter where I was going to go.

The day after I'd confronted my professor, I received a note in my mailbox summoning me to the registrar's office. Most people on campus generally agreed that Dr. Jacobsen, the registrar, was nuts. When he was occasionally seen outside of his office, he walked with a vacant stare and never made eye contact with anyone. He acted manic in almost every respect—his office a wreck of papers stacked on his desk, the bookshelves, on the floor, windowsill, and the chair meant for visitors. His shirt sported a missing button and for once, my hair looked better than someone else's.

"You wanted to see me sir?"

"Who are you?" This spoken without eye contact as he searched for something under his desk.

"Robert Emmett Casey, sir."

"Casey?" He threw an elbow onto his desk and levered himself into a sitting position back into his chair, his other hand holding a folder. "Yes, Mr. Casey, …um, you're expelled for cheating." Still not making eye contact, he opened his folder and started reading the contents.

And that had been the end of it, no handshake, no pat on the shoulder. I turned my mailbox key in at the bursar's office and bought a cup of coffee at the cafeteria in the basement. Now I sat looking out at the river.

Well shit.

Different Problems, Different Solutions

When things turned to shit in my past experiences, I had usually opted for following them right down the shitter. Once I was no longer a student, my previous life experience allowed for a variety of economic solutions. Although I hadn't had any contact with the seedier side of society since coming to the Quad Cities, I had glimpsed the edges of it. For someone like me, it was easy to recognize. To the casual observer, the two women dressed in high heels and standing in the doorway of a low-rent apartment sharing a smoke just looked like ladies out catching the evening air. To me they looked like my old neighborhood, and I knew them just as if they were old neighbors.

The brothers standing at the mouth of the alley, smoking cigarettes and talking too loudly and giving each other secret handshakes, or dap as it was called, usually elicited comments about why they weren't working, and no wonder they lived in this neighborhood. I knew, however, they were already working. They were the connections; the hook-ups and they all had their specialties. If you wanted drugs it was this one, if you wanted a whore, you talked to one of the others. If you needed car parts, there was a different one. The mouth of the alley was a booming economic center. I knew them all. I wasn't fooled, and I knew how to fit in with them—if I had wanted to.

I moved out of the little apartment that I had shared with Shelby. I sold my pickup truck, broken-hearted to leave my old friend behind and to get so little for something that had been so loyal. I bought a bicycle from the guys at the end of the alley, no questions asked, and got a room upstairs. The room was twenty-five dollars a month with a shared bathroom at the end of the hallway that featured a toilet and a three-legged claw-foot bathtub. The distance from my room to the bathroom was two steps, a long hop over the hole in the floor and then five more steps. It was important to know the steps because the lights in the hallway usually did not work. They didn't work because the light bulbs were stolen as fast as they were replaced.

I left the apartment every morning looking for work, taking temp jobs, and selling my blood at the blood bank. On one of those first mornings I forgot something and retraced my steps. At the top of the stairwell I saw that my door was open. Quietly approaching I looked through the crack between the jamb and the door hinges. A solid black fellow was rifling the drawers of the cheap dresser and occasionally dropping items into a knapsack that hung over one shoulder.

"Can I help you find something?"

He whirled around and immediately spread his feet and dropped his knapsack. He looked past me to the doorway. He should have thought about his response a little more as I shut the door behind me, but didn't.

Minutes later, he was going to have trouble negotiating the stairs by himself. A couple of the guys from the alley helped him down the stairs, and deposited him behind the dumpster in the alley. Then they taught me their secret handshakes. I shared a smoke with them in the mouth of the alley and we talked some shit. Although I hadn't made any new friends, I knew things were going to be okay after that.

Eventually, I got a job bussing tables and washing dishes at a supper club. It was close enough to pedal to and the waitresses sometimes shared their tips with me—and occasionally their beds. I even tried waiting tables, but the tips weren't anything like what the girls made. They finally confided that I was a little too imposing to be considered friendly. Instead, I started tending bar at the same place and tips got better.

Three months later, the college was willing to reinstate my status. I kept the job at the bar.

It would be a race to the finish line before my dwindling G.I. Bill funds ran out once they had started again. I would never be a good student, but this had been my hardest test and I had passed it.

Today

lunchtime

I melted some snow in the pot on the stove and opened a little box of macaroni and cheese, thinking about how much the kids had liked this with hot dogs cut up in it when it was cold outside. Most of the other things in the cupboard looked like too much work, and I was out of hotdogs. Something a little salty sounded good anyway and once it was ready, I loaded it up with pepper and a little more salt. I didn't want any more coffee, so I took a cup of snow and set it near the fireplace while I ate. It would be my water for the rest of the day. My doctor would be pleased.

Directing my gaze up at the wall near the clock, I took in the framed documents arranged there in a neat display. Diplomas and certificates, quite a few of them now, collected over a lifetime of study and diligence. Somewhere in the basement, or maybe the attic, a full carton of more of the same, pieces of paper pressed behind glass and wrapped in wooden frames. Milestones with no economic value of their own; landmarks of learning in a lifetime of lessons.

The centerpiece on the wall contained the largest of them. The hardest to earn, and the one I appreciated more than all of the others put together. Once I had it in my hands, I had spent more than a few months expecting someone to arrive at my door and inform me that there had been a mistake, and to give it back.

That little piece of embossed parchment marked the end of one life and the beginning of another. An official document, sworn and attested, on official stationery. I had learned a skill that would bring people to me. It gave me license to serve them, and finally begin to atone for what had come before. I was Dr. R. Emmett Casey, and I had come full circle.

Turning the Page

Memories like these made me smile, and for a short while I bathed in the warmth of them. Some memories deserved to be lingered over, and there were enough bad ones so that my thoughts didn't want to leave the good ones right away. It had turned out that everything that I had experienced up until that time was mere preamble to what was to come later.

Almost like television shows where the subject is placed in a witness protection program, the degree on the wall had granted me a new identity. It carried with it a certain gravitas. All I needed to do was step into it and assume the identity. Like many of those that are placed in witness protection I brought a lifetime of human experience with me. Experience that covered the broad spectrum of human nature, the bad and the worse. I had no desire to return to my past persona but that same persona would prove to be my greatest asset. As a newly minted doctor, there was very little that might walk through the door that I didn't recognize. Patient's conditions vary and diagnosis of those is an art form, but if you know the person hiding behind the condition, you know the cause, and being able to relate, one-on-one with people is the key to becoming a true healer. It wasn't until I graduated with my degree and began a rural practice that my life had begun in earnest.

St. Patrick's Day

I was settling into practice in Tomah, Wisconsin. For someone used to big cities, Tomah seemed a very small town on the edge of civilization at that time. In fact, Tomah was a commercial hub for the county, and for a large part of the region, it was a city with a future already grown to over seven thousand residents. For me, it had felt like home immediately and I allowed myself to immerse in the culture and the people.

In late February I had put a couple months under my belt. St. Patrick's Day was right around the corner. In my family, St. Pat's Day was like a holy day of obligation sent down from the pope himself. It was one of the days that my mother in particular, and indeed the entire extended family celebrated with fervor.

Having saved diligently for it starting right after Christmas, my Ma would have reserved an enormous corned beef from the deli section of the local A&P. She would proudly bring the monstrous brisket home and make sure to display it to the entire family.

Once we had expressed our praise for this year's slab of meat, always noting that it was the best one we'd ever seen, Ma would carefully place it in her enormous blue enamel roasting pan and cover it with a salty brine. The brisket would soak in the brine for an extended period out on the back porch until early morning of the blessed day. That would invariably be the last time the brisket would have any potential. What my mother could do to a corned beef brisket bordered on a criminal act.

The potential for numerous visitors and family members would spark a manic level of activity in our house on the blessed day. Starting in the early pre-dawn darkness, we would be awakened by the roar of the old Hoover vacuum cleaner as the preparations began. My mother supervised the cleaning of the house from the attic to the basement with military precision.

Bathrooms were only judged to be satisfactorily clean after repeated scrubbings. Dusting every surface required the efforts of more than one child and were tested by her with white-glove discipline. Often by mid-morning, all family members were suitably over any jubilant St. Patrick's feelings.

I had learned later in life that a properly prepared corned beef brisket required rinsing the salt brine off and then slow cooking the meat over several hours. In her haste and frantic cleaning efforts, she often put off the brisket until the last minute and there was no longer time for such a tender approach.

Instead, the poor thing was pulled from the brine and put directly onto the stove top, where it was cooked within an inch of its life in haste. The cabbage and carrots were treated with the same level of respect. The result was a dinner that lacked any semblance of flavor, and the meat reduced to being more suitable for shoe repair that ingestion. In later years, my sisters, under the guise of saving my mother unnecessary effort, would offer to prepare the brisket instead. The meals became a decidedly more enticing event.

For her children that could not attend the festive event,

a phone call just wouldn't do.

Only officially written expressions of condolences would suffice to assuage my mother's expectations. Having only recently begun my practice shortly after my graduation, I could not make the trip back to Illinois.

As the blessed day approached, I found myself in the local floral and gift shop to search for an appropriate, necessarily expensive and overly smarmy card to express my regrets.

My search for just the right sentiment ended only after I had spent an inordinate amount of time in the Hallmark section of the holiday cards. Taking my selection to the check-out counter to make the purchase, I was confronted by the store clerk who had sized me up when I entered and didn't appear particularly impressed. For her part, it was obvious that she took pride in her appearance, and the finished product was impressive. I had glanced up from my search frequently to enjoy the view.

Instead of the usual, "Did you find everything you were looking for?", or even, "What a nice card!" her opening was;

"So, you're the new *big shot* doctor in town."

I didn't feel the big shot doctor. In fact, I was more or less apologetic about being the *less than adequate* doctor in town. The first couple of months in the practice had impressed upon me how much I didn't know about handling patient complaints and protocols. The personalities were easy, getting them what they needed had proved to be the challenge. I hadn't considered the true meaning of the word practice and all that the word actually meant. As a result, it was only after I'd begun working that my true education had begun, and I was humbled by how challenging it was right from day one. But I also didn't want to miss an opportunity to grow my practice.

"Yep, but not a big shot, just the new guy up at the

clinic. It's fun." It was fun, sort of, but I was also not above fibbing to a pretty girl. "Being a chiropractor, I get to meet a lot of interesting people who are interested in staying healthy and taking responsibility for their own health."

"Everybody does that."

"Not really, most people don't want to change whatever they do that makes them sick. They just come to the doctor to get a magic pill so that they can keep right on eating junk food, or sitting in front of the TV, until they need the next magic pill."

"You haven't spent enough time up here in the winter yet, have you?"

"What do you mean?"

"It's friggin' winter up here for five or six months. There's nothing to do *except* sit in front of the TV and eat pork rinds."

"There's lots of things to do, but first you've got to make yourself get up and do 'em."

"I know, that's why everybody's got too many kids that are all born in the fall."

"That's not what I meant."

"Nope, but that's what you get. You'll find out once you've been around here for a while." She cocked an eyebrow and made eye contact, "*If* you stay here for a while, anyway."

"I like it here so far. I hear the fishing in the summer is outstanding."

"Fishing around here is outstanding all twelve months of the year—if you've got an ice auger."

"I've never ice fished before."

She handed me the small bag with Ma's St. Patrick's Day card in it, leaned back against the rear counter and crossed her arms and gave me a Cheshire Cat smile.

"Didn't teach you the important stuff in your fancy college then, huh?"

"I guess not."

"I've got my own ice shanty. Got a good spot out on the lake and I keep it set up until ice out."

"You like to fish?" Honestly, a girl, and a nice looking one at that who liked to fish. The world was always full of surprises for me.

"No, I just like to go out and freeze my ass off whenever I can," the sarcasm in her voice matched the downward curve of her mouth. "I like to eat fish, and the ones you catch taste better than any that you get any other way."

"I'll have to try it."

"Yeah? Well you'll learn pretty quick whether you like it or not. Winter around here isn't something you don't take seriously. It'll kill you before you know you're dead."

"Somebody said those exact words to me once before."

"You should listen, especially if the wind turns to the east. I bet they don't teach that in your d*octor* school."

"No, not in my **doctor** school. But my daddy sure did."

She slid the small bag with my St. Pat's card in it closer to me. I had somehow forgotten to pick it up, then handed me a small slip of paper.

"Here's my phone number, if you're gonna call me for a date you're gonna need it." The more I worked with people, the more solitary I had begun to feel. At work, I talked to people all day, every day. I talked about the weather at least a dozen times, I asked about their kids, their cats and occasionally their husbands. At the end of the day I was small talked out, but I hadn't had a real conversation with anyone in a very long time. I called her.

Her name was Greta, most of her friends called her Grit, and I soon learned why. She proved to be an interesting combination of capable, strong, and feminine, with serious tomboy overtones. She could clean a fish, run a chain saw, shingle a roof or swear like a sailor. But she also liked the opposite as well. She could be soft and tender when the situation called for it. She loved romance, and romantic dinners. A dinner reservation at a fine restaurant was an excuse to pull out all the stops and wear something that made her look fantastic and almost always got us seated without waiting. She had a bullshit meter that never missed the opportunity to call me out when I drifted into the realm of fantasy or hyperbole. She had no interest in changing me into anything more than I was, but at the same time expected me to not sell myself short. As a result, I fell increasingly under her spell.

That winter I learned a lot about ice fishing. I also learned that having sex in a fishing shanty was seriously challenging, but doable. When spring came, she showed me the trails into the deeper woods, and the wonders of west central Wisconsin, known as the 'driftless region'.

For my part, I gave her the litmus test. I took her to meet Grandma Casey. It was the first time I had ever done anything like that. On the drive to Madison Grit fidgeted and fussed, looking in the visor mirror repeatedly, nervous and asking superfluous questions.

"Are you sure I look okay?

"Better than okay."

"I should have worn a skirt."

"Jeans are just fine with Grandma. In fact, if you walked in wearing a pair of hip waders she'd probably adopt you. Relax, she's a nice lady."

"Then why'd you say she was a ball-buster?"

"She can be, look; she had nine children and raised eight of them to adulthood. Most of that time she raised them alone. She's a person that's it's well worth getting to know. I'm betting that you'll like her."

I had been wrong about that statement. Maggie Casey didn't like Grit; she adored her immediately. The two were kindred spirits on a level that I was not in touch with. After their initial introductions, and perfunctory brunch, the two of them adjourned to the back porch side by side in the old rocking chairs and talked. None of their conversation had been directed toward me, or required my input. Finally giving up the attempt, I walked around the corner to Willy's Tavern where the reception was much more engaging. Grit had to drive back to Tomah as a result.

A short six months later, we became Doctor and Mrs. Robert Casey in the register at St. Mary's up on the hill. I married my best friend. In the previous twelve months, my life had turned one-hundred and eighty degrees, and I barely recognized myself. The Casey and Quinn clans attended the wedding *en masse*. Even old Willy Donovan made the drive up from the south.

Afterward, we ran out of chairs to seat them all at the VFW. The police were called twice, once for noise violations and the other for a fight in the parking lot. After the second call, they stayed for cake. A good time was had by all, and it became a holiday dinner subject for years to come in my family.

My one-room efficiency apartment quickly became too small. My new wife had been living with her parents. That we needed a new place to live became immediately obvious. One of my patients, a kindly elderly fellow, offered to rent us his cabin in the woods. He said that after his wife had passed away, he no longer enjoyed visiting it. He offered it to us rent free. We insisted on paying something for it, so we settled on free care at the clinic and enough firewood for his fireplace in town.

It was a quaint log cabin well out of town, and deep into the Black River State Forest. It had a large living area and a single loft bedroom and was heated entirely by a cast iron wood stove near the kitchen. It would have been a lonely place for the old gentleman, but for us, it was perfect. It quickly became our home.

The beautiful house was set into a hillside above the vast Black River Forest hills and valleys and the trees below the house had been cut back to open the view. It was twenty minutes from the nearest town. We enjoyed the quiet solitude and the constant parade of the local wildlife across the lane below us while we got to know each other better. Deer were plentiful, along with porcupine, badgers, grey fox, and coyotes. We sighted bobcats, cougars, bears and once in a while a lone and secretive wolf. In the skies above us, we watched red tail and red shoulder hawks along with the occasional goshawk. Bald eagles were frequent along with osprey and turkey vultures, and the woods held rare pileated woodpeckers, flying squirrels, and other tiny creatures.

We moved our things into the cabin on 'Groundhog Day' deep in the cold of midwinter. Previously vacant, no wood has been cut for the cabin's large wood stove in the center of the open space of the great room. Northern Wisconsin winters are long and cold, to say the least, and we faced our first married crisis. Returning from town each night after a long day at the office in the early darkness of winter nights we were compelled to take the toboggan and our ax and flashlight into the woods to gather enough firewood to heat the house for the night and the next day.

Unless you venture far enough away from the lights of civilization one can never appreciate what is meant by the term starlight. In the early darkness of winter, the snow blanketed woods can be surprisingly bright by the moon and starlight and easy to navigate. We only needed the lantern to identify dead and down trees that would be dry enough to burn for that night.

Most of one of my early paychecks was spent on a second hand Husqvarna chainsaw and with it we were able to cut the effort of collecting firewood in half. Even so we spent our weekends slogging through the knee-deep snow to cut and haul wood and at last begin to build a stockpile. It was hard honest work and it brought the two of us even closer together. We hated it and loved it all at the same time.

The Jackpine Savage

My practice had continued to grow as people began to know me. One of the advantages and ironically shortcomings of living and working in a small community is that it is impossible to maintain anonymity. Everyone knows everyone else, and by extension everyone knows everyone else's business. People know their neighbors and everyone else that lives on their street; they know them from their business dealings, school functions, and church. Their neighbors are their bankers, mechanics, grocers, mailmen, and pastors. As a result, it is difficult to be a thief in a town where not only does everyone know you, but they also recognize everyone else's possessions, no matter who is in possession of them. It is the reason people don't lock their doors, and why they leave their car keys in the ignition when they park downtown.

In a small town, reputations are earned in a moment and lived down over a lifetime.

There is a saying that is especially true in a small community. Tel-a-phone, tel-a-graph, or tell-a- friend. All of these are equally quick in getting the word spread about town, and equally hard to refute no matter how unbelievable they may sound. Most people live and breathe by their reputations. It is even possible to get a loan at the bank or credit at the grocery or hardware store simply by who you are and what is known about you. In a town like Tomah, Wisconsin, it is possible to achieve notoriety or become notorious. The first is the result of good citizenship; the second is the result of rigorously pursued and tailored fringe activities.

One such notorious individual that I became acquainted with early on in my practice was Jack Pinter. Jack lived far out of town to the north in the no-man's land created by the southern edge of the Black River Forest, the eastern border of the great Ho-Chunk Native American Reservation, and the vast peat bog swamps of northeastern Monroe County. To everyone in town, he was just referred as Jackpine, after the scrub trees that grew everywhere at the edge of the swamps and fens in that part of the woods. Folk who lived in that area were often referred to as jack pine savages because they drew their primary existence from the land, unemployment, poaching deer, and moonshine.

Jackpine was all of these and more. If I had to sit down and create a fictional character that was the epitome of a jack pine savage, even with the greatest degree of hyperbole that I could muster, it still would not do justice to Jack Pinter. The first time he walked into my office I would have put his age at somewhere mid-sixties, but I discovered that he was barely forty. He had a monstrous gray handlebar mustache with a week's worth of beard on the rest of his face and bushy eyebrows that needed trimming two months ago. He was tall and rail thin, with sharp cheekbones, sunken eyes buried in the roadmap of creases and wrinkles of his face and his eyes were bloodshot enough to change the color of the pupils. A rough patched flannel shirt, worn blue jeans that weren't blue anymore held up by suspenders due to his lack of hips, and a broken-down baseball cap pulled down to his eyebrows. His right eyebrow drooped, giving his left one an elevated appearance, and his head was turned slightly to the right as he regarded me through his permanent squint.

His first action upon entering my waiting room was to quickly stride to the front counter and unbuckle a wide leather belt that held a holster and a good-sized revolver and drop it onto the counter with a loud thunk.

"I need to see the doc."

His voice matched the rest of his appearance and sounded like someone had just pulled a chimney brush all the way up his windpipe. I was so transfixed by his caricature that I hadn't noticed the sudden and totally explainable lack of anyone at the front desk. I was alone. A quick sweep of the area showed that the staff had abandoned ship as soon as Jack had cleared the front door. A second glance showed the few patients in the waiting room were making eyes at the exit and squirming in their seats like they all had to urinate in the worst way. It was apparent that as a recently arrived resident, I was the only person who didn't know who this unique person might be. His appearance would have been frightening enough, but the handgun on the counter completed the surreal feel of danger.

Ignoring the cold sweat that broke out all over my body, but keeping the counter between us and my back against the wall behind me, I spoke up with as much confidence as I could muster. "I'm the doctor, can I help you?"

"You the doc? What happened to the old doc?"

"I'm afraid he's not here anymore. I'm his replacement." The previous doctor in the office had been a good friend of mine, and I had agreed to take his place while he dealt with a serious illness. At the time, I had assumed it was a temporary position, but his illness significantly incapacitated him enough to leave the practice altogether. I had quickly developed a love for the patients and the beauty of rural northern Wisconsin and planned on settling in permanently, but the present circumstance was making me quickly rethink my hopes of staying.

"Well the doc always said that I had to leave my gun at the desk, so here it is." He rasped this out in an overly loud voice and leaned onto the counter with one hand on each side of the weapon.

"Well okay." I quickly, carefully hoisted the holster and belt up off the counter and placed them in the bottom drawer of one of the file cabinets. Turning back to him, I asked, "What can I do for you sir?"

"This here is Jack Pinter and he's got one of his headaches again."

The comment was made by a mountain of a woman, standing just inside the front door. I was so taken up by Jack, that I hadn't even noticed her come through the door, and that was saying something. She and the door were roughly the same size. Upon closer examination, I saw that she was not as tall as she seemed but still stood about five foot eight or nine and easily scaled out over two hundred fifty pounds. She was dressed in another rough flannel shirt on which the sleeves were cut off at the shoulder, bib overalls and high-top work boots that were untied, the laces flapping loosely three holes short of the tops.

"I'm Geri Pinter. When he gets one of his headaches, he can't drive." She added in what basically amounted to an explanation for why he hadn't arrived alone.

I attempted to be professional and went to the file cabinets that stored the patient files and located Mr. Pinter's file. As the new doctor, I didn't know any of the regular patients well enough to work up their case without consulting their patient history. The previous doctor, however, had adopted an arcane practice of making sketchy notes regarding patient visits based upon his foreknowledge of the patient—and I suspected a general lack of professionalism—and this file was no different. As I opened the file, I saw to my dismay that the last five visits that Mr. Pinter had made to the office were all noted with the incredibly descriptive handwritten note that read, *Sick*. That was the total note for each visit. There was no documentation for the action that had been taken, or what Mr. Pinter had been afflicted with.

I asked Jack to accompany me to the nearest treatment room and sit down, which he did. I was not surprised when he did not remove his hat, but I was when Geri also shouldered her way into the room and took up a position in the corner with her impressive arms crossed over her bib overalls. The first thing I noticed about them both was that my initial stereotypical judgment had been wrong because they were both clean right down to their fingernails and their threadbare, mended clothes. They exuded an air of soap, fabric softener, and betadine hand soap.

A quick check of his blood pressure and heart rate revealed that both were seriously elevated, and I said as much.

"It's always up when my head hurts like this."

"How often do you get these headaches Jack?"

"I used to get them once in a while, but lately they've been coming more often."

"In the last couple of weeks, how often?"

"Pretty often," piped up Geri. "In the last week every day. That's why we came today because he says they're getting worse."

"Ok Jack, I have to tell you that I am a chiropractor and not a medical doctor. I want to help when it comes to most things, but I think with your blood pressure as high as it is, I really think it might be wise to see your regular physician for this."

"Well I tried that doc." He finally made eye contact, "I keep calling and they never call me back. Besides it's a hundred miles one way and I can't drive right now and Geri doesn't have a driver's license."

I look at Geri, surprised.

"DWI," she said with a shrug.

"I do my doctoring at the V.A. Hospital in Madison 'cuz of my disability." With that statement he nervously removed the tattered baseball cap and held it between his knees by way of explanation.

I was new to practice and was getting used to being surprised by patients and their histories, but I was not prepared for this new reveal. The symmetry of Jack's head was destroyed from his right eyebrow to his crown by virtue of the fact that his skull was missing. The left side of his face and head was normal, but the right looked as though it had been crushed with a shovel. To add to the incongruity, he sported a full head of hair in spite of the deformity. The missing skull encompassed the right temple and passed above his right ear to the back and crown of his head. Obviously at some point he had had the temporal bone of his skull removed. This certainly explained whatever disability Jack might be dealing with.

After he had removed his hat, I was at a loss to make small talk so I stood up and walked behind him. Toward the back of the flattened area and slightly above the right ear, a barely perceptible elevation could be observed that followed a course downward behind his right ear.

Due to his lack of extra padding, it extended along the lateral side of his neck, curving slightly forward and disappearing beneath his collarbone.

"What's this?" I asked, while tracing the path of the object.

"That's the tube they stuck in my brain to relieve some of the pressure. They said that my brain makes too much fluid."

"Where does it go?"

"Doesn't go anywhere. Just ends up in my gut. They

told me that my body would know what to do with the fluid when it got there.”

“So, this is a shunt that helps take the pressure off of your brain then?”

“Shunt? Yeah that’s what they call it.”

In view of his exceedingly high blood pressure, his blinding headache and the presence of the brain injury with the shunt, I was not sure how to proceed. Because of the aging local physician in town who had been telling anyone he could that I was not a real doctor, only chiropractor, I already had a well-developed inferiority complex. I was concerned to be as comprehensive in my approach to patient care as I could, even if it meant going above and beyond my regular scope of practice. I decided to become an advocate instead of a treating physician and after excusing myself from the room, I took a deep breath and went to my office, picked up the phone and made the call.

Surprisingly Dr. Langston, the local saw bones, took my call. I duly reported my findings and my confusion as to how to proceed. Instead of the expected derision, Dr. Langston responded professionally and with no condescension. His advice was to get Mr. Pinter to the V.A Hospital and report directly to whatever they use for an Emergency Room facility. I thanked him as professionally as I could, relieved.

“Good luck with Jackpine, I hope you took his gun.” After terminating the call, I reported his advice to Jackpine and Geri.

“I figured that’s where we were headed, but I don’t think my truck can make the trip and I got no one to drive me. Geri’s got to get back and take care of the critters at home.”

I told him that I would take him and saw his jaw drop. I left the room long enough to inform the staff that I would be leaving and to clear the rest of the day’s schedule. Their looks of concern were both for the amount of work that would require and sympathy and for my safety with Jackpine in the front seat of my pickup truck. I assured them that the revolver would stay in the file cabinet.

Any drive in that part of the country is well worth it. The views and scenery are spectacular every mile, and the trip to Madison was uneventful. Jackpine presumably because of his headache was not conversational and spent most of his time with his head resting on his hand and his arm braced on the armrest of the passenger door. I assumed he was asleep. Once we arrived at Middleton Hospital, the large V.A. hospital in Madison, Jack was immediately triaged, and with little waiting it was determined that he would be admitted, and I was relieved of my charge.

I had almost forgotten the incident when weeks later Jackpine once again appeared at the front desk along with his entire frightening aura. Without any preamble, he banged a large growler jug on the counter. The jug was filled with a golden liquid that looked like gasoline. It was equipped with a cork and thumb loop at the top to assist in tipping the bottle.

"This is for you doc, some of my best. Thanks for your help, my tube was blocked and so it wasn't draining. Gave me a new one, I'm feeling good now. You let me know when you get through this one, and I'll refill it for you. I'd appreciate it if you save the jug though. Least I can do for you doc. Any time you need a favor, you tell Jackpine."

"I do have one favor to ask Jack," I asked as I reached down and retrieved his revolver and gun belt from the filing cabinet drawer.

"Sure thing, what's that doc?"

Sliding the rig across the counter I dead panned, "What say next time you need to come into the office, just leave this out in the truck."

First there was a look of confusion on his face but as

understanding dawned, he formed a gun with his right hand, his index finger the barrel and his thumb the hammer and pretended to pull the trigger dropping the hammer, gave me a wink with his good eye, and went out the door.

Later I discovered that what was in the jug had a similar taste to gasoline but was effective. My father loved the stuff and asked for it whenever he visited. I discovered that rubbing it on one's gums would temporarily relieve even the worst toothache.

Scandalous

There were patients that just by their arrival in the office, bring sunshine and brightness, whose presence alone lifts the spirits of everyone else around them. Every practice has a few patients that through their unique personalities, endear us to them or conversely, we learn to dread their upcoming appointment. In some cases, it can be the same person that elicits both of these emotions simultaneously. One such person was one of the first patients when I arrived and continued to be a challenge throughout my time at the clinic.

Jean Baker was not ancient but certainly qualified as elderly. Although I knew her age, her appearance belied her actual age. She looked much older. From the first time I met her she was accompanied by a small, wheeled handcart that held a green bottle of oxygen with a nasal cannula to assist her breathing. She was afflicted with emphysema and a well-developed smoking habit. Her already deeply lined round face sported a pronounced groove pressed into the skin of her cheeks and temples where the nasal tube permanently pressed and molded the skin.

The fingers of her left hand were yellowed with tobacco smoke stains. Only her left hand exhibited the stains because she needed her right hand to hold her oxygen tube away from her face while she smoked her cigarettes. She was only a little over five feet tall, had a good-sized pot belly and had an air of authority and impatience. Whenever she wheezed her way into the office, and never with a prearranged appointment, the staff was always on edge until she left.

Whenever I would suggest a reduction in her nicotine consumption, she waved her hand impatiently and told me to just stop. She vociferously maintained that with her condition she would not live one day longer if she quit her habit; it would only seem longer to her. She maintained a dour expression and manner by which I surmised that she had no wish to extend her life any longer than she absolutely had to. She had never married and lived in the house that had been her mother's. She cowed various handymen and neighborhood boys into meticulously maintaining her home, paying them scrupulously. A housekeeper kept up the inside of the house and did her grocery shopping. Jean drove an old and spotless Buick. She would peer through the steering wheel to see the road when she drove with the vent window permanently open to keep the cigarette smoke from blocking her vision.

Over time, as her health weakened, she no longer wished to venture out. As a result, she arranged to see me once a week, on Friday afternoon in her home, whether I wanted to or not. The girls in the office rolled their eyes when I would ready myself to leave for these appointments but in truth, I began to look forward to them. Jean was honest to a fault and never concerned herself with the possibility of hurt feelings. Conversation was frank, and we had many stimulating discussions. As a retired teacher, she kept herself well informed of both local and world affairs and usually came up with some subject to grill me about. She often prepared a light lunch and would place herself in her front window, awaiting my arrival. As soon as I walked in, she would shuffle and deal a hand of gin rummy. As we talked and brunched, she would beat the crap out of me at cards. I kept the enjoyment of these visits a closely guarded secret from the staff.

Eventually Jean had trouble with stairs and her driving. With her breathing difficulties, she finally accepted the eventuality of moving into the local nursing home. She began using a walker to assist her stability, which proved convenient for toting her oxygen tank when she went outside to smoke. Although she let the house and much of her independence go, she did not slack on her sour expression toward the orderly staff, so they were careful not to set her off if they could help it.

The head of nursing, however, was more than a match for Jean. Dorothy Watkins was a tough, wiry woman probably in her mid-fifties, who had no time or patience for nonsense. She kept her own definition of what was nonsense and with almost no exception everyone at the hospital and on the staff referred to her as Nurse Ratchet, after the infamous character in the book, <u>One Flew over the Cuckoo's Nest</u>. I still maintained our Friday card games with Jean, although she was now required to take her lunch in the communal dining room. Nurse Ratchet had no time for me because as she was fond of saying, "I was not really a doctor, not like a real one anyway."

Jean had no respect for authority other than her own, so she took great pleasure in baiting Nurse Ratchet whenever the opportunity presented itself. A fact that did nothing to endear her to either of us.

One night long after I'd gone to bed, I was awakened by the insistent ring of the telephone. Although I never quite gotten used to it, the phone in the kitchen at home frequently rang in the middle of the night. I learned quickly that it should not be ignored. With my busy rural practice, I had begun to perform house calls to reach patients that otherwise could not make the trip to town. As a result, the phone might ring at all times of the day or night. So it was that in the wee hours of this morning, the phone jangled me into wakefulness. I stumbled down the stairs and in my sleep stupor answered, "Hello, this is the Casey's."

"Hey Emmett. This is Jim Kearney." Jim was the young physician that replaced the ancient and trusted physician who had practiced for decades in town.

"Oh hey Jim, what's up?" I said while I rubbed my eyes and scratched my scalp.

"Jean Baker fell out of bed tonight. She doesn't seem to be seriously injured, but she says her hips are out of alignment and she wants you to come and fix her. She's making quite a racket."

Jim was obviously calling from the bedside phone in Jean's room as I could hear Jean's scratchy voice over the phone hollering at some unfortunate staff person even as he spoke.

"I hate to bother you in the middle of the night, but she's disturbing the residents and we can't seem to settle her down. I gave her a sedative and it doesn't seem to be having any effect. It probably won't hurt her but I'm afraid that Mrs. Watkins is about to have a stroke. Do you think you could come in and help me calm her down?"

Jim was not just a good physician; he was a good guy. He had helped me out of some pretty tough situations with patients more than once. I knew he had to do some soul-searching just to call.

"Sure thing Jim. I'll get myself woken up and I'll be right along. It's a bit of a drive so maybe forty-five minutes."

"Thanks Emmett, we'll hold down the fort until you get here. If I tell her you're on the way, she should be a little more manageable."

With that I hung up the phone and climbed back up the

stairs, switching the light on in the closet. My, by now, long-suffering wife gave me *the look* and with a snort turned away from the light and tried to go back to sleep. I dressed as quietly as I could and left the house. The drive to town was seventeen miles but I didn't want to hurry. The deer population in that part of the state was dense, and I had no desire to reduce their numbers with the front of my truck.

Once I had arrived at the nursing home, it took less than five minutes to calm Jean, check her out, and then get her quietly back into bed. The entire floor breathed a sigh of relief and Jim and I adjourned to the front desk, pausing long enough to pour two cups of burnt coffee out of the urn in the staff room. Jim sat in the chair behind the desk and propped his feet on the counter. I leaned over the counter and we quietly toasted each other. Jim was dressed in his on-call scrubs from the hospital and looked exhausted. He had deep bags under the eyes of his young face. For a while we silently contemplated our cups and shared a moment's reflection.

Suddenly Nurse Ratchet was there. With the sour look she reserved for people she disliked the most, she glanced at me and then simpered to Jim, "Dr. Kearney, Jean Baker is out of bed again. She went across the hall and climbed in bed with Mr. Jenkens. What do you want me to do?"

Jim looked at me for a moment and then with a wink turned to Nurse Watkins, (Nurse Ratchett), and in a perfectly serious voice said,

"Close the door."

Today

time and distance

I scratched the sleeping cat in my lap idly, reflecting on the feelings that memories fostered. One of the gifts of advanced age was the perspective that it offered. I had often observed that inspiration had little to do with intellect and was more driven by emotion. In my observation, people who I'd known to possess high IQs could be satisfied with status quo in their lives and moved from day to day without any motivation beyond accumulated possessions. Conversely, I found that when I had been too quick to judge someone as being less than intelligent, they had subsequently impressed me with their creative thoughts and accomplishment.

I had come to realize that ideas and creativity had almost nothing to do with mental acuity. Instead it was driven by the emotional drive that fueled determination and interest. I had seen even the most handicapped individuals accomplish tremendous tasks simply because they wanted to. Every one of them had taught me something of value and to never understand the strength of the human spirit.

The cascade of memories greeting me from the flames in the fireplace were not connected by a desire to think about them; instead by the feelings they engendered. I caught myself smiling into the fire, thankful for the good memories and realizing that my life had contained many events that were both pleasant and remarkable.

After replenishing the fireplace, I made my way to the bedroom to retrieve another photograph from the nightstand and returned to the warmth of the fire. This one photograph held one of my most precious memories, a bright and happy day and a testament to the power of determination. A photograph of what my new life was, and how far I had come to achieve it.

I gazed at it for a long time, the tender feelings it engendered seemed to brighten the whole room to me, in the grey light of the winter morning.

A young mother, holding an infant smiling for the camera, and a tall man beaming next to her. She beautiful and the man—me.

Our children enrich us and age us every day of their lives. My grandmother had many saying sat her disposal that she would use when she wanted to make a point.

"Go outside and get the stink blown off of you." Spoken to lazy children who were idling in the house too long to suit her.

"If it could kill you, I wouldn't have put it on the table." Reserved for children who refused to eat.

Once we became parents ourselves, she modified her axioms of wisdom. "You are only as happy as your most unhappy child." For when we bemoaned how miserable our kids made us. And her favorite; "They're never not your kids."

That statement came to mind over and over again as my children grew and invented new ways to torment my soul and alternate between breaking my heart with love or stupidity. In retrospect, I often relived the torment that I must have created in my father and mother when I was younger. In one minute, to have never wanted to kill a human being so badly and in the next to love someone so unconditionally that you would lay down your own life to save theirs, without question.

Stuck in the Mud

Where we lived you never quite got used to the weather but you learned to expect the unexpected. Living in Central Wisconsin required that with few exceptions, the local weather played an important role in one's everyday considerations. Nice days were cherished but not trusted to last, hot days usually got hotter, and cold days could kill you. Winter reluctantly gave way to spring grudgingly. I had seen it snow on Memorial Day and be in the nineties on another. My wife and I had brought our second newborn son, Sean, home in a driving snowstorm in mid-May. Spring, when it arrived, was brief. The days were cool, and wet. The nights were cold and frost was not uncommon. The transition from cool to hot was sudden and summer arrived in a rush.

After the long winter, most people were anxious to get busy with outside activities after being cooped up in their homes for months. The silence of winter gave way to the out of doors sounds of life; frogs croaked day and night in the woods and ponds, and the birds returned singing their songs of love and territory. You could be sure that spring had at last come to stay when the first bluebirds appeared along the fence rows.

For me, the routine of practice didn't change when

spring came. However, the daily trip to town and the office became less hazardous, and house calls became somewhat easier to manage without the snowy country roads that drifted closed soon after the snowplows passed. As usual, my time was divided between three days of practice in town, and two days of house calls. Saturdays, I usually ended up doing both.

The first spring of our marriage, my wife and I were eagerly anticipating the arrival of our first child in late April. Living as far out of town as we did, my wife became more anxious about being home alone should her labor start, and I was an emotional wreck like all new fathers are supposed to be. My solution to the problem was to take her with me wherever I went as her due date crept closer.

Having her at the office every day was enjoyable as she was both good friends with the staff and also helpful when there was extra work to be done. House calls became even more enjoyable, having someone to ride along and share conversation on the long drives across the ridges of Monroe County. It was a special time as we were both excited about the upcoming event and I was able to demonstrate my skills in front of my biggest fan.

On a cold and rainy morning in the first days of April, one of my stops was to visit a farm where a young Amish woman had just delivered a child of their own. Young mothers were usually confined to bed for a few days before assuming the rigorous work schedule required of Amish housewives, but in this case the local midwife had asked us to stop in and do a wellness check on both the newborn and the woman. I always enjoyed these kinds of visits; they were generally easy and I didn't need to worry about what situation I might be walking into.

Her husband both managed the small farm we were to visit and operated a sawmill situated out close to the gravel road that ran by their place. Their little farm was tucked into a deep valley between two steep hills and far back in off of the country road.

The sawmill was situated near the road and far from the home buildings for two reasons. The first, easily enough, was to allow easy access from the road for commerce, the second was more complicated.

Halfway between the house and the road, a small creek flowed down the valley and across the narrow lane leading to the farm. In summer, it ran dry after the rains of spring finally stopped. In spring, it ran fast and wide as it drained the hills and valley behind it. With mostly buggy traffic in and out, it did not present any problems. For my pickup truck, it was a more important issue at this time of year. Transporting logs or sawn lumber would have been impossible in almost any season; hence the sawmill was located near the road and far from the home place.

On this day, after waving at the men working the sawmill, we swung in off of the road and started down the lane. My wife, in the last days of her pregnancy, leaned forward anticipating the adventure of fording the creek I had warned her about. The amount of moisture had raised the water table of the little valley to only a few inches beneath the surface and twenty yards before we arrived at the creek, the truck began to slew back and forth as we began to cross the spongy wet ground approaching it. Rather than slowing down, I sped up so as not to lose the momentum of the truck. We hit the creek at a good pace throwing water everywhere and covering the hood and windshield with mud as the rear wheels spun and the truck swam through. Arriving on the other side none the worse for wear the look on my wife's face showed that her sense of adventure had vanished.

Once I had parked in front of the hitching rail. I glanced at my wife where she presented a completely different look on her face as she held her belly with both hands and took a few deep breaths. I was immediately on high alert.

"Are you okay?"

Signaling me to wait just a moment while she continued to support her tummy, she took a few more deep breaths and smiled back at me.

"It's another one of those weird contractions. They pass pretty quickly. Braxton-Hicks, isn't that what you said they were?"

"Yeah, but aren't they kinda' more often?"

"Since yesterday, yes, but it's not a big deal. Go on and get this over with."

Leaving the truck running to allow the heater to stay on, I gave her a pat on the leg and grabbing my 'doctor' bag stepped out into the mud.

Inside the mother was friendly and smiling, slightly embarrassed to be found lying in bed and in her nightgown. The baby was mildly undersized, but its heart and lung sounds were good and it was otherwise pink and healthy, with the right number of fingers and toes. I finished my brief examination and was on my way in less than fifteen minutes.

Back out in the chilly spring air, the happy moment that I had been enjoying evaporated in seconds. Wading back to the truck through the muddy front yard, one look at my wife's eyes through the windshield spoke volumes. Even in the gray air of the day, I could see that the color had drained from her face and her eyes were as big as saucers. My first impression was that she was in active labor but with a second look, I realized that we had a completely different problem.

The pickup truck weighed roughly what three full-sized horses would weigh if you stacked one on top of the other and the ground under the hitching rail was used to one horse at a time. In the fifteen minutes I was inside the house, the truck begun to disappear into the morass and now the front bumper rested on the wet ground. There was no way to know how far it could sink, and there was no guarantee that it could pull itself out.

In short order I learned that that was exactly the case. Climbing into the truck I looked across at her. She did not look happy, and I wasn't far behind in that regard.

"I had two more while I was waiting."

"Shit."

Putting the truck in gear I eased down on the gas pedal. Nothing, we didn't move. Instead the rear wheels of the truck spun and the rear end of the truck joined the front, beginning to sink into the slimy mud. I opened the door of the truck in panic and muddy water rushed in over the doorsill and began to pool on the floor under my feet. The weight of the truck was squeezing the water up out of the wet ground. The situation was worsening by the minute.

I stepped out into the mess, oblivious to the ankle-deep water filling my shoes and splashed around to the front of the truck. The broad mass of the front bumper and oil pan was supporting the truck and preventing it from sinking any deeper, but it was already deep enough to prevent it from going anywhere. No tow truck driver in his right mind would venture down this lane to pull the truck out, it was going to take a tractor, and a big tractor at that. One more look at my wife through the windshield spoke volumes. Whatever I was going to do, I needed to do it in a hurry.

The clink and rattle of harness and buggy wheels made me look up. In my excited state I hadn't noticed it approach as far out at the road a small flatbed buggy turned into the lane. In no hurry, the horse walked up and through the mud, the creek, and approached the truck stopping only when the horse was even with the tailgate of the truck. I knew the driver and I dared to hope that he might be able to offer some advice.

"Looks like you have buried your truck Casey." No

emotion, but a truly astute observation.

"Hey Jonas, I'm going to need to get somebody in here with a tractor to pull this thing out. Do you know who's the closest person with one big enough to get this out of here?"

From his seat on the buggy, Jonas looked down at the truck wheels, buried to the rims in greasy mud. Then twisting around on his bench seat, he looked back up the lane.

"A big tractor would ruin the lane pretty bad. I will pull you out myself."

"What? How're you going to do that?" I sincerely hoped he wasn't kidding.

"It will take me a few minutes."

I had no idea what he had in mind, but anything just short of airlifting the truck out to the road would have sounded fine with me.

Jonas pulled back on the reins. The horse's head came up and the little mare started walking backward, pushing the wagon in a straight line. As it neared the creek, with another twitch of the reins, the horse turned and the buggy swung to the right. With very little effort the horse and driver executed a precision 3-point turn and again approached the truck, this time with his tailgate within a few feet of my tailgate.

Unlike me, Jonas had had the forethought to be wearing knee-high rubber barn boots. Climbing down, he sloshed around to the rear of the wagon, unlatched and lowered the 1 X 6 plank that served as the tailgate. Reaching onto the wagon bed he pulled out about eight feet of light chain, the kind you might use on a child's swing set, with a small clasp on the end. With the chain in hand, he dropped the open link at the end over a large nail driven into the wooden bed protruding about a half-an-inch. Smiling at me, he gave me a wink and made two loops around my bumper hitch with the other end and snapped the clasp to an empty link.

"Will work better if you make sure the truck is not in gear."

I couldn't believe he was serious. The lunacy of the tiny chain hooked to the inadequate nail in the wagon bed wasn't enough, but his little horse couldn't possibly be up to the task of pulling the mired half-ton pickup truck. I was almost as big as his skinny little mare so I said so, but I was polite about it. He was already hoisting himself up onto the buggy seat.

"Jonas, the truck will bust the chain. It's really in there."

"She will come out; you should move to the side some."

With that, he gave the reins a flick. The horse's ears flipped back as Jonas gave a quick whistle and then she started slowly forward, pulling the tiny chain tight with a snap. With another whistle the horse threw herself into the harness. At first, there was no movement and the horse stopped and stood with her ears back. I was ready to admit defeat, but Jonas just sat still no expression on his face. With the chain still tight, he calmly spoke: "Heeyah."

This time it was different, the little horse heaved forward. I had never seen a horse hunker down and dig. The little horse leaned so hard into the work that her chest dropped halfway to the ground as she spread her legs and dug in. The truck jerked and began to move.

The little horse was fully engaged in the task at hand and she drew great breaths through her mouth, huffing and snorting. With her chest ever closer to the ground, she began to swim her way forward, throwing wads of mud high into the air in all directions. The truck sucked at the mud as it was dragged slowly backward, at first on a snail's pace but slowly picking up speed.

Shouting through the open window, I told my wife to

grab the steering wheel and keep it straight as the truck picked up speed. Following the wagon and the little horse down the lane, I was soon forced to pick up my pace as I tried to keep up with the procession. Jonas never hesitated and didn't come to a stop until the truck rested at the edge of the road. Wading the creek, I was amazed. If I hadn't seen it, I would never have believed it.

Catching up and a little out of breath after the brisk walk, I expressed my amazement. "Jonas that's the darnedest thing I've ever seen."

He was busy retrieving his awesome tow chain and re-latching his tailgate. I followed him around to the side of the wagon as he mounted up.

"Thank you, Jonas, that horse must be something special."

"She is a work horse; she knows how to work."

"Well I owe you a favor."

"There is no favor. I am thankful that I was able to help."

Only a few hours later, in the warmth and comfort of the hospital maternity ward, my wife and I welcomed my first-born son into the world, Seth.

Thanksgiving Blizzard

After our marriage, Grit's parents had sold their house and moved farther south, having tired of the winters and small-town living. It created something of a dilemma when holidays approached. Both her parents and mine expected us to visit. Their expectations were reinforced once my son Seth was available for cuddles.

Living as far north in Wisconsin as we did, I often said jokingly, "The bad part of living where we do is that my in-laws are four hours away, but the good part about living where we do is that my in-laws are four hours away." This meant, of course, that because of time and distance we did not get to see them very often. The truth was though, I got along well with my wife's parents and family. But as hard as I had tried not to, I had inherited my father's aversion to visiting, and the distance of the trip to see them required the investment of two or three days.

In the fall of that year, my infant son was six months old, and his doting grandparents did not have to insist very hard to have us come for Thanksgiving. We were proud new parents and happy to show him off. Thanksgiving for us was a good time to travel because the Wednesday before Thanksgiving I was planning to take off. This allowed us to pack up and leave for Rock Island, Illinois, Tuesday evening after office hours and be able to stay through Thursday. The office would not reopen until Friday morning, and I could be back to work well-rested after a two-day break. I had begun traveling and lecturing at conventions and seminars by that time and through experimentation, we had learned that the baby slept well in the car if we traveled after dark, so this schedule worked out well. If the baby did awaken, my wife could nurse him while in the darkness and lull him back to sleep quickly.

On this occasion we arrived in Rock Island in good order and spent a pleasant time with her folks. The added benefit of the visit was being able to watch television. We lived too far away from broadcasting antennas to be able to pick up any television stations so we didn't own a television set. My in-laws had a television in practically every room in the house, and one or more of them were always on at the same time. In addition, Thanksgiving Day had football games, which I had truly missed. This Thanksgiving Day, my Green Bay Packers were going to play the much-hated Detroit Lions, so I was anticipating a day of overeating and decadence. The only thing that darkened the day was the constant television broadcast warnings of an impending holiday blizzard.

Making sure that everyone ate too much was one of my mother-in-law's specialties. She was a spectacular cook. A skill she had passed on to her daughter as well. In her tiny kitchen, she bustled about and created a worthy feast of turkey, dressing, mashed potatoes and gravy, sweet potatoes, and on and on. While she worked, she whistled and only interrupted her tune to give us the latest forecast from the little television on the kitchen counter. The weather report became increasingly grim and, for once, exceedingly accurate as it began to snow just before noon on Thursday.

My wife Greta had grown up the youngest in her

family. She had three loud and boisterous brothers who probably helped to explain her tomboy survival skills. All of her brothers had families of their own, which filled the little house to overflowing. The dining room table had so many added leaves that it extended out into the living room, covered from one end to the other with delicious food. Not all of the dinner plates matched, there were just too many of us, but we all sat at the big table. As my wife's brothers and sister-in-laws, nieces and nephews, and mother and father-in-law sat, prayed and enjoyed our dinner the snow swirled past the windows and the football game continued on two of the strategically located televisions. A trailer crawled across the bottom of the screen, continuously reminding people of the danger of holiday travel with the epic storm pressing down from the northwest.

The snow accumulated rapidly and snowfall of well over a foot was forecast. I began to have concerns about our ability to make the drive home, especially as the afternoon progressed. The office was scheduled to open at the seven the next morning and there were usually a few patients already waiting when the doors were unlocked. Already there were at least four or five inches on the ground in Rock Island, so I could not imagine how much must be falling to the north. I knew my pickup truck and I could handle just about any snowfall, but the idea of traveling with my infant son and wife was a major concern. In the end, we decided that I would leave as soon as possible and leave my wife and son with my in-laws. A decision that did not disappoint either of my in-laws. If all went well, my father-in-law would bring them home during the upcoming weekend.

As I got ready to go my mother-in-law bustled about in the kitchen filling a large thermos with coffee and packed a large shopping bag with turkey and ham sandwiches and slabs of pumpkin pie. Her concern for my safety was obvious and she mumbled it to herself over and over as she worked. When I told her that there was way more food in the bag than I could possibly eat, she reminded me that I was most likely going to spend the night stranded in a ditch somewhere. At least I would be able to survive until I froze to death. Although she was being dramatic, she made an excellent point and I accepted the food and thermos with gratitude.

With a quick kiss and hugs all around, I backed the truck out into the street and began the journey north. The snow was light and powdery but it did not relent. There was only minimal wind for which I was thankful because the snow was already deep enough to make driving difficult. The addition of drifting snow would have made the trip impossible. The truck plowed through the snow, blowing it out on either side and creating a rooster tail of kicked up snow behind.

The best route home from Rock Island was to cross the Mississippi into Iowa and take the highway north to Dubuque before crossing back into Illinois. Dubuque, Iowa, was the first leg of the trip and a little over seventy miles of curving winding roads. There was almost no traffic on the highway and I met very few oncoming cars. By the time I reached Dubuque, the snow was fast approaching six to eight inches and showed no sign of slowing any time soon.

My speed was less than thirty miles per hour. When I attempted to go any faster the rear end would break away as the lighter rear end of the empty truck bed lost contact with the roadway. It took a little more than two hours to make the first leg of the trip and during that time, darkness had fallen. Passing through the deserted streets of Dubuque, I soon came to the bridge crossing the Mississippi River and passed into the upper left-hand corner of Illinois and then crossed into Wisconsin.

Not surprisingly, the snow on the east side of the river was deeper. The majestic bluffs that lined the river were as much as seven hundred feet above the water and wind and weather rushing in from the western plains were deflected upward. The air warmer near the ground than above, created convection, which forced the clouds to release even more precipitation—snow in winter, rain in summer. The fourteen or so miles from Dubuque to Dickeyville, Wisconsin, took me half an hour.

Dickeyville is a tiny burg sitting alone in the foothills of the Mississippi bluffs, and although I had no reason to expect any activity, the streets were pristine with no evidence of cars to mar the smooth snow that covered the road and sparkled in the headlights of the truck. Even the lights in the tavern window were not lit. The town was dark and quiet on this Thanksgiving night. Without warning a set of police lights flashed in my rear-view mirror and a squad car pulled up behind me. I knew I wasn't speeding and I was sure I hadn't missed any stop signs, so I had no idea what this was all about.

I didn't know where the shoulder of the road was, and I couldn't be sure that there even was one. Since there was no evidence of other vehicles, I simply stopped in what must have been about the center of the road, or so I hoped. The police cruiser pulled up behind the truck and waited. We were the only ones on the road. Since I had been sitting in the truck for almost three hours, I got out and began to walk back to the squad. At the same time the cop got out and began to walk toward me. In a small town, citizens are not a threat to the police, and this small town was no different. We simply strolled up to each other and the policeman offered his hand to shake.

"Evening sir, pretty rough night to be out on the road. I hope you're not going too far."

"I'm heading for Tomah. Snow's getting pretty deep

alright. As long as the truck keeps rolling, I don't think I can get stuck."

"Yeah, well, about that. The reason I stopped you is because you've got a headlight out."

"What? Really?" I waded through the snow to the front of the truck and sure enough the driver's side headlight was not working. "Dammit."

"My brights seem to be still working but with the snow coming down so thick using the high beams makes the visibility worse, not better."

"Yeah, it's really not a very good idea to be driving at all much less with only one headlight. Listen, I'm not gonna write you a ticket, but I'll give you a warning. You have a grace period before it has to be fixed."

I thanked him and we went back to his car to write out the warning. Because there was nothing else to do, I stood outside of his door and we conversed while he filled out the form, just making small talk. After he finished, he got back out of the vehicle and explained the warning, showing me the specifics and how much time I had to fix the headlight. After that he just stood in the road next to me leaning back with his hand on his big Maglight flashlight on his utility belt. For a while we both watched the snow fall through the streetlight.

"Crappy night for you to have to pull duty being that it's a holiday and all."

"Well I'm new on the force so I get the holidays and the nights too. If you think nothing happens in this town during the day, you should spend some time here at night."

I told him about coming from Rock Island and remembered the grocery bag on the passenger seat and offered him a sandwich and a piece of pie. He gratefully accepted but declined my offer of coffee, saying that he had a thermos of his own.

The snow already deep didn't show any signs of

slowing down and progress on the lonely road was slow but steady. I drank coffee and ate pie and used the telephone poles along the side of the road to estimate where the center should be. Sixty miles and three hours later, I had not met another car as I crossed the Wisconsin River just east of where it empties into the Mississippi at Prairie Du Chien and again skirted the bluffs into the scenic Kickapoo Valley.

Within a mile of crossing the trestle bridge, flashing lights in my rearview mirror informed me that I had another visitor. This time I did not hesitate to step out of the truck and push through the snow to the state police car. As he stepped up out of the vehicle, I addressed him right away.

"Evening officer, I hope you're not stopping me about my headlight. I didn't know it was out before I left home tonight, but I already got stopped for it, and I already got a 'fix it' ticket."

"Nope, I didn't stop you for that at all. I was only wondering if maybe you had any more of those sandwiches left."

I smiled and gladly offered him one and a piece of pie, and we shared a little Thanksgiving spirit in the middle of nowhere in the beauty of Wisconsin. I guess you just can't outrun a police radio.

Today

snowing again

Pulling on my heavy coat, I take the last of my cold coffee and step outside onto the wrap around porch. The cold has deepened and the temperature dropped. The snow has started again in earnest. Fishing in the pocket of the coat, I pull out the crumpled pack of cigarettes and shake one out. Turning to the wall to avoid the breeze, I light it and take a long draw, pulling the smoke into my lungs. As I exhale, I feel the anxiety ebb away that my recent recollections have conjured.

In the end the cigarettes were not the cause; it was Uncle Sam. After all the adventures, travels, and risks taken, after all the danger and hazardous escapes, it had turned out that I was killed fifty years ago. Hearty and vital genetics has bought me more years than it should have, but Irish luck and the U.S. Government had finally accomplished what life could not.

The smokes are a new/old habit recently taken up again after many years of abstinence.

Surprisingly easy to enjoy after so many years, not even a guilty pleasure but rather a self-pitying indulgence. The smoke tastes good in the still quiet and ice-cold air of the winter morning and I lean back against the wall and feel the nicotine rush through my bloodstream and up my neck into my brain. With no wind the cold air lacks the bite of bitter winter and comfortably warm I experience a moment of bliss closing my eyes in the mild dizziness created by the cigarette smoke. I don't hurry the experience. Instead, I take it in, gazing out over the woods below the house and across the valley, acknowledging the beauty of the scenery, at peace with myself.

Once I've finished the cigarette, I push myself up off the woodpile. My knees have had just enough rest to protest weight bearing again, and I rock back and forth on my feet until the pain subsides enough to hazard taking a step. There won't be a warm shower today although I suppose I will need to get dressed at some point, but there is no hurry. There won't be any company today.

Uncle Seamus

"Take some deep breaths."

My Uncle Seamus stood behind me, pressing an ice-cold stethoscope against my back. I'd already taken enough deep breaths to be slightly dizzy. This was his second time around my chest. Apparently, what he was listening for was hard to hear, or he just liked playing with the stethoscope.

"How long have you been coughing?"

"I don't know. It's only recently that I've really started to notice. Maybe a few months?"

He wrapped the scope around his neck and walked back around his desk. Behind him, the bright summer sunshine streamed into the room, silhouetting him. This is another one of those rooms that you return to time and again over the course of your life. Familiar and foreign at the same time. My Uncle Seamus had been our family physician my entire life, and my family never considered going to a doctor right down our street when he was a mere three-hour drive away.

Without turning to look, I could describe every framed photograph on the wall behind me. Most of them in black and white, the men dressed for deer hunting, their wool plaid clothing made black and grey. It suddenly occurred to me to wonder who had taken the pictures, because everyone I knew was already in the photo.

Having never married and with no children of his own, his photos, faded now by the bright sunlight in the room, showed Kodachrome images of nieces and nephews. Mostly with Seamus standing next to them, a hand on a shoulder looking serious. It was not surprising how often Seamus had been tagged to be a Confirmation sponsor or Godfather at a baptism.

Sitting down, he lifted a pack of cigarettes out of one of the drawers, looked at them and then with a sigh dropped them back in again. Seamus had been quitting smoking for years, but had never quite gotten the job done. Instead, he tilted back in his chair and fiddled with his pen while he looked across at me with his doctor face.

"Anything else, shortness of breath? Do you get winded more than you might have in the

past?"

"Yeah, well maybe. I'm not as active as I used to be, and I've put on some weight."

"You've put on lot of weight Emmett."

"Well, I'm married, so I eat better than I used to."

"I don't think it's that kind of weight."

"What kind of weight do you think it is?"

"Your lungs are full of fluid. If I didn't know better, looking at your X-rays, I'd have said you had pneumonia—but I have a different thought."

I had expected that it was something different. I'd been ignoring the growing symptoms for longer than a couple of months, as the concern grew in my subconscious. The shortness of breath was the latest symptom. Any strenuous exercise caused my heart to pound in my ears, and my legs and feet had begun to itch and burn at night so badly that I could no longer sleep in my bed.

"Have you ever heard about Dioxin?"

"Uh-uh, no I don't think so."

"Agent Orange?"

"Oh yeah, who hasn't."

Agent Orange was a chemical defoliant that the U.S. government had sprayed over a large portion of Southeast Asia. The thinking being that it would kill crops and other vegetation and thereby reduce the available food and hiding places for the enemy during the Vietnam era. It was incredibly effective and the government had not been frugal in its use. The smell of it was only slightly more obnoxious than napalm.

"There is growing evidence that contact with Dioxin can cause a variety of sicknesses.

You've been healthy, hearty even, your whole life but the symptoms you're displaying shouldn't appear in anyone until they've reached a much more advanced age. You show evidence of pulmonary edema, your bloodwork appears to indicate that your heart is working too hard, and the problem with your leg's points to neuropathy. I would have a hard time explaining any other way for all of these to show up spontaneously in an otherwise healthy middle-aged man, unless I threw in some sort of outside vector of origin."

"I haven't heard anything about this."

"Well first of all dipshit, you're after all, not a real doctor." Uncle Seamus had never reconciled that I'd chosen a different form of health care than his acceptable norm. "Secondly, the government has refused to acknowledge any correlation between Dioxin and the number of suddenly sickened ex-GI's. So, I can't be sure, but everything I'm reading in the trade journals seems to indicate that they're related."

"Well shit, what does that mean for me?"

"I honestly don't know. The body of growing evidence points to dire consequences, but the research is lagging far behind the outbreak of symptoms."

"Is this something that could kill me?"

"Yes."

"Seriously?"

He met my eyes and nodded.

"So, you're saying that after all the shit I survived over there, I might have come home already dead but just didn't know it yet?"

"Not just you Emmett. There are thousands more like you that are showing up at clinics all over the country with the same symptoms."

"How long do you think I have?" I swallowed. "There's no way of knowing Emmett, I'm sorry."

There had been a growing sense of disquiet somewhere in the back of my mind for a while, as my inner being tried to warn me that something was wrong. Although what my Uncle Seamus was telling me was bad, somehow, I wasn't surprised by it.

"Seamus, I need you to keep this a secret. Please don't tell anyone."

"I wouldn't anyway Emmett, but I'm also not sure of the diagnosis."

"Well shit."

"In the meantime son, enjoy every day."

"That's exactly what I have to do."

Today

cold macaroni and cheese

The drive home from my office visit with Uncle Seamus was in an unconscious tunnel. I arrived home with no awareness of the turns or traffic lights I had negotiated as I contemplated the impact of our conversation. I had looked down the barrel of death many times in my life, each time with absolute certainty of death. At each of those junctures, the awareness of it had not fostered feelings of fear or the seeming unfairness of it. Rather it had brought sadness, and an acceptance that although a shame, it wasn't undeserved. This conversation with Seamus had been different.

The half-eaten bowl of congealed lunch was still in my lap. The spoon a solid mass of stiff cheese. I reached down and set it on the floor. The dogs would be delighted with it once they came in from outside. I had no interest in it anymore.

The fact that I would die and die slowly while my family watched brought elicited anger and fear. Dying was not an ultimate hardship for me. I had become accustomed to knowing I had lived on borrowed time after cheating it so many times. But now that I had turned my back on those ways, and had people in my life that I truly loved unconditionally, it seemed grossly unfair. I had spent the drive cursing karma for waiting so long to pay me back.

I was not angry about my condition, or the inevitability that it might bring. I was angry for the effect on those that must participate in it from the sidelines. The idea that my children would watch me die by inches, to waste away from the robust father figure into a shriveled and fragile fledgling in a hospital bed was such an abhorrent idea, that I had considered not going home, but just driving to the horizon. Almost believing that it might be better if I disappeared altogether instead of the alternative reality that I had discussed with Seamus.

By the time I pulled into our lane, I had resolved the issue. Although Grit needed to know, the children did not. The thought of it galvanized a reinforcement of the love I already felt for them and the preciousness of every event we would share from now on.

I loved my family and I loved what I did for a living. I would go on as before, and by god, I was going to have fun doing it. Even if it killed me.

George

Health care is essentially a people business. The sheer number of different personalities that you come in contact with daily requires you to modify your approach to each and every one. Over the years it would be impossible to estimate the number of patients who quit their personal physician and ended up in our office because they got sick of him or her 'talking down to them' and treating them as if the physician was 'God Almighty.'

Empathy is not specifically a part of any curriculum in any institution of 'higher learning.' You either have it or you don't, and whether or not you have it determines your effectiveness as a health care provider assuming that your skill level is on a par with the rest of the profession. When I was in school to become a doctor, I met many who were anxious to become part of the profession because they wanted to make a difference and help others achieve a greater experience of health. I also met a similar number who spent most of their time fantasizing about the income that the profession would make available to them, and which sub-specialty would be the most lucrative. I could never understand that thinking.

Someone once told me that if a person tells you that 'It's not about the money,' then you can be sure that it is *all* about the money. As such, these latter individuals do not spend a lot of time working on their 'bedside manner' because in their words—they don't have to.

Because patients come in all shapes, sizes, and states of mind and health, some would try the patience of a saint, while others try their hardest to make every visit as pleasant as possible. Their visits are much anticipated and a delight when they arise.

One of these most pleasant patients was Dorothy Prentice. She was well informed, well read, and anxious to do whatever was necessary to help herself stay healthy and active. Dorothy walked to most places she visited in town or rode her single-speed bicycle. She ate healthy foods, and home-cooked all of her meals. Most of all, she was socially active. She went on tours, traveled, volunteered, and sang in her church choir. In short, she was someone you'd like to get to know. Dorothy was a robust seventy-five-year-old.

I had been treating Dorothy for about six months when she arrived one day and appeared not to be her usual effervescent self. She was distracted, and I had to ask her a few questions twice before she understood the question. Elderly people will often show sudden signs of confusion or disorientation, which can be a signal of a silent stroke, or acute dehydration, so I was a bit alarmed. As I began to assess her for either of the two issues, she suddenly came out of her funk and perked up.

"Doctor Casey, I have a problem and maybe you can help me."

I was just glad to see something of the old Dorothy again, "Sure Dorothy, shoot."

"It's George, he's not doing very well and he's got me worried sick."

I knew that her husband George had suffered a crippling stroke almost a year previously.

He had apparently lost the ability to use his left side,

including hand, arm and leg. As such, he had been restricted to a wheelchair and Dorothy was his primary source of care. She rarely spoke of him and I had assumed that his condition was stable, but unimproved, so I had not brought it up in conversation.

"Has he had another episode?"

"No, nothing has changed on that front. He's just giving up. He doesn't want to watch TV, or look at the birds out the window. He even made me put away all his fly-fishing equipment, and that's the worst thing."

"How long has this been going on?"

"It's been coming on for a while, but now I can't seem to cheer him up anymore."

Chronic depression in a chronically ill patient is not uncommon, but it can often lead to worsening of other symptoms as the individual pulls away from life. It is one of the primary causes that leads to a condition known as dementia.

"I was wondering if there is anything you can do. Is there some kind of treatment that you do that can help him snap out of it? You know…maybe crack his neck or something?"

"Dorothy! We don't crack people's necks, shame on you."

"I know, I'm really concerned about him. He's not eating either."

"I don't have anything in my bag of tricks for those kinds of issues Dorothy. It's really a thing for his primary care physician."

"I took him to see Dr. Connors last week."

"What did he say about it?"

"He said that George was seventy-four years old and that that is what seventy-four-year- old men do."

"Really? Not those words I hope."

"Those words exactly, and he said them to George,

which made him feel worse, not better."

"I bet."

"I took all the guns in the house to my sister's. He hasn't noticed yet, but when he does— oh boy!"

"Do you think he'd shoot himself?"

"Not really but I don't want it to be an option. I don't know how we'd get him into the office. He's devilishly hard to get into the car, but if you think you might help him, I'll make him come in."

I was pretty sure that there were not very many things that Dorothy couldn't make George do. Or anyone else for that matter. She was a force to be reckoned with.

"Alright Dorothy, but how about if I come out to the house and see George out there instead."

I swear she positively started to vibrate in her seat.

"You would come to our house and see him!?! That's beyond anything I'd expected, oh thank you Doctor Casey. When?"

"How about my lunch hour, today? Would that be okay?"

"I'll make a little lunch! Oh, that's really special, oh goodness, that would be great."

"Alrighty, afternoon then."

When I arrived at the Prentice home, I couldn't help but notice; the yard was immaculate, all flower beds, weed free, bird feeders everywhere and all full. I had no doubt that Dorothy did all the yard work. I would have been stunned if anything else was true.

As soon as my foot hit the ground, the front door popped open and Dorothy bustled out and across the yard. Taking my bag from me, she apologized for the state of the yard and how messy the house was and the skimpiness of the lunch fixings, but there had been no time to do anything properly. If the front yard was any indication of what the rest was going to be like, I was in for an excellent lunch.

Inside the house was filled with sunlight and plants. George sat stooped over near the far corner in his wheelchair and I immediately crossed the room to shake his hand, which he returned, although without much of a grip.

"Thanks for coming to lunch. Probably be pretty good since we have company."

"It's nice to finally meet you George. Dorothy talks about you non-stop."

"Oh, that's not true Doctor Casey," Dorothy simpered, "I talk about other things too."

"That's my girl, talks non-stop for sure, everything interests her. One of these days, all that stuff is gonna start drippin' out of her ears."

"Oh George, you say the sweetest things." She reached out and touched him on the shoulder.

"That's because I married the sweetest girl." He smiled up at her from under his eyebrows.

Dorothy sniffed and looked at the other end of the room.

"Well I'll get started on lunch, you two can get to know each other a little better while I'm gone."

And she disappeared down the narrow hallway. Shortly the sound of cabinet doors closing and dishes clattering drifted back to us.

"So, you're the quack she's been seein' in town. You doin' her any good?"

"She seems much better than when I first met her. She says her headaches have almost stopped."

"Said the same to me. Guess something helped her, maybe was you." He raised his eyebrows in my direction, "maybe not."

"That's true enough, I'd like to think I helped her, but mostly I'm just glad she's better."

"I like that. So? What've you got for me?"

"I don't know, maybe nothing. Can I ask you a few

questions?"

There followed a short Q&A in which he answered in a disinterested fashion and not looking beyond the floor two feet in front of him. Once I got my stethoscope and blood pressure cuff out, he started to withdraw even farther away. I had hoped we might find some common ground somewhere so he would engage, but I wasn't getting any traction.

While I was listening to his chest, I glanced out the window and saw it was clouding up.

"Well damn, it's gonna rain. I was hoping to get some fishing in on the way home, but I'm wearing my good shoes."

"You like to fish Casey?"

"I love to fish, like fish love to swim."

"I'm not much for pond fishin.' But I like fishin' trout well enough."

"I've got a fly rod; I use it with dry flies and fish for bluegills. It's a riot."

"I bet they feel like they weigh ten pounds on a fly rod."

"Ten pounds and fight like a bear with a cactus up his ass."

"Well shit, if I had a cactus up my ass, the last thing I'd want to be doin' is fightin.' But that's a pretty funny picture." And he smiled.

"Lunch is ready."

Dorothy stood in the hallway and winked.

While we ate with our plates on our knees, George told stories about monster trout and secret fishing holes. He moved his one arm for emphasis, even though his left forearm and hand were trapped in permanent spastic rigor from his stroke. The difference in his disposition before and after we started talking about fishing was amazing. And it gave me an idea.

"George I'll make you a deal."

"I don't make deals with just anybody."

"No, I think you'll like this one."

"Alright, I'll listen, but no deal just yet."

"Fair enough…here's the deal. You let me work with you for a while. I'll come to your house, at least once a week, and I'll work with your hand, arm and your leg. If you are willing to work hard while I'm not here, and you start to improve, then I'll take you to your favorite fishing hole myself, and I'll just see what kind of fisherman you are. Deal?"

"And what if this cockamamie thing that you do doesn't work?"

"Well then you're no worse off than you were before, and I don't get to learn anything about trout fishing."

"Not promising anything but you've been straight up with me, so okay, what are you gonna do."

I'll show you.

Over the next six months I saw George in his home every Tuesday and Thursday. In between Dorothy made sure he did his homework. He grumbled and groused with every new movement, every stretching routine and every new exercise—but he did them. At first there was nothing, then after about eight weeks, he was able to move his thumb, and flex his foot up and down slightly. At four months, he could hold an empty coffee cup. At the end of six months, the day had arrived and we were ready for the big reveal.

"Okay Dorothy, before you go to get things ready for lunch, George wants to show you something."

"George…?"

"Just hold your water. This is Casey's idea, not mine."

I stood behind his chair and he twisted around and looked up at me. I gave him a nod, which he returned. Turning back toward Dorothy, he set his hands down on his knees and with trembling forearms and legs—rose to his feet on his own.

"Oh my goodness, George! Oh George, I'm so happy! I'm so proud of you! What's next?"

"Next? Well now Casey has to take me fishing."

I had worked out an idea of how I wanted to get George to his fishing spot after I did some reconnoitering myself. There was a place that I could back my truck down almost to the water's edge of the trout stream and fairly close to what he had told me was a good spot. It was a game trail crossing and the truck wouldn't have any trouble getting us back out when we needed to go.

On the big day, Dorothy bundled George up in plenty of clothes and wrapped him in a huge quilt. I had borrowed some portable ramps from a neighbor and we rolled his chair, with George in it up into the back of the truck where I secured it and George. Dorothy insisted on riding in the back with him and had brought her own quilt to ward off the chilly spring air. We packed his fly rod and he carried a small leatherette case of 'flies' that he'd personally tied and wore his fishing vest and hat. He had a smile as wide as the Lemonweir River. Trout season had only opened the previous week and George had the fever.

My plan was to set George up in the back of the truck in his chair. Once in that position, I could back down to the stream bank and the chair could rest up against the tailgate. That would afford plenty of room for the fly rod to whip the line out in the typical back and forth action necessary to feed out the tiny 'fly' on the end of the line. I had brought a safety step ladder, and Dorothy had packed snacks. The mood was festive.

Everything went exactly according to plan—until it didn't.

Getting George situated in the back of the truck,

although an effort, went well. The truck was close enough to the river that you could spit into it from the back of the truck. Even with the bed of the truck tipped at an angle on the river's edge, the wheelchair was completely stable once it rested against the tailgate. I stationed myself on the ground near the rear end of the truck and Dorothy stood at George's side ready to hand him anything he might need.

"Any time you're ready George."

"This cold air is making me need to take a leak."

Dorothy gave me a look but spoke to George. "Honey, didn't you wear your special underwear?"

"No dammit! I'm fishing for Christ's sake. Nobody puts on a damn diaper to go fishing."

"Well try and hold it, we won't stay long if you're cold."

"Dot! I gotta go!"

"Hold on George." I climbed up the side of the truck. "We'll stand you up and you can just pee over the side. Nobody will see you."

George's head swiveled in a complete one-eighty, there was no one but us as far as we could see. "Well I gotta go, so give me a hand."

"Here George." Once the plan of action had been decided Dorothy immediately switched into her 'take charge' mode. "Doc you help him up and hold him. I'll get him out of some of these blankets and clothes. We'll get this taken care of in no time Sweetie."

Helping George into a standing position in the tilted truck bed was no small feat. With a quilt draped across the tailgate, I got his knees braced against it and Dorothy reached around to open his trousers.

"I can't take a decent piss with you standing there holding on to me and her holding on to my Johnson."

"Just give it a sec George, try to relax."

"Yes George, try to give it a little grunt. I don't mind

holding onto your little soldier." George gave a grunt and a push with his pelvis.

"Geez-oh-Friday! I think I just shit myself a little!"

"Careful George, just go. We'll sort it out in a minute."

With that George let out with a prodigious stream of urine. The first burst caught Dorothy by surprise and hosed her hand and arm. She flinched and lost her grip on the now wet penis.

"Oh my God, I'm sorry Dorothy."

Urine was now blasting into the tailgate, the quilt and George's shoes. Reflexively he tried to back away from it but the wheelchair behind him tripped him up and he tipped backward urinating in an arc. Because of the wet footing, he dragged me with him. The wheelchair slid out of the way and he fell onto Dorothy with me landing next to him and still producing a fountain of pee up into the cool spring air, dousing all three of us. The sheer volume of his bladder capacity was truly impressive.

"Oh my God!"

"Geezus George." I couldn't help myself.

When he finally finished, there was a long silent pause as we laid in the fragrant wetness. Dorothy, pinned underneath started to chuckle. At first, I didn't understand and then I got it. The situation, if viewed from a distance, was hilarious. I began to laugh too. George embarrassed and soaking wet blustered and fumed but by then Dorothy and I were in gales of laughter. He couldn't help it; he started to laugh as well.

There was no sense taking it the wrong way. George had gotten to go fishing, sort of, and we all had had an experience that none of us would forget. It was also an experience that I would not have had if I restricted my practice to office hours only.

Newspaper Casts and Trouble

The young Amish boy lay between us on the hospital gurney, his face white with pain and stress. Whenever we touched him, he flinched, so I had stationed myself with one hand gently pressing down on his chest while Dr. Castle worked on his left arm.

"This is very clever, where did you learn how to do this?" Dr. Castle was one of the orthopedic surgeons on staff at the hospital in LaCrosse. I had never seen her when she wasn't busy rushing from one place to the next, but for that she was always fastidiously polite. She was somewhere north of forty, rail thin with glasses so thick that her eyes appeared two sizes larger than normal. Tonight, she was nattily dressed in a skirt and silk blouse under her clinic coat, her hair and makeup made it clear that she had someplace else to be. She was busy carefully removing the makeshift splint I had put on the boy's left arm.

"Army. Field dressing."

"They have a lot of newspapers on the battlefront?" She cocked an eyebrow and gave me a small smile. "Wet newspaper, very clever, but a little too tight I'm afraid. See how his hand is swelling?"

"I figured it would probably work. It wasn't tight when I first put it on. I was worried when they told me he couldn't move his fingers."

We were talking quietly while she worked in the Emergency Room bay. Our arrival had been at the end of a long journey to get here and the boy was exhausted, and I wasn't far behind him.

Occasionally, when I was called out to an Amish home I would be presented with a condition or trauma that far exceeded my skills. Although it would have been easy to back away and suggest that they go to a hospital, it was not in my nature to do so. At those times, I became the ambulance driver and transported them to the hospital or doctor's offices myself knowing that any further delay in care could worsen the consequences.

There were times when that just meant a mere fifteen to twenty-mile drive back into town, and there were times when it meant a fifty or sixty-mile drive to LaCrosse. Without an available telephone handy, I often had to make the decision as to which one we needed to head for. Tonight, had been one of the long trips.

The wet newspaper splint removed, Dr. Castle took one quick look and bit her lower lip.

"Both the bones in the forearm are fractured, the swelling and bleeding between them has caused a compartment syndrome. We're going to have to open the arm surgically to decompress it hopefully to keep it from causing permanent nerve damage."

"Dammit, I'm sorry Helen."

Amish children learn to speak and write in English once they start school. Until then, they speak in their "Pennsylvania Dutch' dialect. I glanced down at the boy; he didn't show any signs of understanding our conversation so I continued. I'd have to have one of the parents explain what the next step in care would be.

"It's not anything you did Emmett. It probably would have happened anyway. Your splint actually was a good idea; it kept it from being worse than it already is. They must have waited awhile before they called you."

I didn't bother to tell her that it wasn't because they had waited, it was because of how long it took for them to get in touch with me. It required them first assessing the injury, discussing the best course and finally they would have to hike, or ride, to the nearest farm with a telephone. Once I got the call, assuming that I could come immediately, it had taken a forty-five- minute drive to get to them.

After that there was the improvised casting and loading him and his parents all into the front seat of the pickup truck without further injury and the long drive to LaCrosse. There was simply no other way to shorten the time.

"You know, every time I hear that you're in the E.R. Emmett, I know that it's going to be a long night."

"Sorry Helen."

"It's okay I guess, except that it's my daughter's birthday. I wanted to be there to see her blow out the candles."

"Sorry Helen."

"Stop saying that you're sorry. I've got a suitable punishment for you in mind."

"Seriously?"

"Yep, as soon as possible you're going to start spending at least one day a week in the department. We're going to stretch your learning curve for a while. Okay? As soon as possible." She gave me a smile. "It's a perk Emmett, not a shit-sandwich, stop making that face.

She turned to the nurse who had been standing at the head of the gurney.

"Start a drip, Clindomyocin 15milligrams and morphine point one. Have the Norcan ready as well. I'll get the O.R. ready, we'll prep right away. Come along Dr. Casey, your night is about to get interesting."

The Return of Jackpine

It was the end of another busy day at the clinic. The patient flow had been steady and well managed by the staff. When I had ventured out to the front desk, the waiting room was filled with friendly conversation and laughter. My staff was incredibly efficient at balancing the many trying duties of patient management. I often reminded myself that for every one person I dealt with, my staff had to deal with them twice. Once when they checked in and again on the way out when they made follow-up appointments or paid their balances. On busy days when we were blessed with a full schedule and several walk-in patients, the phone seemed to ring non- stop and yet the ladies never seemed flustered or communicated anything but a serene disposition to the patients, or so it seemed to me.

There was very little that ever threw them, but there was one thing that did it every time.

Jack 'Jack Pine' Pinter. Over the years Jack and I had developed something that could not be classified as a relationship but was more of an understanding of each other. Jack never failed to show his gratitude for his care, not just by squaring his office fees, but in other more colloquial ways as well. Every Christmas season, Jack would barge his way into the office bundled against winter with his hat pulled down to his eyebrows and great leather 'chopper' mittens, and thump a half gallon 'growler' jug of the latest rendering from his still on the counter turn and march back across the waiting room. Then with his hand on the doorknob, he would turn and announce, unnecessarily, and with a solemn baritone voice while making eye contact with each individual in the waiting, leaving no doubt of his unspoken respect.

"That's for the doc."

And with that he would be gone. At other times Jackpine would show up quietly and land a large butcher wrapped bundle on the counter. The bundle would prove to contain fresh venison steaks, or ribs, or roasts. These would arrive unfrozen and obviously freshly prepared and invariably out of season. I once asked Jackpine, in as roundabout way as I could, if he'd shot the deer out of season. His reply had been.

"Jeez Doc, everybody knows that venison tastes best in any month with an R in it. And that includes Argust."

I had left the subject alone after that.

The staff had specific instructions for whenever Jackpine showed up as a patient, for which he never called ahead. (Indeed, I suspect that he never had a telephone.) In that event, he was to be taken back to a treatment room immediately. Jackpine had a negative effect on the disposition of other people in the waiting room, often elevating their blood pressure and heart rates and producing sweaty palms. Once his handgun was checked in at the front counter and he was in a room, staff would come and notify me, no matter how busy I was. Seeing Jackpine as soon as possible was in all of our best interests. His fits of temper were legend throughout the county, and he was known to make a scene with as little as what he perceived as a negative glance. Although I had never witnessed one of these events, the very thought of an angry Jackpine Pinter carrying a handgun on his hip was plenty enough to send chills up and down my spine.

It was one such day when a pale faced Viki from the front desk knocked on the door to the room that I was presently working in. Opening it a crack, in a voice barely above a whisper, she announced, "Jack Pinter is in Room Three." Then she was gone, only to return in a tick, "And Geri is with him."

I quickly wrapped up what I was doing and headed for Room Three. Jackpine in the office was one thing, but if his wife Geri was with him it could only mean that it was serious. Upon entering the room, I gave a cheerful greeting and was met with a sullen Jackpine, and an obviously angry Geri Pinter. Seated next to each other beside the small desk they looked the epitome of Jack Spratt and his wife who could eat no lean. Jackpine never raised his eyes from my shoes and Geri looked like she was ready to chew glass. Which, if she had, I would not have been surprised in the least.

Jack couldn't have tipped the scale at more than one-hundred seventy pounds, give or take a few. Geri was a few inches taller than Jack and outweighed him by almost a hundred pounds, and a lot of that extra poundage was muscle. Together they were a formidable challenge. Trying to maintain my cheerful appearance, although I was uncomfortable with the situation and maybe a little fearful of the two of them together in such a small space, I spoke up.

"Well Jack, what brings you in today?"

"Ask *her!*" With heavy emphasis on the her.

"Well Geri, what's up? Something going on with you?"

"Naw Doc, it's him. Go on, tell him." She emphasized her direction to Jack with a solid poke to his ribs with her left elbow.

"Who you pokin'? Don't do that again dammit." With that he delivered a counter poke with his right elbow.

"Don't poke me you skinny fucker!" This was delivered with a solid right-hand fist to Jack's right shoulder.

With that Jack was on his feet in a flash and with a howl he delivered a solid right to Geri's left cheekbone. The smack of fist on flesh is a sound you only have to hear once. The resulting boom of the back of her head slamming into the wall behind her would have knocked out a lesser woman. Geri exploded out of the chair and with a left-hand upper cut caught Jack right in the stomach. With a whoof, Jack countered and they stood toe to toe trading solid lefts and rights, waltzing around the room, knocking things off the desk, making an incredible racket of profanity and body blows. I quickly opened the door and spoke to the wide-eyed Viki in the hallway.

"Call 911."

I closed the door and decided it was now or never. I was not foolish enough to step between them so as loudly as I could I shouted, "That's enough! You two knock it off and sit down!"

Surprisingly, they stopped immediately and looking a little sheepish returned to their seats. Geri's left eye was already puffy and she was going to have one heck of a black eye. Jack was huffing out of breath, slightly bent over from all of the body blows that Geri had landed. I realized that it spoke to the depth of her affection for him that she had not once hit him in his already seriously damaged skull. I took the time to pick up the collateral damage scattered around the office and rearrange the desk. I retrieved a small disposable icepack from the freezer in the room and handed it to Geri for her eye. As my own breathing and blood pressure returned to normal, I tried again.

"Now Jack, what can I do for you?"

Jack was still trying to catch his breath so talking was going to be difficult. With a wave of his hand he indicated to Geri that she should fill me in on the current situation.

"Well Jack was working on the ladder at home. He was fixing the tin sheeting on the eave of the roof, and the ladder flipped over. I told him that he needed to go to the emergency room at the hospital, but he won't go. He said he'd come here and if you said he needed to go, then he would."

I turned to Jack, "Well Jack, what's up?"

Until now Jack had managed to keep his hat on. This was due in large part to the fact that he kept it jammed so tightly on his head and over his eyebrows in order to hide the missing portions of his skull that it was hard to get off without effort. He reached up and pulled the cap up and off. With the hat gone, most of the right side and top of his scalp slid forward and down over his eyes, hanging like a loose tarpaulin blown by the wind. He used his left hand to push it back up and replaced his hat, looking a question at me.

"I banged my head on the steel roof edge."

If you work long enough in the health care field you get used to seeing things that are truly unnerving. This was one of them. Jack had managed to scalp himself over the same area as his missing skull section. As in all cases where you are supposed to be the 'adult' in the room, you have to act like you've seen it before, dealt with it before and were unfazed by it all. I took a moment to relax my voice and then deadpanned,

"Yep, you need to go the ER Jack. Sooner the better or that skin's going to dry out and you won't be able to get it back together."

"Well okay then Doc."

With that they both rose, and without another word, walked out of the room, down the hall, and out of the office.

I looked at Viki still white-faced standing at the opposite end of the hall. Spreading my hands in a manual shoulder shrug, I just laughed. What a world.

The stressful energy created by the arrival and subsequent departure of the Pinter's slowly abated as both mine and the staff's blood pressures and heart rates returned to normal. Once the excited conversation and general decompression had taken place, we went about the routine of finishing the office day and the preparation necessary for the next day's business. One by one the staff finished their assigned duties and shrugged into their coats, bid good night and left the office.

As I began my last walk-through, turning off lights and the last of the various therapy devices, the phone at the front desk rang. After a long day I was almost reluctant to answer it but also knew that I must. With resignation, I picked up the receiver and answered with as much enthusiasm as I could muster in my voice.

"Good evening and thank you for calling. This is Doctor Casey. May I help you?"

"I'm counting on it." The voice on the other end of the line was gruff, tense, and unidentifiable.

"Excuse me, umm, who am I speaking with?"

"Don't act like you don't know who this is, asshole. This is Tom."

Tom Dunbar to be exact. Tom was one of the first people that I had met professionally when I arrived in town. He was gruff, short-tempered, incredibly competent and probably my best friend. Tom had been a medic in Vietnam and had been shot down in a helicopter while he was evacuating wounded soldiers during a firefight. As a result, Tom had suffered multiple spinal and leg injuries that left him permanently disabled. He walked with the assistance of two canes while he was in the clinic. He lived in almost constant pain from the compression injuries to his spine. I could never be sure if it was this pain and disability that made Tom unusually rough around the edges or if that was just his way. Tom had taken his battlefield skills, and with his disability, bartered it into a hard-won education, and was now a physician's assistant. One of the best health care providers that I would ever meet.

His rough exterior only served to hide his heart of gold and softer than warm caramel interior, which he guarded diligently. Men were usually afraid of Tom, children adored him, and women wanted to hold him to their bosom. As a result, he was in great demand both at the local clinic and during his rounds at the small fourteen-bed hospital emergency room in town. In spite of his infirmities, Tom kept a busy, exhausting schedule. Occasionally, if he could, he accompanied me on house calls. His voice was anything but friendly this evening.

"What is the matter with you, I swear to God Casey, you sumbitch. What did I ever do to you?"

"I honest to God don't know what you're talking about Tom. What'd I do this time?"

"I hope to fuckin' hell, that all chiro-fucking-practors are not as goddamn dumb as you are Emmett." Even with all of that education under his belt, Tom has managed to not only maintain a healthy military vocabulary but also honed it to a fine point. "You have got exactly ten minutes to get your sorry ass the fuck down here or I'm coming to get you myself."

"What? Honestly Tom, what'd I do? What's going on?"

"Ten minutes." Click went the other end of the line.

With a final sweep of the area, I shut off the lights, locked the door, and reluctantly hurried out to my truck in the parking lot. Tom was not much of a social creature and was a firm believer that you could never have too few friends, so he usually reserved his rough and mean voice for people who didn't know him. That way he never had to worry about making a new friend and having to be nice to yet another person. He and I had developed something of a loose and easy friendship, and so for him to be angry with me, it must be something that was probably going to require a lot of apologizing on my part. Although he had given me ten minutes to get to the hospital—I was in no hurry to face him just the same.

I pulled into the parking lot and drove around to the emergency room entrance. Indulging in one of my secret guilty pleasures, I parked in one of the spaces marked Doctors Only. The old and venerated physician, Dr. Langston, had finally retired a few years back to a well-deserved rest. I never parked there that I didn't think about him. My presence in this space alone would have been enough to finally push him into a massive stroke. Thankfully, he no longer lived in the area, having deserted the six-month winters for warmer climes. The thought always made me smile to myself. With that tiny satisfaction, I sighed and girded myself up for whatever was waiting for me beyond the double sliding doors of the emergency room entrance.

Once inside, it didn't take long to find out. As soon as I cleared the second of the two double doors, I could hear the ruckus. The all too familiar gravelly voice of Jack Pinter was raised to a shout, and accompanied by a background of rattling equipment. Rounding the corner, I was met with a sight I had never seen before in the ER. The two nurses and Tom Dunbar all were seated in the nurses' alcove. The nurses, eyes wide and faces pale, had their eyes fixed on the spectacle in front of them. Tom, on the other hand, his bad leg propped up on another chair was sitting with his chair rolled back from the desk. Arms folded on his chest and chin down, eyes closed. To the casual observer, he would have appeared to be taking a nap. I knew better though, his time in the army had taught Tom how to wait.

As I approached the desk, Tom immediately roused, and smiled an evil smile at me and to no one in particular announced, "Well okay, Doctor Casey is here, we can get started. Doctor Casey, we are going to need you to scrub." With a wave of his hand toward the wash station on the opposite wall, he grabbed his hand crutch and heaved himself up off of the chair and started for it himself. Once we were side by side he muttered under his breath, "Don't know why you hate me so much. What did I ever do to you, asshole?"

"What's up with Jack?"

"He says that he won't let me shave his head, doesn't want me to be messing around with it. He thinks if we do anything, he'll start getting his headaches again." He paused mid-scrub to glance back over his shoulder then leaned in closer. "Can't say I blame him about that, but he's got himself wound up to a high rev and the missus can't seem to calm him down. Whatever magic you do to these people, and for the life of me I don't know why, but he trusts you. So, you're going to help me wrestle him to the mat."

"What? I'm not going to do anything that will piss Jackpine off. He'll kill us all."

"You should have thought of that before you sent him over here. I can't use general anesthesia on him because he's on every kind of medication known to man, so I can't be sure he'd ever come out of it. We're going to have to use a local, and it's going to take four hands to get this job done, so tag, you're it."

"Gee, thanks Tom. What about Geri, she's big enough to hold him down?"

"No can-do dipshit. She said that if we kill him, she'll need an alibi, so she took off."

"Nice."

"Well she did take his gun with her, so that's one thing in her favor. We'd probably be doing her a favor if we killed him, but there it is. Besides, this is a procedure that you should learn so you can put it in your bag of tricks. Especially because then you won't send this shit in here to me."

Washed and gloved, Tom pulled back the curtain to the treatment bay and we approached a very agitated Jack Pinter. His head wound had seeped enough blood that most of the right side of his face was painted with rivulets of red and brown. With his half-flattened skull and raised skin flap of scalp, he presented a truly gruesome figure as he paced the small space rearranging everything in sight. As soon as the curtain was retracted, he turned his angry face toward us, ready to take up his previous argument. When he saw me, his eyes widened for a brief moment and then relaxed.

"Goddammit Doc, you sent me over here to get this thing fixed and they don't even have a doctor on duty. This little weasel says he can do it, but I ain't trusting some glorified nurse no how."

"Take it easy Jack, this isn't a glorified nurse. He's a corpsman, so he's better than a doctor."

"Corpsman? No shit?" Turning to Tom, "Army or Marines?"

"Army."

"Army? Shit then you can't be that good. I was Marines, Mekong Delta. You see any action?" Then he looked at Tom again in this new light and noted the crutch and his crooked posture. "No way, you were in the Army, walking like that."

"Central Highlands, just like the Doc here. I didn't always look like this. Had a little accident, got stove up."

"Well, bet you ain't seen nothing like this." Pointed to his head.

"Listen candy ass, I've seen worse than you before

breakfast. Now can we fix this and let me go back to my nap?"

Looking back to me, "Shit Doc, this guy's alright. Shoulda told me he was a medic." Without any more hesitation, Jack hoisted himself back on the gurney and laid down on the pillow.

Turning the gurney around so that Jack's head faced out, we adjusted the height of the head portion to arm level and Tom called in the nurse and said to me, "We can't shave the skin flap, it's a little too loose and too big, and he's not going to sit still while we do it. We can't risk too much pressure on the tissue underneath either so I'm going to teach you a little trick. That way I won't have to have your sorry ass in here any more than I have to." I couldn't see Tom's face behind the surgical mask, but the roughness had gone out of his voice, he was all business now.

With the stainless-steel table rolled up close, the nurse, armed with a bottle of saline braced herself with hands that only shook slightly. Tom brandishing a small hypodermic syringe, began injecting the area with a local anesthetic of one percent Lidacain and Epinephrin. Working carefully, he covered the area from front to back and while he worked and waited for it to take full effect, he tried to engage Jackpine in small talk.

"So? I guess you live pretty close to the reservation. Do you have much contact with the Injuns?"

"Nope, they don't have nothin' to do with me. But I hear they taste like chicken."

That exhausted the conversation possibilities. With a nod from Tom, the nurse began to rinse and hydrate the area. We didn't bother trying to clean up his face but instead, once we were sure the areas were numb, very gently with cotton gauze and forceps, cleaned the accumulated blood and sera that had begun to crust the edges of the cut. Once that was done, a sterile drape was placed over the entire head with a hole that exposed the work site. The flap was replaced in the approximate position where it belonged and it was rinsed again. Tom took a small tube from the tray and holding it up for me to see said, "Normally we'd staple this wound shut, but I really don't want this guy to come back in to have them removed so this is my secret weapon. I found out about this stuff from another medic at a triage station. It's like Loctite that they use in industry but this one is made for medical purposes, once you mix the two compounds together it sets up in less than a minute. We'll start at the front, you pull and hold the two sides together about a half an inch at a time, and I'll glue it in place. If there's a wrinkle or space, it'll wind up at the back."

From under the drape Jack piped up at that point, "Hey, you know I can hear you two. I don't want any wrinkles in the top of my head."

"Don't worry Jack, more than likely we'll kill you before that happens." Tom's sense of humor left something to be desired.

I recoiled ready for Jack to rocket off the table after that remark.

Instead, "God, if that were only true. Doc, I'm starting to like this guy."

Over the next hour, while I pulled the loose flap of skin tight and held it together, Tom would place a tiny drop of the clear, intensely smelly glue on the tear. Each time we would wait the necessary minute and a half to make sure that it had hardened before we moved on. It was a constant challenge for the nurse to keep the area dry enough for the glue to bond with the skin, so the three of us worked in close quarters and the hour seemed like ten. Once we had the entire area in place and secured, Tom went back and ran a long bead of the glue from front to back, effectively sealing the wound from outside contamination.

"The Loctite will fall off on its own in about five days, by that time the skin will have pretty much healed together unless dumbass here does something else to it."

"I can still hear you."

Today

a smile and a chuckle

It was proving to be a good day. I smiled at the memories. Tucking the afghan blanket around my feet and legs, I took a drink of the melted snow that I had scooped from the bucket near the fire.

I smiled at the thought of how many 'extra' years I had gotten. Years of crazy patients and wonderful kids. Sometimes they were both of them at the same time. The experiences were deepened by my secret realization that each one should be cherished because each one had been stolen.

Sometimes the ones that could have been the most tragic had also been the most fraught with substance, and deepened my understanding of the wisdom with which karma dealt out its fate.

Measles

As the Wisconsin winter deepened into February, Groundhog Day often ushered in a brief warm spell. Sometimes the temperature would rise all the way into the high 30's. The brief respite could be as short as a day or two, but sometimes almost a week. When that happened, the fisherman rushed out onto the ice to bask in the low winter sun and catch buckets of panfish. No matter how long the spell would last, everyone was reprieved from the often joy crushing cold that would follow again.

The sudden rise in the outside temperatures however also gave rise to multiple respiratory conditions. February is the prime month for colds and flu's; nuisance illnesses that primarily sap our nation's GNP, but there are worse things that follow in the footsteps of these conditions.

Opportunistic diseases that prey on the weakened immune systems of those already sick with something else. Our society today takes most of these conditions seriously and should perhaps, but in our hurry for a quick remedy we have unwittingly created strains of bacteria and virus that no longer follow the old rules. These strains are learning how to develop immunity to the usual antibiotic and vaccine. When these two worlds collide, the subsequent maladies that they bring are truly frightening and the consequences dire.

The usual cases of colds, flu's and winter injuries kept us busy throughout the month of January and February promised more of the same. The office hour schedule in winter was abbreviated so we could accommodate the rise in our house call schedule made necessary when the hard winter weather made travel difficult. So it was no imposition when I answered a phone call and discovered an anxious Tom Dunbar on the other end. I was always grateful when Tom called me, his competence and level of empathy were only matched by his character, and I greeted him with a smile on my face.

"Emmett would you walk over here. I think you need to see this."

Not can I walk over…would you. I left immediately and made my way over to the medical side of the building. Grabbing a lab coat off of the hook inside the door I hurried down the hall to Tom's corner suite of examining rooms where Tom met me in the hallway with a chart in his hand.

"Hey Emmett, look, I've got an Amish family in here, the husband, wife, and two kids. I think we've got a problem and I need to know if you've seen any of this up on the ridge."

Well whatever Tom was talking about, he had my full attention, and I was immediately wishing that Tom would make a wider scope of friends to share news with.

"I want you to gown up before we go in there, and I want you to look at the kids before I share anything. The throat culture and blood tests will help but the lab's been slow."

After gowning, gloving and masking, I entered the room with Tom right behind. I knew the family right away so pulled down my mask and offered both parents a handshake. Then inquired of the parents, what had brought them into town today. After a look at Tom over my shoulder, the husband related that the two boys had complained of sore throats for a few days and became hoarse, yesterday they spiked high fevers and after trying everything they could think of to bring down the fever, they relented and brought them into town.

Turning to the boys I did the best examination I knew how, and then turned back to Tom. "Diphtheria."

"Roger that. But it gets so much better, listen to this." Tom made a face, then grinned at me, "both boys had measles last week. Fevers, chills, photophobia the works, not much doubt about it, and they were at the 'measles house' whatever that means."

"The 'Measles House'? What's a 'Measles House'?

"I was hoping you'd know, you spend a lot more time with these people than I do."

Together we turned back to the family and asked for clarification. We got a lot more information than we had bargained for and the situation went from important to critical in minutes.

Like many religion-based sects the Amish people do not avail themselves to mainstream medicine if they can avoid it. This included routine vaccination such as the MMR used to prevent measles, mumps and rubella. Instead, when someone contracted a condition like measles that person, usually a child, would be wrapped in a blanket and warmed up to the point of causing them to sweat. Once the viral condition had sufficiently impregnated the blanket—the blanket was then circulated. Measles are incredibly contagious with the victim becoming contagious a full three or four days before they show any symptoms and about the same amount of time after their own malady clears up. Children that had never had measles were wrapped in the blanket to infect them. Once you have had the measles, you are granted a lifetime immunity and this, in their way, was how they dealt with the condition. Those that contracted the measles were gathered in a single house where they could be treated and monitored collectively—the 'Measles House.' The result was that the entire community suffered the disease all at the same time and subsequently obtained lifetime immunity as a result. That is if they survived the condition and all of the opportunistic diseases that hovered at the edges of a depleted victim.

Measles itself, causes fever, chills, diarrhea and of course red spots. The chief danger during the course of the illness is dehydration. But a very significant portion of those that suffer this condition develop a secondary infection—pneumonia, which attacks the compromised lungs. For the general population it can be serious, but for infants and the elderly, it is dangerous. Older adults who have never achieved immunity are often already in a state of compromise due to advanced age and limited mobility. For infants and toddlers the high risk of dehydration quickly depletes their reserves and they are quick to worsen. Most of the fatalities that occur as a result of a measles outbreak are the result of pneumonia and not the measles. In the United States diphtheria is a rare condition unless the entire community does not participate in the routine immunizations. Although measles is a viral condition, pneumonia and diphtheria are bacterial, and aggressive.

The bacteria is treated with strong antibiotics and in the case of diphtheria, an intravenous injection of anti-toxin as well to arrest the bacteria that is already in the bloodstream. With these treatments patients usually achieve full recovery in a few weeks; if these treatments are not made available, fatalities are an almost sure thing.

Once we were back in the hallway, Tom turned to me.

"How many Amish families would you guess on the ridge?"

"About three hundred seventy or eighty, I've got a map

of them all, but I've got no idea how many people that is Tom."

"I've got to report this to Public Health and the shit is going to absolutely hit the fan. They are going to be knocking on doors up there. Shit, this could accelerate into a real big deal. Look Emmett we've got to get up there, and I'm going to have to get some more anti-toxin. Do you know where the houses are?"

"Well I know where this one is, but there's got to be at least a couple more."

"I'm gonna talk to Jim, (one of our local medical doctors), he'll have to vouch for the requisition anyway. We're going to be busy for awhile. How soon can you get clear?"

It was already after lunchtime and the afternoon was advancing toward early evening darkness. At three o'clock I usually picked up my son after school. Seth would come back to the office and busy himself until the office closed and we then went the seventeen miles home together. Today I was in a hurry, so after school we immediately headed out of town and toward the higher ground of the ridge.

Both of my boys had contracted measles a few years back and except for feeling miserable for a couple of days, had emerged from it without any apparent ill effects. The 'measles house' that I needed to visit was between town and our home. Although I was not worried about Seth getting measles, I was concerned that he might be exposed to something else. However I was also feeling the urgency of need and decided to at least stop by before taking him the rest of the way home. For Seth's part, he was completely used to house calls and enjoyed the time of seeing so many different and foreign things, usually enjoying the uniqueness of the event. Tonight though, he was going to stay in the truck.

Crossing the ridge, we began to descend down the back side and into the deep cut valleys and steep inclines that sheltered many of the Amish homesteads. The combination of warmer air and frozen ground produced a fog that hung in the air and condensed onto the windshield and made the road surfaces slippery. The sharp turns of the winding ridge roads becoming dangerous as the early darkness would soon bring on freezing temperatures. As we continued our destination appeared in the mist below us and I immediately noticed several buggies parked about in the yard. I turned into the yard and nosed the truck in between them, careful not to spook the horses who stood quietly, hitched to various posts, trees and other stationary objects, most of them covered with heavy blankets to protect them from the wetness and cold.

I knew that I was not expected, but I had no reason to believe that I would not be welcomed. I took a few minutes to explain to Seth that I was only here to see what the situation was and that I would be back in just a little while. Seth was dressed for winter, with a heavy parka, boots and snow pants, but just in case I left the truck running with the heater on low.

Cautioning him to touch nothing, I climbed down and into the frozen mud of the yard and made my way to the back door where the door stood open and one of the women stood wiping her hands on her apron. She was none other than Esther Yoder, the midwife and herbalist whom I had worked with on many occasions. After a handshake, she opened, "We have sickness in this house, but were not expecting you."

"I'm sorry to come unannounced Esther, but a couple of children in the community were in the office today, and they are very sick. It is a sickness that is different than measles and it is very contagious. I thought I should at least warn you to look for it. It takes pretty potent medicine to treat or else it can be a bad thing."

"What sickness is it?"

"Two of Jonas B.'s have diphtheria."

She turned away from me and gazed out at the truck idling in the yard. "You should bring your boy inside. I think you will be here for a while."

"He had measles last year that turned into whooping cough, I don't think he can catch anything you might have, but let's have a look first."

Stepping into the kitchen from the back door, I was blasted by the intense heat being put out by the massive cast iron cook stove that occupied most of one wall in the kitchen and the overpowering odor of kerosene from the lanterns scattered about. The room was busy with the bustle of several women, their hats loose on their heads and faces flushed by the heat of the wood burning stove. Pots on the stove steamed and bubbled, adding to the weight of the hot air in the room; the overall effect was one of concentrated busyness.

I bent down and removed my shoes, leaving them near the door and Esther immediately led the way around the corner and into the main room in the house. The open room spanned the entire length of one side of the house, fully thirty feet from one end to the other and fifteen feet wide. All of the furniture had been removed from the space and in its place, mattresses had been placed side by side along both of the long walls with space down the center to walk. The heat emanating from the kitchen was no less overpowering in this room and the windows had all been draped with heavy hangings to block the light from the outside. The low light of several lanterns gave a somber view of the occupants.

Each mattress was occupied. Most were children, but some were adults. Two cribs near the kitchen doorway also contained infants. Some of the children sat cross-legged on the mattress and looked up at our arrival, but most took no notice. Even in the low light of the room, the spotted faces of the nearest ones were clear enough to assure me that indeed measles had come for a visit.

I understood the need for the window coverings. Aside from their deeply protective need for privacy, measles often caused a condition known as photophobia, which is a strong aversion to bright light. The coverings offered some comfort from that uncomfortable aspect of the disease, but the heat in the room was overwhelming and so I asked Esther why they were keeping it so hot.

"The children complained of the chills, and we could not keep them warm enough."

"The fever is what gives them chills Esther, but the heat is not good for their lungs and breathing. The two boys also have pneumonia, and if the air is too dry and hot along with the sickness, it can cause that to happen."

"So you think we should let it become cool?"

"If you are asking me, I would recommend that you keep it very cool, and that you open windows at both ends of the room. Air moving through will also prevent some other sicknesses. I have seen some get meningitis when the air gets too full of germs."

"I will talk to David," (the home owner), "he will decide."

I stayed in the doorway while she went to the kitchen and spoke with two of the women. One threw on a shawl and left out the back door, the other stepped to the stove and turned down the chimney damper, to begin to lower the intensity of the fire in the firebox. After she returned, I asked her.

"How many are here?"

"We have twelve children and two babies. Also, Amos B. and Jonai H. who are both older. You will have a look at them."

"Yes, I would like to, if you don't mind."

With my stethoscope around my neck, we began with the infants. Both of the little ones had high fevers, each over one hundred and two degrees, but instead of being fussy, they were lethargic, lying still without protest while I listened to their chests and examined their bellies, checked their eyes and ears. One also had a raging ear infection in one ear. Lethargy is a bad sign, and Esther said as much.

"They have become worse since this morning, and now in the late evening, they have become quiet."

"How much fluid, water and other things have you been able to get into them Esther?"

"They can not nurse easily; they are too stuffy. They do not like to drink because it makes them cough."

These are all bad signs. Dehydration is the opening for trouble, and both infants were in peril. Keeping this in mind, we moved through the room, examining each child with the same procedure and finished with the two elderly gentlemen who both offered lively responses to my questions, but who were both already demonstrating almost certain signs of pneumonia. I lost all track of time, and my distress at the magnitude of the situation completely occupied my thoughts, until I suddenly remembered that Seth was still sitting out in the truck. Straightening up, I said as much to Esther.

It is alright, the boy is in the kitchen. Sarah brought him in and gave him cookies and milk."

I thanked her and finished with the examinations. There was going to be a long phone conversation with Dr. Dearing and Tom after this, but my real concern at the moment was the four already compromised people that were in need of immediate medical attention. Making our way back toward the kitchen we were met by David Schrock and another of the women. David offered his massive hand and I gave it a shake, then nodded to the woman.

"The children seem to be doing well. There's no reason that they won't all get better fairly quickly David, but I really recommend that you get some air moving through the room. It's better, even if it gets a little chilly than having air that is too hot and not moving."

"I will open the windows, but the stove heats the house so that must stay hot."

"The two babies are very sick. Both are dehydrated, and at risk for worse. If you want my opinion I would take them into the clinic and get some fluids into them as soon as you can manage it. Its pretty important, otherwise they can worsen very quickly."

"I will speak to their parents when they arrive after chores are done."

"The two men both have pneumonia. They need antibiotics, but you should move them away from the children. I will speak to the doctor in town, and I should be able to get the medicines for them and then bring it back to you, but for now move them somewhere else before they infect the other children."

"We have no other beds in this house. We can move them in the morning to another, if that will be alright."

"I would say the sooner the better. I am going to go back to town and see about the medicine, but those two babies are in need David."

"I will speak to the parents, as I said."

I headed back out to the kitchen to put my boots back on and was stricken with the image that greeted me as I turned the corner into the room. It said something about how preoccupied I had been because once again I had forgotten all about Seth. There he sat, still in his snow pants, boots, that only reached halfway to the floor and parka with the hood tied under his chin, immediately next to the blast furnace of a kitchen stove. A half-eaten cookie dangled from one hand as he stared vacantly at the far wall of the room, his face almost scarlet the only thing visible in what must have been a steam bath inside of all that clothing. I was mortified by my poor parenting skills, and apologized profusely to him as he nodded.

I swept him up in my arms and headed out to the truck in the yard, now equally concerned for his welfare as I was for the occupants of the house. The air had turned cold again with the setting of the sun behind the hills, and I feared he would catch cold in his sweaty clothing.

Starting the truck, I opened his coat and pulled off his hood and then wrapped him in one of the blankets that I kept in the back seat during the winter months. Once I was sure he was reasonably comfortable, we turned out of the yard and made the run for town and Tom Dunbar.

Forty-five minutes later, I was once again on my way out of town. This time with another friend Jim Kearney, a young medical doctor who was extremely competent and very likable.

Once he heard the story I had related, Tom had placed a call and Jim had insisted on making the return trip. Seth had fallen asleep almost before we had pulled out the of the farmhouse yard and Tom's wife had insisted on keeping him at their place while we returned to the ridge. He had not roused even when I carried him into the house and laid him on the couch.

Back at the house, Jim deferred to me to make introductions but his agitation was obvious in his haste to enter the sick room. After the requisite handshakes and introductions, he went to work, moving from bed to bed, much as I had, but this time administering medications along with injections. The room was decidedly cooler since my last visit, and the air much fresher, making the oppressive feel of sickness seem less intense. An hour later he straightened from the last sick bed and motioned us into the kitchen.

"The older gentleman on the left is very ill. His lungs are not working well, and the pneumonia is in both of them. He needs to be in the hospital as soon as possible."

"He will not go. He has already said he will not."

"Are you sure? It is almost certain that he will worsen if he doesn't."

"It is his wish."

"I also agree with Doctor Casey, they need to be moved away from the young people because they are contagious with a different kind of illness, that the children can catch from them."

"They are going to go to Amos T's who is the next farm from here down the road. Amos is coming for them in a short time, but they will not go to the hospital."

"All right, but the two infants are also very sick, and for them the need is greater. They are very weak and both of them need to go to the hospital right away."

"The girl will go. The boy's family will take him home, and care for him there."

"Mr. Schrock, this is very serious. The boy needs intravenous fluids and antibiotics; he is very close to not being able to recover."

"The family has decided that it would be best if he went home."

"If you would like, Dr. Casey and I will take the one child back with us then, but I seriously wish you would ask the other family one more time."

"I will ask them, Esther will take the baby and go with you. The parents will follow in their own way so that they can bring her back once she is recovered."

In short order the limp baby was wrapped against the cold of the winter air, and we once again returned to town. Going directly to the hospital, Jim directed Esther into the Emergency Room and began the heroic measures it would require to save the poor child. I returned to the truck and went to retrieve Seth, struggling to clear my head of all of the tragic potential of this latest turn of events.

Within the week, two more 'measles houses' were identified, and the necessary care and precautions were given. In all thirty-two children, six infants and five senior citizens were treated. Tragically, both of the elderly gentlemen succumbed during that time, and two of the infants also perished. It was a horrible episode that could have been worse, but was bad enough.

It was my privilege to be allowed to assist in the digging of the two tiny graves and I am not ashamed that I wept the whole time I worked.

Walter Dunn

"Do you think he'll be there?"

Grit spoke into the blackness of the room. We had made love slowly enjoying the intimacy, dragging it out, in no hurry to end it. Now we both lay on our backs quiet with our own thoughts. The absolute darkness of the deep woods was intensified by an overcast which blocked any star or moonlight. It was the kind of darkness that your eyes couldn't become accustomed to. It was the best kind of darkness to speak from the heart.

"There's no reason to believe that he would. He's never showed up before. Except for that one time."

"Would you still be afraid of him?"

"I was never afraid of him."

"What kind of bullshit you pedalin' boy? You told me you were. You even told me more than once."

I had been afraid of Walter Dunn from the first time I'd set eyes on him. Actually not really afraid of him, but the kind of healthy respect that keeps you from climbing into the pen with a fifteen hundred pound bull. He was physically imposing enough, but not in a way that I hadn't seen countless times before, but Walter Dunn radiated an energy that made your 'fight or flight' mechanism kick into overdrive. He couldn't hide the fact that he was a tough guy because the realization arrived way ahead of him.

"I'd kinda like to meet him."

"What in God's name for?"

"Cuz' if he's half what you say he is, I've never experienced those kinds of feelings before."

"He's everything I say he is, that is if he's still alive. Nope, I can honestly say that if I never set eyes on him again in this lifetime, it would still be too soon for me."

"Jeez Em. Well tomorrow's the day anyway. The last one. Excited?"

"Not really. Just glad that it will be all over finally."

Although I had diligently changed everything in my lifestyle to this point there was one aspect of it that constantly gnawed at my consciousness. The bi-annual reminder that the life I lived now was not the life I had once lived, my semi-annual review with the probate court. Once a month I called in and gave them an update on my whereabouts and whatabouts but twice a year, I had to physically present myself at their office. It dragged at me from behind like a giant sea anchor slowing our progress forward always somewhat aware of it in the back alley of my mind, never allowing me to forget the sins of my past.

At the time of my separation from the Army it had been largely accepted that I would immediately embrace a life of crime once my feet hit the civilian sidewalks. There had been no real reason to believe otherwise, I had demonstrated a talent and apparent skill set that had supported the hypothesis. My separation in fact, had only occurred once it had become clear to the military that they could not imprison me for a laundry list of felonies. Their only satisfaction had been the consolation that I would be monitored rigorously for the next five years and that it would annoy me. Tomorrow would be the last time.

I had met Walter Dunn while I was in the military. He was at the time a hybrid type of policeman. Our initial meeting had been in the middle of an emotionally charged drug deal. He had conscripted me and I had risked my life at his direction. It had been a harrowing experience and for it he had thanked me in his own closed-off way. Which means not at all.

Dunn appeared again at the very end of my service time. This time as an ally, but not out of affection or even as compatriots. Instead, as in the first instance, the person or persons that he wanted were standing on the other side of me. The only way to them was through me, or in his case directly over the top of me. I had been imprisoned on the charge of murdering a police officer, the jailers were police officers. The police officers in the jail had a particular opinion about cop killers which they demonstrated nightly in the showers.

The fact that a police officer had been killed was unarguable. The fact that the cop had been killed while participating, in fact directing, an illegal black market scheme was what had interested Dunn. I was merely the end to the means. As a result, I had spent thirty-seven days in Stuttgart Military Prison; ironically the same number of days I had survived in the central highlands of Vietnam. Both situations had not ended well, and both had taken a massive physical and emotional toll.

At the end Walter Dunn had disappeared into the woodwork. I had been released and separated, and although there is some evidence that the military justice department was justified in their initial suspicions, I had avoided most flagrantly illegal activity. I had dutifully reported for my probation hearings, and I had maintained an address and a job—usually.

Then at one of the hearings, Walter Dunn had inexplicably turned up instead of my usual P.O. In very short order he had conscripted me again, leveraging my apparent current criminal behavior against me and the roller coaster had begun its' ascent. The outcome had been the same, people had been found deceased, money and drugs had exchanged hands, and I was incarcerated. I had once again been jailed under circumstances that the jailers had a particular opinion about— and one which they felt compelled to express—again.

In the end, I had reluctantly been allowed to walked away. The hand of Walter Dunn was evident if not visible and once again, he had disappeared.

After that episode I had decided to look for a different line of work.

Tomorrow my parole officer would inform me that my required time was up, he would stamp the top sheet in my file with an official government stamp, maybe give me a copy, and close the file. I would officially be a free man. No cake, no congratulations, no streamers, but done.

"Well just the same, I'd like to see the guy." Grit flounced the bed covers and turned onto her side. "Good night Em, it's gonna be great. You'll be free at last."

The last P.O.

After much bureaucratic wrangling it was finally decided that I no longer had to go into the Chicago Loop for my sit-downs with the parole officer. Once I'd gotten a permanent address and duly licensed in the State of Wisconsin, the state had taken a personal interest in my probationary status. Subsequently, I now reported to their office in Milwaukee. The drive wasn't any shorter, but the parking was a lot cheaper.

The building was older, and the elevators were slower, but the air in the office itself seemed fresher, and all of the windows seemed to be filled with sunshine. A vast improvement over the brick wall and overcast skies that had been the featured view in Chicago. The countertop was still formica, and there was still a little stand with plastic cards on a spike and a sign above that read, 'Take A Number'.

The office had the identical feeling of a lazy mid-summer buzz with the heat too high and the activity at a bare minimum. I took a number, it was #3. Turning to the chairs every single one was empty. Before I could sit down a secretary walked over and in an unnecessarily loud voice.

"Number 3?"

"I'm number three."

"Name?"

"Casey, Robert E."

"Step through the gate at the end of the counter please. Interview room two."

Once in the room I sat in the stiff green chair facing the desk. I had no reason to expect immediate service, but the officer entered almost before my butt had compressed the plastic seat. Stepping briskly around the desk he dropped my file on the desk with a soft slap and practically threw himself into the seat.

The sunlight from the window behind him was intense enough so that his face was shadowed, but he was obviously not interested in making eye contact. It was eight-thirty in the morning and his shirt was already wrinkled with sweat stains in the armpits. His top button was undone and his tie loosened. He flipped open my file and got down to business.

"I've stamped your file completed. You can pick up your copies at the front desk when you leave. At some point in the next ten days to two weeks someone from the office will contact you to see if there are any further questions."

He looked up from the paperwork he was randomly shuffling and fixed his gaze on the framed photograph of President Gerald Ford over my left shoulder.

"Do you have any questions for me right now?"

"Is that it?"

"That's it."

"Well, um, …thanks." I put my hands on the armrests of the chair preparing to push myself up and out of it.

"When you exit the interview room, turn right and proceed to the conference room at the end of the aisle. There's a minor formality."

"I thought you said that was all?"

"As far as I'm concerned, it is Mr. Casey." He sighed, the last thing he wanted to do was invest any personal energy into me or the circumstance. "Just jump through the hoops please."

I made my way out the door and turned right. No one looked up from their desks, some that were on the phone swiveled away from my eyeline. No thumbs up, or winks just business as usual. Once I got to the open door of the conference room the final question answered itself. There was no mistaking the person sitting at the end of the long table.

He was leaning back in his chair gazing out the window which was open to the outside air. He appeared completely relaxed, and in no hurry twisting a silver Zippo lighter in his right hand, apparently lost in thought. His suit, impeccable as usual.

"You're the last person I would have expected to see today."

"Come on in and close the door please Mr. Casey, or may I call you Emmett? We do have some history together."

"I don't honestly care what you call me." I was actually a little pissed off that I was needing to talk to him at all. Walter Dunn had nothing to hold over my head anymore, I didn't need to be afraid of him, and that meant I didn't need to be nice to him either. Because of him I had very nearly been killed on multiple occasions.

"Please have a seat? I drove up from Chicago this

morning just for this; I wanted to congratulate you in person."

"What the heck for Dunn, you really are someone I want far back in my rear-view mirror."

"And for that matter, I am. Today ends my ability to keep tabs on you *legally.* You're officially on your own, and I'm *officially* out of your life. I'd say that qualifies for some sort of celebration, don't you?"

"You and I have never been friendly, now seems like an odd time to start if you asked me."

"No, we've never been friendly, but never adversarial either. In the world I live in and the one you used to, that's saying a lot.

Look, cards on the table. I still do my job every day, and I keep my ear on the ground. Every once in awhile, something pops up, only one perpetrator, a crime where intelligence and cleverness play a big part. Luck is sometimes involved as well. Those kinds of crimes can be hard to solve and the list of usual suspects is usually short. Very short really. With what I know about you, the natural tendency for someone like me is to put your name right at the top of that very shortlist. The probation office has proved to be an easy way to keep track of your movements and whereabouts. So my apologies if I didn't entirely trust your rehab.

But with that consideration Emmett, I'll also admit that I've admired you, and your uncanny abilities, from the first time we met. Your ability to create a separate reality, think on your feet and somehow get the result you intended is rare. On top of it you always displayed an overabundance of personality. It made it hard not to like you.

Most people have a hard time walking away from more illegal lifestyles. You've not only done that, but you've done an entire one-eighty. You are by-god respectable. You've certainly earned my admiration, and I wanted to come here this morning and tell you personally.

Dunn reached into the inside breast pocket of his impeccable suit and drew out two fat cigars. Leaning to his left he fished out a cigar cutter from his pants pocket. Cutting off the tip of the first one he handed it to me, then repeated the operation for the second.

"Cohiba Behike, incredibly expensive. Picked them up in Madrid a couple days ago."

He flipped open the lighter and held it to the end of his, turning the cigar but not puffing on it. The aroma of the fine tobacco was intoxicating. Once he was finished, he took a puff and let it out slowly.

"Now that is some fine shit. Go ahead Emmett, this is a celebration."

He slid the lighter across to me.

"By the way, keep the lighter when you're done. I think you'll recognize it."

I turned the battered Zippo in my hands, there was an engraving on one side.

'PFC R. E. Casey, 173rd Airborne, 1970'

"Where the fuck did you get this?"

"Evidence locker in Chicago lock-up. I took a look a few weeks ago now that that case is completely wrapped up and there it was."

"It's wrapped up?"

"Finally, didn't go easy, and there was a lot of pavement pounding, so to speak, but yes, wrapped up."

I had never known Dunn to be talkative, but now he had my interest. I didn't want to think about it, but I had always wondered what had happened after I was no longer a part of the proceedings. I lit the cigar, copying his technique.

"Wrapped up in a good way?"

"Some good, some not so good. Yes. The part you played early on cracked the foundation, there was a lot of scrambling that took place. It's not very often that two of the brains of the outfit take each other out. It made for a lot of initial confusion, and a lot of jockeying for position. Their flanks were exposed.

"Charles?"

"Deceased. Apparently he was not a part of the master plan."

"How about the Chicago people?"

"We were even able to take down a couple of higher ups in Joey Dove's gang."

"So job well done, three cheers for Special Agent in Charge, Walter Dunn."

"Three cheers for the U. S. of A. you mean. There's always work for people who want to protect the American way of life.

"Well that's me these days. I'm living the American way of life."

"So it would seem," he took a long pull on his cigar and flicked the ash onto the polished table top. Looking at me he shrugged, "A little social disobedience."

"You know, there are a lot of advances in forensics these days. It really makes my life a lot easier in some respects. Things that were a little questionable, say only five or six years ago, nowadays take a few hours in a lab someplace and the story changes immediately. Crime scenes tell different stories, hearsay evidence becomes easy to corroborate—or disprove. Double murder scenes can be particularly informative."

He gave me a wink and then shrugged.

"Yes, you are living the American dream now and congratulations on the family. Two strong boys, and a pretty wife."

"No offense Dunn, but that's none of your business anymore." I knew what he was hinting at about the crime scene, but I wasn't taking the bait.

"Nope."

Reaching into his side pocket he drew out something and held it up to his eye. He looked at it for a minute and then passed it across to me.

"I wanted you to have this. You may have earned it or you may not have in the eyes of the bureau, but in my opinion, you've earned it and more."

I looked at the thing in my hand. A lapel pin, heavy and obviously solid gold. In the center, on an onyx-like background, the gold letters F.B.I. Around the outside edge, three words in elevated relief, *Fidelity, Bravery, Integrity*. I looked back at Dunn honestly touched.

"That's who I think you are. I take those three words seriously."

He rose from his chair and walked to the window. Pausing briefly with his back to me he tossed his cigar out. Turning back to me he added.

"When you do this kind of work for very long you learn to expect the worst, even from the fun ones. You start to believe that nobody is anything more than a piece of shit on two legs. Thank you Emmett for proving me wrong."

Today

the little pin

Bowing to my own self-imposed rule, I had finally made my way to the bedroom to get dressed. I didn't need to make the bed, because I had slept in the recliner in front of the fireplace. Instead I dressed in front of the closet, randomly choosing whatever was clean, not slightly concerned with whether the items matched. Cinching my belt I discovered that I now could use the next smaller hole for the buckle. Lettie Shcrock wouldn't be happy I thought.

Stopping at the oak dresser, I opened the small wooden box sitting on top. Inside miscellaneous keepsakes competed for a visible spot in a jumble of glitter. Poking around with my finger, I pushed my old pocket watch out of the way and uncovered the little lapel pin. The gold had dulled a little, tarnished with time, but the lettering was still bright against the black background. I still marveled at it. What it represented to Walter Dunn was a far different thing than what it meant to me.

Dunn had been impressed with my integrity, whereas I had been just trying to tread water. I had never considered whether what I was doing had been right or wrong. As far as I had been concerned, they were just two sides of the same street, different ends of the same stick. What was good or evil seemed to be more related to which end of the stick you had grabbed. To the winner went the spoils.

I had once showed the pin to my father. He knew the story from one end to the other, and had even participated in a chapter of it. After turning it over in his hand, he handed it back to me and after lighting his pipe, he fixed his gaze on the horizon for a long pause.

"Make you a better father?"

"Those are two different horses."

"The little shiny bribe is just a way of reminding you not to step off the mark. Having a fancy stick-pin doesn't have anything to do with whether you're a better father just because you have it. You aren't that punk anymore, so the medal is from another life, but you *are* a father right now, in this life."

I couldn't believe I was listening to the same Father that I had grown up with. It had never seemed to me that he might give a damn about whether he was a good father. Once I had come to adulthood, he suddenly was now capable of wisdom and compassion. I was so stunned by the revelation in those few sentences that I could only manage; "Yeah, I guess."

The pin had lived in the wooden box on my dresser from that day forward.

I don't know if I was a good father or not. Even though I lived a different lifestyle now, I still brought the old Emmett Casey with me from time to time. I was entirely certain that my children had plenty of stories to share as a result.

Childbed Fever

It was a splendid late June evening. The light was muted as the sun began sinking toward the horizon, and there is a hint of an Aurora in the sky that sometimes occurs in the northern latitudes. The sun was far from setting, although it was already past six o'clock.

With the yard mowed and my tools put away, my home chores were finished. I took a seat on the back porch relaxing and listening to my two young boys busying themselves with a major highway project in the sandbox out beyond the porch railing. There was not a breath of a breeze but the temperature was perfect. With a tall glass of iced sun tea, alfalfa, and red clover blossom, I felt myself at peace with my surroundings and content.

I was jarred from my reflections by the phone on the wall in the kitchen. Evening phone calls are not usually family members, evening calls are more often patients, and for a brief moment I considered not answering almost too relaxed to feel like being responsible. Instead I hauled myself up out of the chair, pulled the screen door open and reaching inside picked up the phone. Even before I could answer a too-loud voice on the other end spoke.

"Casey?"

"Yes, this is Dr. Casey. How can I help you?"

"My wife, Letty, has been to bed now three days. Her mother says that you should come out."

"Who am I speaking with please?"

"Yes, this is Amos Schrock. The baby is fine, but my wife is fevered. Her mother says it would be best for you to see her."

"The baby is fine? Did she just have a baby?"

"Yes, she had the baby Monday morning. It is not the baby, but my wife."

"I understand. Was your mother-in-law there for the birth?"

"Yes. She and Esther Yoder were here."

"I will come along shortly Amos. I will need to bring my children with me, though as I can't leave them alone."

"I will tell Esther that you will come then."

There is a sharp click as the phone receiver was hung back up. Any telephone conversation with an Amish person can be a little iffy at best. They use the telephone system only in an emergency and then are not familiar with the niceties of what one would consider normal telephone etiquette. For Amos to call, he would first have to hike to the nearest neighbor with a phone and then ask permission. A hard thing in itself, but he would also have been required to ask for assistance in acquiring the proper phone number and then making the connection. It is unquestionably important or he would not have gone to the trouble.

I had gotten used to being asked to care for patients that had conditions beyond my chiropractic scope of practice. The mere fact that I was usually willing to help, even if it was only to bring them to town where they would be treated by a physician more versed in their condition, was reason enough for them to call. I had often been called out for issues, both large and small, only to be presented with a serious condition. For the Amish people, the decision to seek help often required the consultation of a midwife or other more knowledgeable person. This was followed by the necessary trek to the closest telephone, and then the wait for help to arrive. If the injury or illness was serious enough, the additional delay, sometimes hours, frequently complicated the situation to dire levels.

As a result, the local physicians in concert with some of the specialists at the large hospital had taken it upon themselves to teach me some basics that my chiropractic had not provided. It was in their interest that many conditions were somewhat stabilized and appropriate first aid had been provided before the subject arrived on their doorstep. Some things were simple enough on the surface, basic wound care, and where appropriate suturing. Beyond that was the absolute necessity that I expand my knowledge so that I could perform the triage necessary and determine what and where the person would need. Whenever they could spare the time, and my schedule allowed, I had been tutored one on one, scheduled to observe surgeries, or simply to accompany on rounds in LaCrosse. Over the years, I had my overview of health care knowledge expanded far beyond the horizons of my original scope of practice.

As my scope increased and the shortage of local professionals continued, I had been asked to assist in care at the local clinic, or even the hospital. It had never ceased to make me nervous, but it had also expanded my knowledge of the many things that can befall people. Knowledge is the most important thing that a doctor can carry in his medicine bag.

I drew a deep breath. A woman who is five days 'post-partum' and too weak to get out of bed is a bad thing. It is the Amish custom for the woman to stay in bed for a week after birthing no matter what so just the fact that she is in bed is not a terribly serious consideration. The fact that the midwife is concerned though, is proof enough that something is wrong. The further fact that it is important enough to call for a doctor, even if it is me, tells me that the trouble is worse than bad whatever it is.

I called for the boys and told them that we had to go out on a call. Their mother had kept her job at the local floral shop to 'keep from going crazy' and would not be home for a few more hours. To their credit, they didn't even hesitate but curtailed their project and immediately climbed the steps to the kitchen door. Sean, who was five, announced through the screen door.

"I'm hungry."

"Yes, well we will have to eat in the truck. I will pack us a picnic. Will that be okay?" Seth, who is eight years old, asked. "Can we have a soda?"

"How about some sparkling water instead, your mom bought some of that with fruit juice in it."

"Okay, and cookies too?"

"Sure, I'll pack it all up and you guys can sit in the back of the truck and eat while I see this woman. It's a long ride though, so you can ride inside the truck until we get there. We have to go to Amos S.'s and that's on the other side of Dorset Ridge, away out beyond the sawmill. Remember though, you have to stay in the truck while I am in the house. I don't want you messing with the horses or anything. Okay?"

"Yes Da," they agreed in unison.

I pulled bologna and cheese out of the refrigerator and quickly slapped together a couple of sandwiches a half bag of potato chips, and slice a few carrots lengthwise. Reaching back into the refrigerator, I grabbed four cans of sparkling water and dropped them all into the picnic basket that we kept on top of the refrigerator. Swinging it in my hand, I left the house and told the dogs to 'stay' as they sat expectantly at the truck door, anxious to go for a ride too. I lifted the boys up into the truck and Sean climbed over the front seat and into the small 'jump' seat. Seth, who considered himself a grown-up, sat in the passenger seat and took the basket on his lap.

The drive across Middle Ridge was picture perfect. The evening was beginning to cool and ground fog was starting to blossom out of the low spots between the cultivated fields, as the day's humidity began to settle on the ground. The corn was well beyond 'knee-high' and the oats, still a light blue-green, gave contrast to the deep green of the corn and woods as we passed them. Here and there families were still hard at work in the hayfields gathering their loose hay onto the wagons that were pulled by their teams of patient plodding draft horses. Hurrying to get as much hay up off the ground before the evening dew moistened it. As we wound our way along the road with the windows open, it was a perfect night and I was with my two favorite people.

Passing the large sawmill, I noted that the mill was quiet. No engine noise from the massive Volkswagon engine the Amish had rigged to run the entire operation. The saw blade itself fully three feet in diameter, the great moving carriage and the auger and chain that pulled the sawdust away from the saw and up a long tube pouring it out twenty feet above the ground into a great pile beyond the shed that housed it. Ever observant Seth looked it all over and in a moment reflected; "They must be all bringing in the hay if the even the sawmill is shut down."

I nodded and began to watch for my turn in to Amos'. With the good weather there was no need to switch into four-wheel drive, but just the same the Amish lanes could be treacherous. Usually nothing more than a track from the house to the road, they had little need for grading or smoothing. They often joked with me that their vehicles had four-legged drive. Amos' drive however was well maintained with fresh gravel all the way from the road to the barnyard. I swung in and parked next to the hitching post closest to the house. Even before I shut off the engine and reached for my bag from the back seat, the screen door swung open and I recognized Esther Yoder, the midwife, as she stepped out of the house carefully shutting the door behind her. She waited on the entry step with her hands folded in front of her. Her presence and posture signifying there would be no strange children allowed in the house while a woman was down in bed in her nightclothes.

Turning to Seth, I said, "Take the basket and climb into the back. You can sit on the wheel wells and eat but stay in the truck."

I then took my bag and met Esther at the door. With a stern last check of the boys, she turned and opened the screen door holding it for me. The house smelled of fresh bread and floor wax and something else—sickness. I looked at Esther, noticing the lines of worry and fatigue around her eyes. Esther was one of the first women I had met in the community and one of the few who had been welcoming from the beginning. She was a first-rate midwife, an herbalist and she liked to read. We had both learned a great deal from each other. She had common sense and I had resources. We had teamed up more than once over the ensuing years and I respected her completely. Where you found trouble on the ridge, you would also find Esther.

Raising one eyebrow, I looked a question at her. She was all business.

"The baby was born Monday night, closer to Tuesday. Baby is healthy, a girl and gaining. It is Letty's seventh alive." The implication being that some had been born not so alive. "She did not pass the afterbirth until Tuesday around noon and it was not whole. The fever began on Thursday and has been building. At evening today, she passed to sleep and will not wake. There has been no milk.

I fear it is the 'child-bed fever.'"

Post-partum sepsis, truly bad and horrifyingly fatal if allowed to run its course. I had been afraid it was something like this and the worst of my fears. The condition created by an incomplete separation of the placenta from the lining of the uterus and probably worsened by the midwife's attempt to dislodge the remainder of it had caused a bacterial infection of the genital tract. The rich environment of a raw and bleeding uterine lining creates the perfect medium for fast growth and eventual development of puerperal infection. A systemic infection that left unchecked would rage through the woman's body and eventually cause massive organ failure and death.

"No milk?" Nursing the baby immediately after childbirth triggers a hormone release in the woman's body. This release of hormones then assists in causing the uterine's muscular walls to contract, assisting in shrinking the swollen organ and dispelling the placenta. If Letty had no milk, then this had not had a chance to take place.

"Yes, Martha B. has been nursing the child for her."

Esther led me to the bedroom in the back and immediately there is no question as to the origin of the odor of sickness. Lying on the bed between the two windows was a smallish woman, deathly pale with colorless lips and sunken eyelids half open. Letty was completely unresponsive to our arrival. Another older woman sat in a straight back wooden chair by her side placing a damp cloth across her forehead. It was her mother and as she met my eyes, the sick dread of worry was plain on her face. I tried to assume my most professional demeanor and crossed to the other side of the bed and touched her forehead; it was burning.

A small commotion at the back of the house was followed by the slam of the screen door and the arrival of

Amos. His thin blue cotton shirt damp with sweat and he was covered head to toe with hay dust and smelled of the clean fields. He slid into the room as quietly as he could and leaned his narrow shoulders against the wall, present but trying not to interfere. I met his eyes and he gave a very slight nod of greeting but his eyes immediately went to the woman in the bed.

Her fever was extremely high. An oral thermometer was out of the question so I had Esther pull down the bedsheet and place the thermometer in her armpit. I asked Esther if I might examine her and her lips pulled into a tight line as she considered what that meant. She turned to Amos and made a shooing gesture with her hands and the mother got up from the chair and closed the door. Pulling down the sheet further, I saw she is in a light cotton nightshirt that was soaked with sweat.

As I continued my examination, I suddenly became aware of a noise that I have been hearing for several minutes, the sound of a car horn beeping, not a constant beep, but a beep followed by a long pause, then another beep. There was only one 'car' around here and that would be mine, my truck more accurately. I had not noticed it before because my attention was focused on the dire situation in the bedroom.

Crossing to the window, I looked out into the farmyard at my truck. The boys were no longer in the bed of the truck, instead they were both in the cab, shoulder to shoulder in the front seat, Seth behind the wheel and Sean standing and leaning over toward the driver's side. Directly next to the truck, Amos has tied the team of horses to the hitching rail. They were still hitched to the hay wagon that had a full load of hay piled fully twelve to fifteen feet above the ground. The boys' attention was on the horses and as I watched the horn beeped again.

Although the reaction was predictable, the effect was

striking. With the beep of the horn both horses jumped straight up in the air. Were it not for the wagon which must have weighed several tons and the fact that they are secured to the hitching rail, I realized they would be in the next county by now. The reaction of the boys was also predictable; they collapsed into fits of laughter that I have no trouble hearing from my vantage point. I slid the window down from the top and shook my fist at them and then waggled my finger in a definite "no-no" message. They dove through the back window of the truck into the bed and composed themselves on the wheel wells, still giggling. I closed the window went back to my examination.

Turning to Esther, I told her that we must get Letty to the hospital immediately. She would require a medical procedure called a D&C and if we were going to save her life she was going to need some very serious medicine. She nodded and let Amos back into the room and they lapsed into a discussion in their own "Dutch" language, excluding me. Amos' shoulders drooped with the news and I know that barring a miracle the expense would break them for years to come. I stood waiting for the inevitable outcome, and then I heard the 'beep' of the truck horn again.

I took my leave of the bedroom and hurried outside to the truck. As soon as I came out the screen door, the boys repeated their hasty retreat to the back end of the truck and collapsed into giggling idiots. My face stopped them in mid-chortle and they attempted to compose themselves as they assumed their seats on the wheel wells both cradling their cans of sparkling water. They had already finished a can apiece as I saw them rolling around in the truck bed and it was only now that I noticed that the cans were not 'sparkling water,' but wine coolers! In my haste to leave the house, I had inadvertently gotten both of them tipsy. What kind of father must I be? In as few words as possible, peppered with threats of bodily harm, I scolded the boys and told them to behave while relieving them of the unfinished wine coolers.

In order to move Letty to the hospital, I was going to have to put her in the bed of the truck. There was no ambulance service in this part of the county. The nearest hospital is almost forty miles and we have no time. To take her from the house to the truck, Amos and I took the pantry door off of its hinges and padded it with blankets. Laying it on the bed next to the unresponsive woman, we gently transferred her to the door and secured her with long strips of a torn cotton sheet. Securing her to the door allowed us to turn the narrow corners of the house. Once we slid her into the truck bed, we covered her with quilts and placed a small towel over her face to protect her from the wind and the chill of the evening air. The boys were put in the jump seat in the back of the cab, and Esther climbed into the passenger seat with her own bag. Amos climbed in and laid down beside his wife to keep the blankets in place, and we eased away from the horse rail and into the lane.

Once we climbed back up over Dorset Ridge and into the valley beyond, I pulled into the small Lutheran Church that housed the congregation of the few "English" families that also called the ridge home and stopped at the tiny parsonage. Quickly striding up the stone path to the front door I pulled the brass door knocker and immediately heard the sound of approaching footsteps on the other side. The door swung wide open with no preamble and Pastor Krause's kindly face smiled out to me. With a glance over my shoulder, he took in the picture before him. He was no stranger to my quick stops and need for a telephone, and without hesitation, he waved me in and led me to the wall phone in the kitchen.

As I dialed the phone number for the hospital in Tomah, his wife of many years breezed into the room and immediately opened the refrigerator and began to take out sausage, cheese, vegetables and other supplies. My phone call was brief, but it was important that the small emergency room staff be alerted to my impending arrival. We would also need to have the surgeon that covers our hospital present and he would need to be notified if he is not already there tonight. In the short time that it took for me to complete the call, Mrs. Krause had created an impressive supply of sandwiches, fresh vegetables and apples. She also added a half-gallon jug of ice tea and handed them to the pastor.

"They will need food if they are going to be at the hospital for any amount of time." She said matter-of-factly. "…and I see that you have the boys with you so I added some cookies for them." She gave me a smile, patted my arm and bustled out of the room.

Pastor Krause accompanied me out of the house but not all the way to the truck. Handing me the foodstuffs he smiled,

"They are lucky to have you Emmett. Drive safely."

"I hope you don't spread that sort of talk around Pastor; I'm busy enough as it is."

It would take another thirty minutes to make the drive into Tomah and the hospital. Once there I backed the truck into the ambulance bay and the Emergency Room team, along with Raleigh Kendall, one of the best general surgeons I knew of, came into the bay at the sound of the overhead door opening. One look at Letty Schrock was enough to change his casual demeanor to one of severe professionalism. Even before we had pulled the pantry door stretcher far enough out of the truck bed to transfer her to the gurney, he is quietly giving orders.

"Take her straight to the O.R., start I.V. drip Ringer's and Gentomycin, Clindomycin and Ampicillan, contact Hayes so we have anesthesia. He looked at me and gave a wan smile.

"You do this just to test me don't you Emmett? You should scrub in; the family will want to know what went on."

"I can wait in the hallway with them."

"No we will probably need you anyway, I'm not sure we will be able to find Hayes on a Saturday night. Besides, it's the only way I can get even with you for ruining another quiet evening at home with the missus." He released the brake on the gurney himself and started to help push it toward the double doors. Over his shoulder, he added, "She hates you by the way."

As he was talking, Paulette Downey bustled out through the wide double doors that lead to the Admitting area and the Emergency Room. Paulette was a no-nonsense woman of indeterminate age and the unquestioning "Master Sergeant" of the Emergency Room and Admitting Desk. At five feet tall and well in excess of two hundred pounds, she cut an imposing figure and would be terrifying if everyone didn't already know she had a heart of gold.

"Where are your boys Doc?"

"Still in the truck, they have had their dinner, so please don't let them tell you differently."

"Everyone needs a little something to tuck in around the edges. I'll take them down to the vending machines and I have some new coloring books and crayons that they can have after that."

I am sad to say that this was not the first time that the boys had gotten stuck at the hospital for what might prove to be a long time. The standard practice was for Paulette, or someone else to take them in hand. She would see that they were fed if they needed to be and then entertained, and if it was late, she put them to bed in the chapel. We had done this on a few occasions and the boys adored Paulette.

After she left, I was whisked into the ER and began the

process of washing, scrubbing and gowning for the upcoming care. I had no active role to play in the procedure. I would function primarily as an observer and interpreter for the family waiting outside. They were private people with a distinct discomfort when it came to the hospital environment, my presence in the operating room was a small comfort to them and I could also describe in more pedestrian terms the process and prognosis than the doctor might. Unless Dr. Hayes could not be located, then I would operate the oxygen and monitor the patient's vital signs for the other and much busier professionals in the room. As I was holding up my hands to be gowned by the surgical nurse, I received a very sharp rap on the back of my head. Surprised, I turned to see what it was and was greeted with a spitting mad and very puffed up Paulette Downey.

"Those boys have been drinking!" She fumed, "they are both about 'three sheets to the wind. You and I are going to have a talk later on mister."

Then she stormed out of the room. I turned back to the rest of the staff in the room to see every one of them frozen in suspended animation, their eyes wide even over their surgical masks, then the room erupted in laughter.

Much later that night, after Letty Schrock was resting peacefully in her hospital bed and I was just starting to feel the fatigue in my neck and shoulders, her husband Amos and the midwife Esther were finally admitted to see her. They thanked each staff member individually for their help before approaching the bedside. Amos then turned to me and I was expecting the same thank you but instead.

"Your boys are snoring very loud in the church room."

With a snort of laughter, the nurse and her assistant exited the room, and I headed down the hall to take my children home.

Calf Roping and Bull Dogging

One early summer, while the boys were still small but fancied themselves men, I received a call from one of the local farmers who lived at the other end of the ridge. It may have been one of the oddest calls I had ever gotten and that was saying something. His name was Harold Pritz and I had seen him in my office on occasion but not frequently so that we were on a more or less first name basis.

"Hey Doc, I've got a problem with one of my calves. I was thinking at first that it might have gotten into some bad paint off of a fence or something, but it is acting pretty strangely."

I didn't see any connection to me yet, but I just had to ask. "Did you call Doctor White?" Doctor White was the local large animal veterinarian and I knew him by reputation, and well enough to say 'Good Morning' to on Sunday's after church.

"Yep, I did. He came out and checked it out from head to tail and said he couldn't find anything wrong with it. But then he said, why didn't I call Doc Casey and see if he might be able to help."

I knew Doctor White well enough to know that he could display a quirky sense of humor.

I didn't know though if it was that or if he was in a

roundabout way trying to give me a hard time. But I still couldn't see how it applied to me.

"I'm sorry Harold, but I don't know what I have to offer. What's wrong with it anyway."

"Can't walk. It was fine one day and couldn't walk the next. It's a puzzle for sure. I was really hoping that Doc White could help cuz' I got a lot tied up in the calf already and I sure hate to put it down."

I have to say at that point I was a little interested. It really couldn't hurt, I thought, to come out and examine a calf. So, after expressing my reluctance in a couple of more ways, I agreed that I would come out to his place after dinner that evening. It was going to be one of the evenings when the boy's mother would be working late in town anyway so I thought it would be fun for them to tag along. Something that they were used to doing, and it often proved to be very educational.

As it happened, as evening approached, one of the famous 'driftless area' storms boiled up out of nowhere and brought with it sound and fury and torrents of rain. As was usually the case in no time at all, the power went out at our place. The loss of power was a regular occurrence, the consequence of living out at the end of the power lines. Power lines that ran through miles of heavy woods and often fell victim to limbs and whole trees blown down by the storms.

The boys were seasoned veterans to power outages and each had their own flashlights and it took no time at all to light the lanterns and secure the flashlights. I picked up the phone to call Harold and inform him that with the power out on the ridge, perhaps we should reschedule my visit. The lack of dial tone told me that the phone lines were also down. Harold was already expecting me and without being able to tell him otherwise, I got the boys ready to go out. We all had good rain slickers and rubber barn boots and the air was warm in spite of the rain so shortly we were on our way.

The rain had slacked off from the downpour of the previous hour and the lightning had drawn back to a safer distance with the thunder starting to take a more distant rumble. As we wound our way across the ridge, we could roll down the windows and take deep breaths of the freshness. The ride wasn't long and we turned off the road into Harold's place. The large house on our left showed gray in the darkness and a large much darker barn took up most of the space on our right. Various farm equipment were neatly parked along the fence in front of us and the standard pickup truck was pulled close to the house.

As soon as our headlights swept the darkened yard, a bright two-mantled lamp emerged from the backdoor of the house and floated toward us. As it got closer, we could make out the man carrying it. Wearing his rubber barn boots and with his pant legs stuffed inside of them, Harold held up his lantern and greeted us. A large hulk of a man, in the darkness, he seemed even bigger than I knew him to be.

"Didn't know for sure if you would come out tonight. Sure have had plenty of rain and now the powers out too." If he was surprised or concerned to see that I brought the boys along, he didn't mention it.

"The power is out down at our end of the ridge too. I'd guess it's probably out all the way down to Wilton."

"I wouldn't be surprised. I hope you've got boots. I put the calf up in the farrowing house up above so it wouldn't be out in the yard with the rest of the cattle where they might get in your way. I was also kind of worried about it lying in the mud with all that rain coming down."

"The boys both have their boots and I've got mine on too. If the mud's pretty deep, I can carry Sean though."

"We can cut through the barn, it's not as short but we'll avoid the worst of the mud out in the cow yard."

With that statement, he turned and with the lantern in hand strode off toward the barn leaving us to keep up. He didn't have anything else to say, so he didn't fill the air with useless talk. We walked through the empty barn down the main aisle of what must have been the milking parlor as the ghostly stanchions for the milk cows still lined both sides of the long aisle. At the end of the barn the large doors opened out into the barnyard and the huge shadowed backs accompanied by the huffs and lowing of the cattle in the yard could be just made out in the inky darkness as their dark masses milled about moving slowly out of our way. It was too dark to count how many of them there were but it seemed like quite a few.

Striking out across the cow yard, Harold led the way slapping cow rumps to move them out of our way as we did our best to get through the crowd. The mud and manure were deep and sticky, sucking on our boots with each step. In no time Sean began to have trouble keeping up so I swept him up and carried him the rest of the way. We could just make out the silhouette of the dark low square of the farrowing house ahead of us sitting just beyond the cow yard fence.

A farrowing house is used to birth pigs. As far as I could see Harold kept no pigs on the place, so the farrowing house was probably unused. As we entered, the lantern illuminated a typical farrowing house setup. The building was obviously very old. It was built out of stacked stone and roughly thirty-five or forty feet long and thirty feet wide. The roof beams were made of stripped logs, round and still sporting some bits of bark after all these years. There was a regular barn door at each end of the long aisle along the left wall as we entered with the top half of the doors fastened open. On the left side there were small windows that lined the top of the wall at regular intervals and the roof slanted down away from above the windows toward the right side. To the left side of the aisle were the slats of a long four board fence of the pen enclosures. In a farrowing house the pens are arranged in narrow sections where the female or sow is contained while she births her piglets. I could see in the darkness the narrow individual pens on the other side of the aisle fence as they disappeared one after the other into the depths of the large interior space.

"I took some of the dividers out of the pens so that the calf wouldn't be too crowded and put down plenty of straw," said Harold as he walked down the aisle holding the lantern up even with his head. "Here he is, he still isn't standing though."

We all looked over the aisle fence at the animal lying in the pen, and couldn't help but draw a deep breath in surprise. Lying in the deep straw was eight hundred pounds of Hereford 'calf.'

"Jeez Harold, when you said calf, I was expecting something a little smaller. You know, like a calf."

"This one's almost finished out, was gonna try and ship it next week or so. Takes a while to get them to this weight, I fed him and the others all winter so I'd hate to lose him this close to payday."

As he lifted the lantern up to get a better view, the poor animal attempted to stand up. He was only able to get his hind legs under him though. His front legs lay useless on the shed floor so he was resting on his chest with his hindquarters in the air. With a deep bellow that was answered in kind from his cohorts out in the cow yard, he tried to run but only succeeded in pushing himself around the pen on his chest, snowplowing the straw into a huge drift ahead of himself. Once he pushed himself into the corner of the shed facing away from us, he stopped and rested content that he couldn't see us anymore.

"You gonna be able to do anything Doc?" Howard

whispered.

"You said you had the vet check him out?" I asked, stalling for time.

"Oh yeah, Doc White was out here yesterday late. He said that he couldn't find anything wrong with it though. That's when he thought of you."

I made a mental note to get even with Doctor White at the first opportunity. This had his sense of humor written all over it. I regarded the 'calf' in the lantern light and decided what the hell, let's give it a go, but Harold needed to hold the lantern and this was a two man job.

"In for a penny in for a pound," I sighed. "Okay Seth, climb on in there with me and let's see what's what."

Seth was going on ten years old and already exhibited strength and a can-do attitude. Already a big boy, he was going to be a bigger man one day. Once I climbed into the pen, he eagerly clambered over the fence in his high rubber barn boots and heavy raincoat slicker. He looked at me the eagerness to do a man's job obvious in his eyes.

"Okay. Listen carefully okay, we'll see how this works out but let's also be careful. Cows have trouble kicking if you bend their tails up over their backs. This one's not going to be able to kick much anyway cuz' he's only got two working legs to start with. But if we hold his tail up he might not try to run either, so I'm going to pull his tail up and once it's up, I'm going to give it to you to hold. Okay?"

He nodded, both excited and also aware of the size of the beast in this small of a space.

Inside the farrowing pen, the steer seemed larger than he had on the other side of the fence.

The steer had conveniently plowed himself into the far corner of the pen so his escape possibilities were more limited. I strode over not at all sure of what I was going to do but now determined that whatever it was, I was going to give it my best. Making it up as I went along but open to the experience. I had learned long ago that if you jumped in with both feet you stood a good chance of learning something you didn't know before and at the same time limited the chances for injury. I grabbed the steer's tail just above the tassel at the end and without hesitation pushed it straight up over its back and creating as much pressure as I dared, pressed it toward the animal's spine. The animal showed the whites of its eyes but did not move.

Indicating to Seth to take hold of the tail, he walked up behind the critter and bending over grasped the tail with both hands. After releasing the tail, I stood back and contemplated what to do. I reasoned that the lower half was working fairly well in that those legs worked but the upper legs did not. If it were a human being, I would naturally assume that there was something in the neck or upper shoulders that might be blocking the nerve pathways to the arms. I also reasoned that if anything I tried worked or didn't work, the patient was doomed either way, it was just a question of timing.

With that I decided that I should probably check the patient's neck. I stepped over the steer's head, straddling its neck with the head behind me and facing the rear of the animal.

Surprisingly the steer did not protest and became still. Using my knees and legs as levers, I moved the head and neck back and forth while trying to get some sense of the movement of the neck vertebra through the muscled neck with my hands. As I approached the withers, the side to side range needed to be increased in order to achieve any movement in the bones farther down the neck.

Suddenly from beneath my hands at the base of the steers neck, there was a very audible 'crack.' With a bellow, the steer threw itself to its feet, all four of them, and began frantically searching for an escape. I found myself astride the animal's neck with its head extended behind me and facing the rear where I had an excellent view of Seth, his concentration total, determinedly hanging onto the tail and being dragged around the pen. The low timbered ceiling was suddenly a real hazard and I had to duck down lying along the animals back to avoid being brained by a passing timber. With each lap, the animal bawled out its distress and so did I. It also emptied its bowels, increasing Seth's dilemma. His concentration never wavered, nor did his grip much to the misfortune of his raingear.

Unable to escape the pen, the animal became more and more frantic and our situation switched from comedic to dangerous. Suddenly the answering bellows from the cow yard were no longer distant, and with a crash, the first beast came up and over the half open barn door and the second one came straight through it followed by the others stampeding down the narrow aisle. Thanks to my preoccupation with our current dilemma, I couldn't react to the possibility of Sean being trampled to death in the narrow aisle under the oncoming onslaught of eight hundred to one thousand pound cattle.

"Son of a bitch!" yelled Harold.

With no hesitation, he reached down and grabbed Sean by his coat between his shoulder blades, hoisted him in one hand and the lantern in the other over his head and scaled the pen fence hands free. The stampede poured down the aisle bellowing and slamming into the fence and the stone wall on either side with Sean suspended above them, Harold's yells adding to the already incredible din. When the herd reached the door at the other end of the building, they first began to pile up against it and then with another crash broke it down and disappeared into the stormy night beyond.

On the next lap around the pen, I was able with the use of the centrifugal force of the turn to exit my perch, albeit not very gracefully and landed hard up against the pen fence. Jumping to my feet, I waited for the next lap and grabbed Seth and with a single motion, lifted his legs and swung him up and over the pen side. Climbing out myself, I bent over and grabbed my knees trying to catch my breath. Slowly collective hearts started to slow and breathing returned to normal.

Sean still hung from one of Harold's great arms almost forgotten in the moment.

Suddenly becoming aware of him, Harold lowered him to the ground and with relief I could see he was none the worse for wear. Seth, however, was another story. Covered from chest to toes in manure with what appeared to be half of a bale of straw clinging to him, he looked like a poorly stuffed scarecrow. But it was nothing a hose wouldn't fix. Other than my own bruises, surprisingly no one was injured. I looked into the pen and regarded the now placid steer standing with its legs spread and head lowered looking back at me.

"I've gotta' say I've never seen anything like that before Doc." Harold managed to whisper.

I would have to come up with a very special Christmas Card for Doctor White this year.

Today

more wood in the fire

I threw a few more logs into the fireplace. Taking the small fireplace shovel from the stand next to it, I shoveled some of the ash out from under the grate, dumping it into the steel ashcan next to the wood stack. The firewood breathed better now.

Sitting back down, I reflected on my parenting skills, wishing I'd been better at it, but knowing that my kids had turned out alright in spite of them. My father had taken a different approach, and I had come out okay as well—eventually.

My boys had grown into men of stature and integrity, and I was proud of them as sons but also as men. There had been times when their lives had been more precious than my own and I would have given mine in exchange for theirs without hesitation.

That realization may be the most humbling realization that parenting bestows. When it is tested, your fear of death is not for your own, but theirs.

Hickory Nuts and Bedlam

Living in the Northwoods in our log cabin, we were settled into our new lives. To this cabin brought our first son home. I have many fond memories of my young bride carrying armloads of firewood balanced precariously on her big pregnant belly, making her all the more beautiful to me. The long winter nights were spent snuggled in the loft bedroom cozy in the warmth of the parlor stove heated with our hard-earned firewood. The bassinet placed close by in the complete silence of Northwoods winter, broken only by the occasional howl of wolves or bark of the coyotes.

The only 'fly in the ointment' came when I was called out in the middle of the night for a house call. The Amish community that I served was nestled in the high hills fifteen miles south of town. Our cozy cabin lay in the woods more than twelve miles north of town.

Any house call, even if it was a simple one, required a round trip of over fifty miles often in less than optimal weather and often in near blizzard conditions, and at least three hours travel time counting the call itself. Although I trusted our little pickup truck to handle the roads as the calls became more frequent the strain of time, fuel, and loss of sleep began to take its toll. A decision was made that we would have to leave our cabin and look for a home on or near the ridge. Luckily the search proved to be a short one. We found our next home, an old one hundred and thirty-year-old farmhouse with a few acres and a forty by sixty pole building, in the middle of the Amish community strategically located on Middle Ridge.

Although the drive to work in the morning and home at night was now seventeen miles, the scenery as the county road wound its way along the top of the ridge looking down into the valleys below was magnificent. I never grew tired of it no matter what season it was.

There are many joys and advantages to living that far out in the country. The night skies are blanketed with stars so bright that you have no problem seeing your way wherever you could choose to walk. The air is so clear that you can see and count the weather satellites as they pass overhead in their orbits and we soon welcomed another son home. With the fresh air and countless adventures of the country, the boys flourished and grew strong and healthy. To my wife's constant embarrassment, the boys soon became adept at removing their clothing once they were outside and she was often obliged to drop whatever she was doing when she viewed two naked young boys racing each other across the yard.

For the children, there are no busy streets to cross. Passing vehicles are a rarity, in fact almost an event. There are no jungle gym playgrounds or municipal pools when it gets hot in the summer. Instead there are countless trees to climb and a creek to swim and wade in. The woods and hills are forever filled with multitude species of birds, plants, and critters to watch and learn from. There are toads and frogs and worms to catch and hide in their pockets for their mother to find at bath time. The kids can explore and play in endless games of their invention, climb trees and pretend to be pirates, pick wild berries until they can hold no more, and learn the basics of self-sufficiency. By the time the boys were school age, we had had as many pets as they were willing to care for. There were goats, who took tremendous delight in eating my roses, and pet pigs, dogs and a constantly varying population of cats.

Country dwellers live without the luxury of running to the corner store for milk or bread, or McDonald's when you just don't feel like making lunch today. The weekend chores of mowing the yard or minor household repairs increase tenfold with the increase of acreage and additional buildings and there is no hardware store or home repair 'big box' store that is less than an hour's round trip. If you need to borrow a tool or mower, even the neighbors are a mile away and not just on the other side of a comfortable suburban fence. When there is trouble, you are on your own.

It was Sunday, a glorious fall day. One of those last warm days when the sun shines so bright that on the multi-hued trees glowed with their colors and the distant hills and valleys looked as if they were shot by a talented photographer; the air so clear that they seemed close enough to touch. The morning grass now frosted with the first of the cold nights to come and the afternoon air was filled with the smell of dry leaves and the freshly turned earth of the harvested farmland that surrounded us.

The last warm days of autumn provided a last chance to finish outside chores that would prepare us for the cold days and deep snow that would arrive in early November and stay until Easter. The nearness of winter added a sense of urgency and I was hard pressed to keep up and finish what needed to be accomplished. The large kitchen garden had been tilled and mulched with the compost that had fermented throughout the hot summer. The basement stairwell was lined with the glass "Ball" jars filled with pickles, jelly, fruits and vegetables that we had canned throughout the season. The woodpile, almost completed, was stacked neatly in the shed and added its warm scent of freshly split oak and walnut wood to the aroma of the leaves. The garage had been cleared of tools and toys so that both the car and the truck could shelter from the ice and snow to come.

The boys, now seven and ten, were anxious to 'help' and they pitched in readily to stack the split firewood and operate the handle of our gas-powered log splitter. Seth, now ten and growing taller by the minute, took great pride in being able to reach the pedals of the yard tractor. He used every excuse to hook up the small trailer and putter around the yard and neighboring fields gathering corn missed by the combine harvesters, or to collect the raked leaves and haul them to the now empty compost bin. Sean, similarly enjoyed riding in the trailer and 'helping,' although his seven-year-old attention span lacked a more diligent commitment to labor.

On this day, the boys hatched a plan to collect hickory nuts that fell in abundance from three mighty trees at the top of the hill above the house. The trees stood side by side along the country lane that brought us from the blacktop road a mile away. Their plan was to collect enough nuts to sell in town and make a fortune. It was an ingenious scheme designed not so much for mercenary goals but to be allowed to take the tractor and trailer up the hill by themselves, making them feel independent and grown up. Since I was going to be busy mowing the front yard I reasoned that they would be in sight the whole time, and their plan would keep them out of the way of the mower. They were actually dancing from one foot to the other in their excitement to carry out their plan as I agreed. I was not surprised when they rounded the house with the trailer already loaded with buckets and pails for the nuts. Sean riding among the buckets along with his currently favorite dog and the other two trotting alongside eager participants in whatever adventure the boys invented. When treated with trust and respect, the boys responded, usually in kind, and I was not worried and I went back to my own chores.

Later as I was pushing the mower up the slope in front of the house, movement in my peripheral vision caught my eye and I looked up to see Sean, the younger of the two sons, racing down the hill toward me waving his arms frantically. Shutting off the mower as he arrived, his face white as a sheet, he panted, "A bear! The bear is killing my brother!"

Without the noise of the lawnmower, I could hear the unmistakable ruckus of animals locked in combat even at this distance. The scream of injury and the snarl and bark of the dogs was impossibly loud even from a quarter of a mile away.

"Get in the house! Now!

I didn't have to tell him twice and he bolted for the house, starting to cry, as he met his mother coming out to find out what the commotion was about. Sprinting to the shed, I turned the key and unlocked and pulled open the cabinet above the workbench. Inside lay my twelve gauge double barrel Stevens. Grabbing it and a handful of shells, I turned and ran toward the sound, breaking the gun open and jamming shells into the twin barrels as I ran. Terrified by the implications I could not seem to make myself run fast enough. I was afraid for my son but not of the bear. The fear clutched in my throat and heart hammered in my chest already dreading what I would find at the top of the hill. Panting up the hill, the noise grew louder, the screams of the beast and the incredibly vicious snarling and yelping of the dogs only fueled my anxiety. There were no accompanying sounds from a boy.

Cresting the hill the scene lay out before me and my breath caught in my throat. On the shoulder of the road sat the small tractor and trailer, Seth, deathly pale, stood on his toes alone up on the highest part of the tractor hood paralyzed by the scene in front of him. Between the tractor and the middle hickory tree, a life and death battle raged with unbelievable fury. Backed up against the tree was not a bear at all, instead, a huge feral boar screamed his fury as he fought the full-on fury of the three dogs. The three dogs, teeth bared and hackles raised were the vision of nightmarish rage as they defended their boy, working in concert and fighting to the death if necessary. In and out they darted. The monstrous hog would turn to the right to fend off an attack and the dog on the left would lunge in. If he turned to the left the dog on the right would seize the opportunity to avoid the already red stained tusks. My dog Shirley faced him head on and dared him to step out from the tree. The sound and fury of it filled the air.

The boar, an escapee from some domestic barnyard had transitioned into a huge feral monster. His shaggy humped shoulders and lowered head sporting three-inch tusks screamed his anger as he lunged out at his attackers protecting what he thought was his own private hoard of hickory nuts. His vulnerable hind quarters were backed up against the trunk as he took on the three dogs that bracketed him. The dogs gave no quarter and it was obvious that they would give their own lives if needed. Already they were showing the dreadful cost. Phoebe, the golden lab on the left fought on three legs, her left front bloodied and held against her chest.

Copper the golden retriever, her muzzle bloody and torn waded in again and again from the right. Shirley their leader and alpha setter/spaniel mix, had her side laid open from shoulder to belly. It would not be a standoff for much longer, the boar, protected by the tree was going to outmatch them, and soon.

Glancing at Seth, I could see that although terrified he was unharmed. For a brief second I gave thanks that he was smart and did the right thing instead of trying to outrun the beast. It is said that pigs can reach speeds of thirty miles an hour. With the intensity of the fight and the constant swirling movement of combatants, I could not shoot without hitting one of the dogs. Instead I pulled the trigger and fired one of the barrels into the trunk of the tree just above the hog. The explosion of the 12-gauge was incredibly loud above the din of the fight and caused all of them to freeze for a split second. Shirley, my best friend and hunting mate, immediately looked over her shoulder, acknowledging the reinforcements and slid to the left, opening a space and I didn't miss the chance. Firing from the hip, I emptied the second barrel into the face of the beast.

The skull of a pig is incredibly thick and has been known to deflect a bullet when fired from a distance, but there are very few creatures I can think of that can take a full load of twelve gauge shot in the face at point blank range and not drop on the spot, but that is exactly what happened. He staggered and shook his head, losing his footing for a moment, dazed. There was no time to reload the shotgun but the girls did not miss their chance and dove in to catch him from behind. Still shaking his head and obviously thrown off by this new assault, the pig was unable to defend his back legs and hams. The dogs doubled their efforts and the pig decided that retreat was a better strategy. Turning away from them, he dove into the standing corn of the field behind the hickory trees, grunting and crashing through the stalks. The sound of his squeals growing farther and farther away.

To their credit the dogs did not pursue. Exhausted and too smart to risk ambush in the tall corn, they dropped to the ground, whimpering. Panting from the pain, Shirley lay on her side, the gore of where the tusk had laid open her side, looking even worse than I had thought. Phoebe's leg was twisted and obviously broken and only Copper seemed to have avoided the need for stitches, but she was badly cut up just the same. Breaking open the shotgun, I pulled to two spent shells and reloaded noticing only then that the shells were number eight bird shot, not the double 'B's' that I thought I had grabbed. It was no wonder they had not stopped the pig in his tracks. I didn't make the same mistake this time.

I dropped to my knees next to Shirley, my eyes misted. I thanked her with all my heart. I told her she would be okay. I told her she was beautiful. Turning her head, she made eye contact, panting, proud of herself and her friends.

Rising, I turned and lifted Seth down. Up to now he had held up under the stress, but now he clung to me and began to cry. Setting him down, he knelt and wrapped Copper in a hug and I let him hold her and cry. Down the hill our truck roared out of the driveway, spraying gravel and squealing the tires onto the pavement of the road. The truck raced up next to us and jolted to a stop, my wife pallid and tearful, jumped out of the truck and grabbed Seth bawling her eyes out and crushing him in her desperation.

"I heard the shots, did you get the bear?"

"Wasn't a bear. Was a wild hog." I said as my knees began to shake. "The girls are pretty bad off, I've got to get them to town and see Doc White. Help me load them into the truck will you, then go back to the house with the boys and call him at home, tell him to meet me at his office please. Then call Jim Peters, (the county sheriff), tell him or one of his deputies to meet me there. I wounded him pretty good, now he's going to be doubly dangerous, they'll need to get some hunters after him." I was talking fast, agitated by the scene and adrenaline pounding in my ears.

A week later, a county police car came down the hill slowly and turned into the yard. The dogs all still recuperating did not race out to greet it as was their usual custom, but instead lay on their various rugs and watched from the porch. After a moment, Jim Peters crawled out from behind the wheel and rose to his feet behind the driver's side door. Jim, never in any hurry to get anywhere, took his time stretching his back and regarding the view out over the fields. Finally, he made his way around the front of the squad car and moseyed up the walk and eased his long legs up the steps. Eyeing the dogs, he squatted down beside Shirley and examined the long-shaved line from her right shoulder down to her belly with its neat line of stitches. Scratching behind her ears, he said, "Well old girl, I hope he bought you the best steak he could find. You surely earned it." "Believe me Jim, there isn't enough steaks to thank these three enough."

"I believe that. Especially after what we found Doc."

"Did you get him?"

"Yep, we got him. Really big son-of-a-bitch, almost three hundred pounds. Got himself one of Doug Tanner's dogs before we could catch up to 'em. Took more than one shot. These dogs of yours, they must be hell on wheels Doc. How's the boy?"

"He's okay I guess, probably not gonna want to go up by those trees again for a while though."

"Can't blame him there. That guy was the devil." He looked up at me. "Well I wanted to stop myself and tell you that it was safe again and to bring you these."

Unbuttoning his shirt pocket, he reached into it and brought out two three-inch tusks, handing them up to me while he continued to scratch Shirley behind the ears.

"Thought you might want to keep them. Probably make a good story someday, I would guess."

I would guess indeed.

Today

dads

Leaning back in the chair, I looked hard into the fire. With every bump, bruise and small cut our love and care for our children is deepened. In retrospect, the internal bumps and bruises seem the deepest, and I wonder whether those emotional traumas are ever totally recovered from. In their young lives, my two sons and later my daughter had witnessed things that would have left an enduring image on their hearts and minds.

They had grown up, become adults and had families of their own now. I wondered at how the terrors of their youth colored their own parenting skills. I wondered if they recalled the specific event that elicited the emotional response. Did they look at the event objectively or still regard it from the emotional vision of the child that was present. These little moments that altered their trajectory toward self-awareness. Most of all, I wondered if they had found it in their hearts to forgive me for allowing them to happen.

My father had done his best to raise a family, but in later years I had begun to see the similarities in our individual parenting techniques. In those same later years, I learned more about him on a deeper level when he gave me glimpses into his own childhood.

The Wolf Packs

The morning had dawned cold and crisp with the low sun not bothering to warm the landscape. At dusk we'd crawled into the tent, but as the cold deepened during the night we'd given up and crawled outside to sit near the fire where we had dozed wrapped in our sleeping bags. Across the fire ring from me, I regarded him.

The black stocking watchcap on his head hid the thinning hair and accented his ever- growing ears. The sleepless night had formed bags under his eyes and they joined the creases and wrinkles that crisscrossed his face. The eyes that looked back at me though were bright and sparkling. My father loved this—he loved all of it.

Mostly to the fire and no one else in particular, he said, "Air smells like snow. Sometime after noon probably."

The sun was shining brightly and there was no wind to speak of, but I didn't doubt him.

He knew his weather like he knew these woods.

Indeed, the snow started just after noon. We had stopped and had our lunch on a sawn tree stump on the edge of a clearing sitting back to back, not needing small talk. The first flakes small, almost invisible, drifted across my vision. The sun that had slowly given up the fight as the skies had progressively grayed was now invisible behind the haze. The breeze had picked up.

"It's startin' sooner than I thought. We'd better head back; it's gonna get bad—quick."

Once again, I didn't doubt him. I quickly got up and packed our lunch wrappers and thermos into my knapsack and then helped him to his feet. He reached down and picked up his old Steven's 12-gauge shotgun.

"We'll cut across Bell's Mound, shorter that way."

I met his eyes.

"Storm's coming, gonna need to shuffle." His eyes were still bright, but his lips were a thin line and his eyebrows were drawn down. He was worried.

"We might'a waited too long." He added.

This was going to be his last hunt in the big woods. Well into his seventies, his balance was no longer trustworthy as he shuffled along in the fall leaves. The last of his brothers, he had insisted in spite of his doctor's warnings, and I had reluctantly agreed to accompany him. Now his stumbling disappeared from his walk as he struck out up the steep slope, cutting the corner toward our camp and into as straight a line as we could manage.

Within a quarter of a mile, the snow started falling in earnest. The wind swung around to the north-east, and began coming in off of Lake Superior. In a few minutes the footing became slippery, covering the twigs and branches that pulled at our boots and threatened to trip us up.

Twice he fell, unable to break his fall with the heavy gun he carried in his hands. His stocking cap whitened in the falling snow.

"This isn't gonna work—too far. And too steep. Let's head downhill. Head for the old lumber camp. We'll ride it out." He spoke while wiping the gun off with his sleeve. Then he squatted down and levered the shells out into the snow. "Can't keep fallin' on a loaded gun.

Gonna get bad."

He didn't have to tell me twice. The old camp had been abandoned decades ago; the forest had long ago reclaimed the site. By my reckoning, the old camp was at least a mile, maybe more, but probably closer than last night's campsite, and it was mostly downhill.

It was a rare thing that we would go to the old camp and then only to pass by it.

Approaching it you could feel the ghosts that walked among the broken-down log buildings, not to be disturbed. The light around it seemed dim and even as full-grown adults, we stayed clear.

I took the lead, breaking trail, but listening behind me for his progress. I was no spring chicken either, in my mid-fifties. My lungs had stopped cooperating years ago and my pace had slowed accordingly. In all, we were a good match for each other, physically anyway. Right now, it felt like hurrying was in order so I pushed myself and him.

With the concentration required to make our way, the time it took to hike to the old lumber camp didn't seem to take as long as it probably did. By then the snow was already inches deep. I was a little proud of myself for being able to find it and I stopped at the edge, marveling at the appearance of the old structures. Trees had grown out through the blind windows and broken roofs. The dark buildings whitening in the driving snow gave it almost a Christmas card appearance. The old man pushed past me.

He shouted above the wind, "The old cookhouse, most of the roof looks like it's still
intact."

He didn't break stride but headed at an angle to his right, toward the largest of the disappearing structures. The snow was now blowing straight across, the wind whipping the heat from our faces. Once there, he leaned through the nearest window frame and set his gun down inside and unshouldered his pack and dropped it next to it. Turning he immediately began gathering downed limbs and branches, shaking the snow off of them and throwing them in through the window. I followed suit, working as fast as we could, dragging the larger ones close, then breaking them with our heavy boots, throwing them through the window, and finally following them ourselves and out of the worst of the weather.

"Give me your shotgun." He hollered.

I looked at him, he was starting to shiver but his eyes seemed lucid. Sort of curious I reached back for my Remington and handed it to him. Without hesitation, he swung it to his right and fired out the window. The report was impossibly loud in the relative quiet of the old cookhouse—and the dead silent woods. Twenty yards away, a snowshoe rabbit jumped once and laid still.

"Dinner is served." He leaned the gun against the inside wall and waved me out to fetch the rabbit with a finger. It would go with the one grouse we'd gotten this morning. How he'd seen that bunny in the middle of the raging storm, I couldn't guess but he was like that even now, he didn't miss much when he was here in his woods.

Later, with the fire burning near the hole in the roof where some previous fire had taken the back half of the building, we sat with our backs to the inside wall. The wind howled outside and blew snow in through the burnt out hole in the roof, piling it evenly on the floor near our feet. We had plenty of firewood, we'd eaten well and Da pulled out his pipe.

Once it was packed and he had a good cloud wafting away, he leaned forward and twisted, looking past me and around the large gutted room.

"I spent a few winters here when I was a boy, you know."

I hadn't known that.

"Times were hard back then. There was no work for

Pappy; it was the depression. But he was always welcome in the camps, wasn't too many jobs he didn't know how to do there. Us boys all came with, worked in the saw shop, or in the cookhouse and tended the horses. Me too, I was too young for most of the man work, mostly I was just a mascot, I guess. Ma stayed home with the girls and kept up the farm, but we'd spend the winter months up here. Was easier on the home groceries that way, and the camps paid cash money."

"Winter up here ain't like winter down there. Up here they can kill you, and you don't even know your dead, freeze ya' solid in no time flat. Snow gets so deep, the deer 'yard up' down in the tamarack swamps. Makes 'em hard to get to. Food'd get pretty scarce unless you liked salt pork and beans."

"When middle winter came," he took a pull on his pipe and stared into the fire reliving the memory, "the wolves would come."

He stopped and stared into the fire for a full minute.

"At night we'd hear them howling in the distance, 'singing to the moon' Pappy used to say. Then they'd come —they'd come a'howlin'; howlin' into the camp; just howlin' and eating everything they could find. A lot of 'em. Anything made outt'a leather, scraps, anything they could find, they ate. Gloves, harnesses, they'd even chew the leather straps that we used for door handles. They'd pull the deer hides we'd nail up to dry on the barn no matter how high we nailed 'em. They ate anything and everything."

The pipe in his hand was forgotten as he struggled with the emotion that tightened his voice.

"I was terrified. We all slept in small bunkhouse together, and I'd hide under the beds. I can still remember the ice-cold floors on the side of my face while I was lying under there. Once after it had been real cold and the snow was too deep for the men to work, they came, howling and a poundin' into the camp, snarlin' and fightin' each other for the scraps. I could hear other kids crying in the other buildings and the horses in the stables screaming. I hid under the bed. I put a sock in my mouth so I wouldn't cry —so nobody'd think I was a baby."

He relit his pipe and looked into the fire for a long time. I thought that was the end of the story, the goosebumps on my arm had goosebumps. He took the pipe out of his teeth and pointed across the open space.

"All of a sudden a blast of cold air hits me in the face. I can hear the wolves scratchin' and howling even louder, they were so close, right outside the window. I couldn't get any farther under the bed, my back was up against the cold wall behind me. I was sure they were comin' for me."

"Boom, Boom, …Whoom, Boom!" He waved his arms over his head so wildly that sparks from his pipe flew everywhere.

"Right over my head. Four shots, all at the same time. It was not just loud, it was like cannon fire. I opened my eyes and saw four pairs of stockinged feet an arm's reach from my face. I peeked out from under the bed; the window next to it was wide open and the Casey boys all stood at the window with their rifles still up."

He tapped out his pipe on the floor and pulled his heavy coat up around his face.

"Everyone else was afraid and hid under their beds, but not the Casey boys." He pointed the stem of his empty pipe out into the darkness of the room, "The Casey boys stood up to those wolves. I learned what it meant to be a Casey that night. That night that the Casey boys stood up against them starving wolves, and I was one of them, I was a Casey by god, and that's all I've ever wanted to be since then."

Tomorrow

Tomorrow will be a different kind of day. Tomorrow will be Thursday and Thursdays are baking day in the Amish neighborhood. Every Thursday afternoon a black buggy will slowly climb the hill below the house and pull into the yard. After tying the horse to the old basketball hoop post in the driveway, the Schrock's, Amos and Letty, along with one of their many daughters will climb down. Their arms will be full of fresh baked bread and other food stuffs.

Once inside Letty, an old woman herself now, busies herself in the kitchen while her daughter dusts and cleans the empty house, putting things away where I can't find them and rearranging the pictures on the fireplace mantel. Letty will then stand over me while she sternly oversees me choking down a disgusting concoction of Lobelia and Chamomile tea that she insists is good for me. I, on the other hand, am sure that she's trying to poison me on the installment plan and tell her so—every week, which makes her smile. She leaves me a small canister of her poisonous tea that I'm supposed to drink daily. I thank her for this and later I will burn it in the fireplace, destroying any evidence of absence.

Amos will shovel the walk from the house to the shed

where my old truck is wintering and refill the woodpile on the front porch. Never one for conversation, once he's finished with these outside chores, he will busy himself in my small shed but refrain from entering the house. I've always liked Amos.

I love and hate Thursdays.

Last Night

the nightmare

Last night the dream had come again. The first time that it had visited was shortly after my rotation out of Vietnam. I had been on a medical flight back to the states, my body shattered by the violence and my brain high on pain medications. I had various nightmares ever since I was a child, just as all children do, but after Vietnam the childish fears were all superseded— replaced by only this one. This one specter had reached back into my past lives, coalescing into a horror that was terrifying, yet familiar. Since that time, the nightmare emotions that the dream created had become a constant source of dread and had created in me a fear of sleep.

The frequency of the nightmare slowly receded after I married and entered fatherhood. Only visiting when I was running a fever or physically ill in other ways. Now in my later years, it had become an infrequent visitor, never failing to catch me by surprise when my guard was lowered.

In these later times, this unwanted visitor had not changed. Always the same. Wrapped in a ruthless dread, the light of the dream is dim and grey, where I can see nothing. Akin to driving a car on a densely foggy night, impenetrable, but 'It' is there, somewhere within it. With absolute assurance, I feel the presence of it just beyond my field of vision. A palpable presence, just beyond the threshold of perception, breathing, pressing in—coming. 'It' is huge, an immense shapeless mass, unstoppable, relentless. Paralyzing dread flows from it and it is near, always coming ever nearer, coming for me. Its' malevolent progress inexorable, the slow unrelenting speed of fate itself.

In the dream, the air surrounding me is hot and moist, suffocating. My arms and legs are trapped, paralyzed, wrapped tightly in a blanket of flannel air that I cannot breathe, claustrophobic, and defenseless. The 'something' is coming, always coming—coming for me. It wants to engulf me in misery, suffocate, and drown me with fear and grief. A specter of my unforgivable past sins. The embodiment of the horrors of a steamy jungle night where the screams of the dying and those still afraid to die, echo together and trap me in a tangle of agonizing anger and mayhem. A reminder of when I walked into the darkness— and had embraced its ways.

There is no escape, and there is no defense. I feel it approaching a crossing point in the timeline of my life, a crossroads, somewhere in the near distance where we must inevitably meet, approaching at the agonizing pace of the hour hand of a clock. In that one single night, so very long ago, the nightmare had become the Rubicon in my life, marking the departure of any remaining childhood innocence, fantasies or fears. From then on, it had laid in wait for me whenever I closed my eyes—the horror and terror of it, haunting my nights and days. Eventually, I had accepted the evil it represented as my own identity. The guilt and the shame of death and violence that I had experienced and embraced became my mantle of darkness, and for a long time I had descended into evil ways and had become the darkness itself.

When the nightmare comes, for a time even once I am awake, my thoughts turn to my darker memories and my road through the purgatory I once walked.

The Specter of Darkness

It was the last few days of 1973. The winter already seemed to have gone on for too long; cold, wet and lonely. Two of us were hunched in a shop doorway trying to avoid the worst of the winter weather that swirled around us. Icy sleet whipping down the narrow street collected in the alcove around our feet and made the frozen sidewalk slippery under my boots.

My full-length duster stopped the snow from going down my neck but could not prevent the bone-chilling cold from penetrating. With my hands shoved deep into the pockets, I flexed my fingers to keep them from stiffening and patted the small automatic stowed inside my belt for reassurance.

The cobbled street was deserted in both directions. Dimly lit by period street lamps spaced far apart that added ambiance but no significant illumination. The sound of the gusting wind gave noise to the otherwise silent city street, occasionally interrupted by the periodic tolling of a distant church bell. We had been waiting for some time, and the cold wind added a bleak aspect to our planned evening's activities.

There was barely enough room for the two of us in the small space as we crowded together. I'm not a little guy, but Martin Biddle dwarfed me by half. I was also dressed for the weather; Martin was not.

Martin Biddle was my latest partner. He was a product of the pine woods of Mississippi, with no experience in cold weather preparation. He was a large man by any measurement, imposing by size but not by demeanor. A gentle giant, he had demonstrated good decision making, and was smart and clever, but also had shown inklings of a hot temper. He had all the qualities of a good second hand, but I didn't trust him entirely yet. Tonight was going to be a watershed evaluation. Paired not by choice but by the attrition that followed our line of work.

Our attention was focused on the small gasthaus, in suburban Nuremberg, Germany, a half block distant. It was well after closing time and the lighted windows in front had gone dark ten minutes ago. Now the small metal sign hanging above the front door swayed in the breezy half-light, adding a faint discordant squeak to the otherwise silent street. We were the only souls out in the frigid post-midnight air.

Finally, the sound of latches being thrown was followed by the front door below it slowly opening. A head appeared and peeked around the door, then a figure stepped out into the street and gestured with a wave in both directions.

Separating ourselves from the shadows, we stepped out onto the bricks and moved briskly forward. Catching sight of movement, the man in the doorway signaled for us to hurry and then ushered us into the entrance. Once inside he closed and locked the door behind us and then preceded us up a few darkened steps and into the small saloon.

Stepping behind the bar he pulled down two heavy beer steins and filled both from the tap. Setting them on the bar in front of us, he gestured with a tilt of his head toward the back of the room, then turned and exited through a small door behind the bar. Throughout the encounter he had neither spoken nor made eye contact.

Lifting the two beer mugs, Biddle made his way to the back of the house and a table in the corner. The table was big enough to accommodate the five chairs arranged around it and still have room to maneuver. We each took a seat with our backs to the adjoining walls of the corner, so that we both faced the rest of the room.

The place had none of the ambiance that marked it as an enjoyable establishment during business hours. Instead, the room was dimly lit with the lights of commerce turned down. The heat had been turned down for the night, leaving the atmosphere filled with the stink of cold ashtrays and stale beer, both chilly and unwelcoming, surreal in its lack of substance. Neither of us wanted to get too comfortable.

I was within one hundred days of rotating back to the States after my U.S. Army tour in Germany. Marten Biddle had been groomed to be my replacement. We knew enough about each other already and didn't need to speak; we weren't here to socialize. We were here on business and both of us were on edge. It was not the type of business that the Army would have been happy that we were involved in and we hoped to avoid them finding out about it.

Tonight, we were here to deliver a package of some value. The value of which had already been agreed upon. We were only the delivery boys—but delivery boys with teeth. In a very short while there was going to be a lot of money on the table in front of us and we had no idea who we would be meeting or how safe our encounter would be. Both of us had done this before, and both of us had experienced what happens when things didn't go as agreed upon.

Halfway through my second cigarette, we heard the sound of locks being turned at the back of the building and heavy boots on wooden floors. I moved my beer glass out of the way, opened my duster and loosened the automatic in my waistband. Biddle stood and removed his coat to clear his shoulder holster.

Three men entered through a back door and approached the table, slowly spreading out across the open space. None of them appeared unique. I wouldn't have remarked on them if I had passed them on the street, but they radiated a tension that was palpable.

"Pretty warm for July." Spoken by the clean shaven one in the middle.

"Pretty hot for December." Was the rehearsed response.

"You're Casey." I nodded. "What have you got for us?"

I reached into the inside pocket of the duster and pulled out two hefty 3.5 X 8" decks of computer cards. Each weighing well over a two-pounds apiece and dropped them on the table in front of me.

In 1972 the United States Department of Defense had shouldered the task of stepping into the twentieth century by beginning the monumental task of computerization. It made sense for a global military power to find a way of coordinating the massive logistics of supplying all of the necessary equipment, food, and weapons required of an international policing force. The effort was laudable and necessary, but it didn't come easy. It would still be decades before a computer would be miniaturized enough to sit on a desktop. Or under a desk. Silicon microchips and microprocessors were a long way off, Steve Jobs and Bill Gates were still in high school. A single computer that the army employed was moved about in an environmentally controlled semi-trailer and weighed several tons. It required a second trailer housing input terminals, storage, and replacement electron tubes. A third trailer contained a large 30-40 KW generator to power both the computer and the air conditioning system.

For all their high intent, these computers were basically just adding machines that counted inventory. They were not sophisticated enough to communicate with one another, even if there had been the technology for it. Instead, all units, companies, battalions, and brigades logged their inventories. Everything, food, equipment, trucks, trailers, and weapons were punched onto little cards that were fed into the behemoths, where it was sorted, counted, registered. A days input would often require an equal amount of time to process the information once the computer had it.

Once complete, the computers would dutifully produce a deck of cards with all of the compiled information. These decks would be placed in a secure pouch and hand-delivered to the nearest radio broadcasting station maintained by the Army and then broadcast by teletype to a headquarters location to be further compiled with other input. The process required many hands, all of which needed security clearances.

The clearances were necessary because of the confidential nature of the information. Anyone interested in knowing troop strength, equipment buildups or placement could gather valuable sensitive intelligence from a single deck of cards. One deck of cards was produced by each computer once a week. On the table in front of me was two weeks' worth of inventory, troop strength and supplies for most of the Czechoslovakian front. The Cold War still occupied the attention of both NATO and the Soviet Union.

"Is that all of it?"

"Yep. Let's see what you've got."

The man on the left raised a fat briefcase onto the table and unzipped it. Then shoved it toward me. Inside were bundles of bills, each in one-inch stacks. Some were deutsche marks, others dollar bills. Each stack had a bank wrapper around it that testified to the amount in the bundle.

It took only a few minutes to separate and compile the total amount. It didn't add up to the amount that we had been told to expect."The count is short." I wasn't upset; I was open to an explanation. Biddle was less conciliatory.

"What the fuck!"

"It's short because the last set was short, and the deck was out of sequence."

"That's not up to us. You take that up with your boss. I'm here to deliver and collect. I don't negotiate."

"This isn't a negotiation Casey, take it or leave it."

"Doesn't work like that. I take the correct amount, or I walk out. Simple as that." "This is the amount you get, and we'll take the decks."

"No—you won't. I don't have any wiggle room in this; it's an all or nothing arrangement. I just make the deliveries and pick-ups."

"The last set was incomplete; we don't trust this one to be any different."

"Then you should be doing business with someone else. It's not my deal, it's just my job."

Biddle had been struggling to keep quiet, but finally he'd heard enough.

"This is bullshit! You sons-a-bitches either cough up the rest of the bread, or I'm gonna kick some German ass, take the money, and finish my beer!"

The man closest to me was quick. Very quick. A nice big Sig Sauer .45 was in his hands instantly as he stepped forward.

"No more talk!"

"Motherfucker!" Biddle erupted out of the chair, pushing the heavy table away from himself with his left hand while his right one reached for his shoulder holster.

Before he was fully upright, the first shot caught him just below the chin. The second shot hit him in the left shoulder, spinning him away and into the corner. It was unnecessary, the first one had done the job.

I was caught by surprise with the beer mug halfway to

my mouth, but the beast that slept with one eye open wasn't. The beast that had first awakened far back in the jungle of Vietnam and never fully slept again. The red mist flashed into my vision, the formidable strength of it took control of every fiber of my being, making me a spectator in the violence it was capable of.

With all the strength I could muster, I slammed the heavy beer stein into the outstretched hand that held the gun, as I leaped to my feet. Finishing the first blow that crushed his fingers, I brought the mug back in a backhand stroke that caught his right ear, smashing his skull. He was dead before he hit the floor.

The sheer rage and joy of the fight were beyond rational thought but instead instinctual, remorseless, and without mercy. I rose from my crouch and turned to the other two. Both men were fumbling for their weapons, but I gave them no time. The heavy duster coat that I wore was too clumsy to find my own in the billowing cape-like garment. In a fight, my first impression had never been to reach for a gun. When the beast was in control, it wanted more violence than a gun provided. It wanted physical contact. It wanted only to kill.

I rushed them both. Catching the man on the right with my shoulders, raising him off his feet. I carried him all the way to the far wall, slamming him against it and raising my knee into his crotch. The wind flew out of him, and he sagged. Without hesitating, I turned back to the last one.

He had recovered and had a small automatic in his hand. The shot passed through the duster under my right arm. I brought my foot up and caught him on the outside of his left knee, driving it sideways and folding his leg backward. As he fell to the floor, I finished my spin and used the same boot to kick him in the head.

I turned back to the other man. He was using his hands to slowly climb the wall.

Catching him by the head, I smashed it against the wall again and again, until he dropped into a sodden pile.

I turned back to the room and the carnage that hadn't been there seconds before. Pulling the table out of the way, Biddle lay in the corner. The wound in his throat bubbling blood and air. His eyes communicated his fear, he had only seconds and he knew it. I looked him in the eye and nodded confirmation. His struggle ended. I closed his eyes.

The fire in my veins burned slowly away. As if in a haze, out of the corner of my eye, I glimpsed the little bartender. His eyes were huge with fear and surprise. I sat next to Biddle with my back to the wall and his head in my lap and stared at nothing. Gradually realizing that I was also hurt as my body again began to take stock. I could hear the approaching sound of the polizei sirens. I knew they were coming for me. I didn't care. Let them come.

Some memories are good and some are hard. Apologies to ghosts serve no purpose; reparations today do not revive the dead. I no longer fear the crossroads where the nightmare and I must finally meet. Perhaps it is because the crossroad of this final judgment is nearer at hand than ever that the terror that seized my heart in past times, no longer exists. Perhaps it is because my penance for past sins finally has accumulated enough to level the scale of judgment. Perhaps it is only because there is nothing left for me to fight against and the beast can finally sleep.

And perhaps it is because karma always balances the scales of justice—eventually.

Baby's First Book

I was restless, tired of sitting in the old wing chair but without anything else to occupy my energy. I fidgeted, trying to find an excuse to keep sitting and at the same time not wanting to sit any longer. Finally, in frustration I rose to my feet and paced a circuit of the room, away from the heat of the fire and back again. My damaged knees protested the first steps as they always did, but gradually gave up the complaint until the next time I challenged them.

Encouraged, I shuffled another circuit, idly brushing my hand along crowded bookshelves, full to bursting with tomes of knowledge and children's old storybooks side by side. Any empty spaces that might have been, filled with keepsakes, mementos and outright junk collected over a lifetime of endeavor. All of them reminders, each one harkening back to the memory that fostered its place on a shelf of distinction.

Memory, especially old memories, have a way of fading the color of the picture. Bright hues of summer become pastels of memory. The happy times, bring equal parts of happiness of times's gone by and sadness that they are no more. The hard times and the sad times have their sharp edges smoothed, so the contrast of sorrow becomes more grey than black. Even at a distance, the pain of the hard times is unmitigated even at the great distance of time gone by and the greying of memory.

Each piece on these shelves represents a learning experience. A small piece of knowledge that at the time did not instantly transfer to wisdom. It was only over time that the knowledge could ferment, combining with emotions to become wisdom, often too late to serve anything but a rue-worthy moment of reflection.

Near the far end of the shelves, in the darkest corner of the room, one book draws my eyes with each shuffling revolution of the room. I know it by heart, its feel and the undeniable weight of it. Pausing, I glide my index finger down the spine, slowly mouthing the title, <u>Baby's First Book</u>.

Sliding the leatherette album out, I carry it to the chair. With it resting on my lap, I look at the filigreed beadwork cover running my fingers over its texture.

I woke the boys before daylight.

"C'mon guys! Mom says it's time.

In an instant they were both out of bed and pulling on clothes. We had been ready for this, the last two weeks, a seeming eternity. At last, it was time and my excitement was equal to theirs.

Once downstairs shoes and jackets were pulled on near the back door. Only then did my wife appear coming down the stairs. The look on her face did not match the excited anticipation of the three of us. She grimaced as her foot struck the floor, and her eyes were wide with something else.

"Something's wrong Em."

"Wrong how?"

"I don't know, just not right. We need to go."

The boys were dancing at the door, eager to go. I lifted the small travel bag that we'd packed days ago and I helped

Greta out the door and down the back-porch steps. Once situated in the truck, we started the thirty-minute drive to town so we could meet our newest family member.

I understood her trepidation. There had been other babies. Other little ones that had not made it to the finish line. Each one, loved from the moment of conception, but ultimately not ready for this world. Each one grieved for once they were no more. For their mother, it was a bottomless feeling of loss and failure that relentlessly ebbed and flowed like the tides with the changing of the moon. For me the father, a struggle to locate the grief and deal with it on a conscious level. Struggling with the inability to console my wife, because nothing can fill the hole that such a loss creates. There had been other little souls.

My hands tightened on the steering wheel, mitigating the concern with the excitement of the potential moment. Encouraging the boys with their suggestions for names of the new arrival.

"Skuzz-bucket" Seth was wide awake and looking for a laugh.

"How 'bout Cheez-Wiz?" I said. "With a name like that, he'd be sure to be a major NBA Superstar."

"How 'bout you shuddup? It's gonna be a girl." Grit was playing along between contractions.

"I know, I'm all set. Wilhelmina is my vote."

"You are such a dipshit. We already decided, it's gonna be Jennie. Jennifer Lee."

"You decided, you mean."

"Same difference."

I had called ahead to the hospital. I had been working in and around the hospital for the last ten years so I wasn't surprised when no one but my very good friend Paulette Downing met us as we entered through the ER doors.

"I'm so excited for you Doc! Grit how'ya doin' baby? Your folks are gonna be so excited. Come on honey, I'll take you back. Doc take the kids into the chapel I already laid out some snacks, and pillows so they can sack out once they're done."

"Thanks Paulie, any word on Doc Southerland?"

"He passed the puck Doc, you got none other than Doctor Kearney tonight. He insisted."

Paulette and Greta headed through the double doors and into the hospital proper just as Jim Kearney was getting ready to step through.

"Hey Emmett! How about this? Another delivery, only this time its yours. I'm thankful that I can be a part of it. He narrowed his brows and put a hand on my shoulder. "Especially after the others."

"Grit says there's something wrong."

"What? What do you mean?" He was immediately on the alert.

"She said she doesn't know. Just not right?"

"Okay, I'm heading back right away. Go scrub up Emmett. I'll catch you up once you're down there."

There is no way to hurry scrubbing and getting into scrubs but I shaved the corners a little anyway. Even so, as I turned down the hall leading to the one maternity delivery room, I met Paulette and Jim coming the other way.

"Get Raleigh on the phone right away, and also Doctor Hayes we need anesthesia too. Call in the surgical team and prep the room Paulette."

Turning to me, "Sorry Emmett, I can't let you go down right now. We've got some issues and we need to move quickly. Babies in stress, and Grit's B.P. is off the charts. Two hundred ten over one-seventy. We need to take your baby right away."

"Eclampsia." I didn't have to guess. I had seen first-hand what kind of hell it could cause.

"Exactly. We need to go; I'm going to scrub up. I hope they find Raleigh in town, I don't know what his surgical schedule is these days.”

“I’ll check on the boys then. Are you sure I can’t help calm her down Jim?”

“She’s afraid you’ll be more upset than she is. The last time was bad enough Emmett, she’s afraid and this time she’s right.”

“That’s nuts. Sorry Jim, I’m going to go see her.”

“Okay, we’ll get ready.”

Holding her hand while she tried to control her breathing, I met her gaze.

“This is like before Emmett. Oh God, we’re so close. I can’t do that again.”

She was mirroring my own feelings. We had suffered miscarriages in the past, more than a few. Each one had been hard, but none had gotten beyond twelve to fifteen weeks. With this pregnancy everything had gone right. Grit had gotten more beautiful with each passing week, and we had laughed and enjoyed the planning and preparations. Now we were at forty weeks, full term, the finish line.

“It’s okay my love. It’s just a speed bump. I won’t let anything happen to you or to the baby. It’s gonna be alright. We’ve got Paulette and Jim right here, and I wouldn’t be surprised if that dipshit Tom Dunbar doesn’t blow through the doors any minute now too. We’re in good hands.”

“I know, but I’m still scared. And I feel terrible.”

Paulette entered briskly and once the door was open wide a surgical gurney followed her into the room pushed by one of the surgical team.

“Doc, sorry but you’ve got to scrub again. We can’t find Hayes. Raleigh’s already here, so we’re gonna need the extra hand.”

“No Paulette, I can’t. I just can’t do that, c’mon, what about Tom.”

“I tried that, I talked to Janet. She says he’s had to take his pain meds twice tonight and he’s finally resting. We can't use him."

A shuddering gasp came from behind us. This from Grit.

Everyone in the room was immediately galvanized to the spectacle taking place on the bed. My wife was in full rigorous spasm, her shoulders and lower legs the only thing making contact with the bed itself. Her pelvis and swollen abdomen thrust toward the ceiling. Her eyes rolled back in her head.

"Code Blue!" Paula yelled and pushed a button above the headboard.

Immediately a calm female voice spoke over the hospital intercom, "Code Blue, maternity. Code Blue, maternity, Code Blue, maternity."

"Let's go!" This was not her first rodeo, Paulette was in command. "Doc, other side pull the sheet. On the count of three lift, One, Two, Three. We lifted her and heaved her onto the gurney. Almost before she had settled the sides came up and the surgical nurse headed for the door.

"Doc go ahead of us. We'll see you in there. Hayes's gonna have some serious hell to pay once I find him."

Hours later I quietly entered the little hospital chapel. Pausing at the altar in front of me I looked up at the benevolent gaze of the Man on the Cross for a long moment as he looked back at me. Turning to the two small boys asleep on the pews in front of him, I sat down between them, and touched Seth on the shoulder. He immediately opened his eyes, rolling them in sleepy awareness.

"Is she here?"

"Yeah, Dad, is it really a girl?" This from his brother Sean.

"It is a girl, boys." I idly stroked Sean's hair as I smiled down at him.

"Can we go see her now?" There was excitement but sleepy excitement.

"I'm afraid she couldn't make it all the way out of heaven boys. I'm sorry."

Sitting back down in the chair near the fire I open the little book. Turning from one empty page to the next, all of them blank. A study in cream colored heavy bond paper. The little Baby's First Book has no entries, no babies first tooth, no recounted life events, no landmark dates, no first dance pictures. The pages still blank after all these years.

Today

afternoon, and after tears

The day has melted into afternoon. The light outside is the same with the overcast, but the feel is close to quitting time. Although I hadn't worked for a number of years now, I could still feel it when happy hour approached.

Rummaging through the refrigerator and freezer, I find a whole box of Thin Mints leftover from some distant and forgotten Girl Scout cookie sale. Chuckling at my good luck, I make a fresh pot of coffee and feast in front of the fireplace. Ha, win some, lose some. Hard wins and hard losses.

The Bad Foot

It is the end of a busy day and with the last patient casually leaving the office I lock the front door and assist the staff in the end of the day duties. The evening darkness that comes so early has already brightened the stars outside the windows and adds to the haste we all feel to finish and go home to our families. After walking the staff out and helping them brush the afternoon snow off of their vehicles, I brush several inches of new powdery snow off of my own truck, climb in and start the seventeen-mile trip up onto the ridge and home. The night will be cold and beautiful with uncountable stars and not a breath of wind. A true northwoods winter night, with the air so clear that you can smell the snow and stars so bright you can see almost as many features in the landscape as on a cloudy day. I look forward to the drive out of town and through the woods after work. Climbing the eight hundred feet to the high ridge that bisects the county east to west is always beautiful no matter the season. It always puts my day into perspective and helps to put the daily pressures behind and the anticipation of a warm fire, dinner, and time with the children ahead.

I pull off the blacktop and onto the gravel road that wanders back through the snow blanketed hills until eventually passing the little house over the next hill where I live. I stop in the middle of the lane at my mailbox, one of many sitting side by side and nailed on a weathered plank and set on two fence posts near the entrance of the lane. Each mailbox has a number and some other distinguishing mark to tell it apart from its' counterparts. Mine, the second from the right, has a bright yellow splotch of paint on its door. Due to encounters with wind weather and the snowplow over the years, or just age, the whole assembly leans slightly east as if into a strong wind but it has stood at that angle as long as I can remember. The bank of plowed snow stands almost as high as the posts on the mailbox. I climb out of the truck and scale the side of the snow pile squatting at the top to yank the door open and remove the day's mail.

Among the bills and flyers, there are a couple of Christmas Cards from family members and a postcard. Actually, not a postcard at all, rather it is a 3 by 5 index card with the name 'Casey' written on the blank side. Under my name are the words, "Leave on the Rte." In the upper right corner, the finish of the card is marred and there is a dirt smudge in the size and shape of a quarter. The sender obviously had taped a coin to the card and left it for the postman with those instructions. The return address in the upper left corner says "Borntrager, Rt. 1, Wilton, WI. I pause for a moment before I turn the card over wondering what the rural delivery mailman must think of this type of mail. This is not the first time I have received a post addressed in this fashion. I will have to remember to have my wife make him some cookies, (and maybe a pint of whiskey or six-pack of beer), to leave in the mailbox this Christmas.

The back of the index card is lined. Printed in pencil and using all capital letters it says, "Can you come out, Eli has hurt his foot. Don't come on Saturday as we have a wedding." I sigh as I climb back into the welcome heat of the truck and head up the lane toward home. It is late Friday night now, it has already been a long night at the clinic, and it is near bedtime if you are Amish. If I don't go tonight, I will not be able to see Eli until Monday due to the wedding plan and the fact that the Amish are unavailable for contact on a Sunday.

Eli is definitely Amish, in fact, I know of five Eli Borntrager's or Borntreger's that live on Route 1. There are only two mail routes in Wilton, Route 1 runs from Middle Ridge in the west across the top of the ridges and down off of Dorset Ridge in the east before it winds back up along the Kickapoo River and into the little town of Wilton. There are three hundred and forty-eight Amish families that live on or below one of the ridges that surround Wilton, Norwalk and LaFarge Wisconson and the Borntrager name is one of the more frequent family names.

Once home, I shake off the cold and weather, the enthusiastic onslaught of wild boys, too many dogs, and the knowing look from my wife. I go to my desk and pull out my map of the Amish communities. It was provided to me by one of their elders; a bishop, with the express instructions that I not share it with anyone. The map is almost two feet square, hand drawn, surprisingly detailed and somewhat to scale. Although there is no topography, all the roads and lanes are duly noted in dark solid lines. Between them are dotted lines that indicate 'short cuts' through the fields or woods that the Amish avail themselves to with their buggies or wagons. Each school house is painstakingly drawn at their exact locations along with the various cemeteries indicated by tombstones. Every family is shown in their location and labeled with the sires first, middle initial, and sir name. By my count, there are seven E. Borntragers, with various middle names.

It is my experience that the men's middle name is the

same as that of their father, so all of Daniel Borntrager's sons have the middle name of Daniel and the middle initial of 'D.' The nearest E. Borntrager is about five miles, two miles east of the Ridgeville Store and on County Trunk 'A'. I check my valise to assure that I replenished it with the necessary supplies after the last 'house call' and make myself a peanut butter and jelly sandwich. Standing at the kitchen sink, I wolf it and wash it down with cold milk. I have learned that there are no simple house calls and many times the simple has turned into a dire emergency. It is best to prepare.

After the short drive out to the highway and back through the ghost town that once was the Ridgeville Settlement, I pull onto County 'A' and follow the crest of Middle Ridge until I arrive at the homely house that is Eli A. Borntrager's. Switching into four-wheel drive I pull into the lane and drive the quarter mile distance to the small cluster of buildings, stop at the horse hitching rail and shut down the engine. The night is dark after the glare of the truck's headlights and there are no yard lights at the Amish homes but there is plenty of starlight to navigate with and after a moment, my eyes adjust to the light. The buildings all appear black in the starlight and the whiteness of the snow makes them all the darker. I take my flashlight and 'doctor' bag and climb down from the truck and hear the clank of milk pails and soft singing coming from the barn that tells me that the family is still finishing evening chores.

My breath comes out in great clouds of vapor that hangs in the icy still air around my face and I pull my hat down over my ears as I find the shoveled path toward the barn. Entering through the milk house, I enjoy the familiar smell of warm cows and dried hay listening to the crunch of cows chewing and their soft lowing as they begin to settle down for the night. As soon as I enter the barn aisle, the singing stops as does all other activity. The children are unused to strange English visitors and the sight of me freezes them in their tracks for a moment before they scatter in every direction. The smallest ones are sitting in a cardboard box that just fits in the bed of a red wagon to keep them safe and out from under the cows as the rest of the family busies itself with finishing their tasks. From between two cows, a woman's voice addresses me,

"Casey, Eli is in the house; he cannot chore for his foot."

There is no break in the steady squirt of milk into her pail. That tells me that she has told me as much as she intends to. I do an about face and exit back out into the cold and make my way to the house. From this angle, I can see a lantern is lit in the kitchen and I let myself in through the mudroom at the back of the house and slide my four buckle overshoes off before entering the house. The house is beyond warm, it is hot and the smell of kerosene oil and wood smoke emphasizes the temperature. Seated in front of the stove is Eli, whom I now remember from previous meetings. With his hat off even in winter, there is a line across his forehead that shows where the headband keeps the upper part permanently whiter than the lower and he is prematurely balding on the top of his head. His appropriately long beard is black as coal and his eyes are lined by his work ethic and his pain. His left foot is propped on a chair in front of him and has a towel draped over it. On top of the towel is a large plastic "baggy" filled with snow. He looks up and fixes me with a pained countenance,

"It is my foot Casey; it does not seem to be healing on its' own."

No "thank you for coming" or "glad you could make it." The Amish are not big on small talk.

"Well, then let's have a look, and maybe we can get you some relief."

I lift the bag of snow from his foot and even that change in pressure makes him wince. Removing the towel, I look at his foot. It takes all my training not to wince myself. The foot is wrapped from toes to ankle in gray duct tape; the toes are swollen and darkly purple. Above the tape, the ankle is swollen and puffed out and over the top edge of the tape. The tape is too tight and the swelling is cutting off the circulation to the entire foot. I am shocked at the grotesque swelling in the toes and worse by the blood and serum leaking out of the end of the tape, staining the towel on the chair. Masking my concern, I try for an attitude of professional deference.

People never cease to amaze me with their foibles and quirks. I am in over my head and I have not even begun to work.

"We need to get you to the hospital Eli. This is not something that I can deal with."

Instead of looking directly at me, his gazed is fixed on the wood stove. "There is no money for the hospital. The children doctored for measles last fall and the bill is quite large. I cannot pay again."

"When did this happen?"

"This past Monday after lunch, I wore my boot laced extra tight but that did not seem to make any difference, so we put the tape to it."

"I am going to need to take the tape off Eli before I can do anything else, so I will need you to sit very still while I do that. I will be very careful, but some of this is going to hurt."

"That will be something different," he says grimly, "it hurts hard already."

Reaching into my bag, I find the sharp razor blade 'Exacto' knife that I keep for things such as this and carefully cut slits through the tape at the top of the foot and on both sides. As soon as I complete the cuts, the tape springs away from the skin below and just falls to the floor. I am surprised by the ease of separation until I examine the foot further. With the tape gone there is nothing to hold the two sections of the foot together and it splits open from between the first and second toe along a remarkably straight line into the foot midway to the ankle. The surface of the foot is crusty and there is a white substance that falls to the floor in flakes as I watch. The cut is almost completely through the foot from top to bottom and gives it a cloven appearance to the top of the foot. Checking the pulse in the foot, I am relieved that it is still there for starters and that it is relatively strong. I take a breath. I have never heard of an Amish man with one foot, but Eli is close to becoming my first one.

"What is this white stuff all over your foot Eli?"

"That is powdered sugar. We put it on to prevent the 'proud flesh'."

"Proud flesh?"

"Yes."

What he means is that the powdered sugar will prevent the formation of keloids, scar tissue. Often, especially with deep or ragged tears to the skin and the tissue below the injury, the healing process will form large, raised areas at the injury site and produce an angry reddened scar that never goes away. In the case of a foot injury like this one, it would result in a lifetime of foot pain whenever the person wore a tight shoe. Once again I have been taught one of the Amish healing remedies that have been handed down family to family, which I can add to my 'bag of tricks' the next time I am in need of something the simple folks can do on their own.

I carefully spread the wound, which elicits a slight gasp from Eli. I can easily see that although the foot is cleanly cut, it has miraculously missed the toe bones, although I can clearly see them and the joints along the cut line.

"How did you do this Eli?"

"With the splitting ax. It is good that it was very sharp. Yes?"

"Yes, a duller ax would have torn it up pretty badly and we would have a lot more trouble than we do now. Didn't this bleed a lot?"

"It did until we poured the kerosene on it."

"Kerosene! I bet that really stung."

"It did…yes."

"And then you put the sugar on it?"

"Yes."

Already the foot looks somewhat better after the restrictive tape has been removed. The flesh is remarkably soft and pink. There is no sign of the usual drying that takes place along a laceration. Often with a deep cut the edges of the skin dry out quickly and pull back from the injury making suturing impossible and lowering the chance for a good outcome from the repair. Open wounds in a farm environment also increase the risk of infection and sepsis. I explain to him that I am going to numb as much of the area as I can with Lidocaine and then I must clean out the wound. His raised eyebrows are enough to caution me to be careful.

Once when I was young, my cousin and I had been shooting bottles up in the pasture and I had stepped on one of the bottles that we had previously killed. It went up through the bottom of my sneaker. The resulting cut had required almost twenty stitches and although the intern at the emergency room had repeatedly injected the area I had felt every excruciating stitch as he meticulously sewed. In order to fill the time as I work, I tell Eli this story as a means of explaining to him that although I am numbing it as well as I can, it will probably still hurt quite a lot.

I prep the foot by washing the entire area as best as I can with Betadine, foregoing the sponge and using gauze instead and working with as much care as possible. Meanwhile Eli observes quietly, never flinching or making a sound. Propping his foot on a towel, I bend over and begin the process of closing the wound. First pulling the opposing pieces of tissue together with quarter inch wide by three inch, 'Steri Strips' to secure as much approximation of the opposing sides of the wound. Between the strips, I begin the stitching process with 3-0 silk and my last FSL needle.

Like many things medical, I have never taken a "stitching" class. This knowledge like my medical supplies comes by way of various 'real' doctors. Many who understood the very real and uncomfortable position that I was often put in had taken it upon themselves to make sure I had Lidocaine, suturing supplies, knowledge of some medical procedures. Stitching was one "class" that I had been given on a few occasions. The stitching is slow going, I had never mastered the standard square knot used for interrupted suturing so my stitch of choice, and consequently, necessity, is a 'running' suture. To anyone who sews clothing, they would call this a 'loop stitch' with a twist. I have to adjust the foot often to access the top and bottom but in less than an hour, the work is done as best as it can be in the light of a single kerosene lantern.

As I was working, I have slowly been surrounded by the entire family as they completed their evening work and returned to the spectacle in the kitchen. They stand shoulder to shoulder in a tight circle, silent and wide eyed, the older ones holding the smaller ones. No one moving. There was no other activity as they leave me to my business. The wood burning cook stove is cranked to full on and the proximity of so many bodies has kept me perspiring profusely. Mrs. Borntreger, Ada, has a cloth diaper in her hands, which she has used repeatedly to wipe my forehead while I work. I suspect it is as much to protect her shiny waxed floor as it is to keep my vision from becoming blurred.

Once I am done and the foot is dressed, I stand up and stretch my aching back. I give the missus a set of instructions, including no weight bearing on the foot for as long as he is willing to sit still, crutches if he needs to move. No shoe or boot, especially not one that has been in the barn, any type of anti-inflammatory that she has in the house and preferably Tylenol or Ibuprofen every four hours. He is to see me at the clinic, weather permitting at the end of next week for evaluation; otherwise, I will stop on the next "call day" which is usually Tuesday and Saturday. She nods and reminds me that they have a wedding tomorrow and plan on attending, so he will be on crutches.

When I do see him again, two weeks have passed. He comes into the clinic wearing a tall jack boot that laces to just below his knee and walks in without crutches. After the boot and stocking are removed the wound is remarkably clean. Mrs. Borntreger, Ada, tells me that for the last week they have soaked it every night in "Johnson's Foot Soap" and rewrapped the foot in gauze. (I am very familiar with the remarkable healing capabilities of "Johnson's Foot Soap" and have recommended it for years for many types of lacerations.) She also proudly confides that he has been doing barn chores for a week and does not seem to limp. They both thank me sincerely and hand me a fresh loaf of bread and two dozen fresh eggs. I am impressed by the healing and healthy skin surrounding the wound. He can wiggle his toes, although it is painful but cannot flex his foot yet. After removing the stitches and reapplying new 'Steri-Strips' I tell him to let me know if he has any more trouble with it and he shuffles out of the office. I don't see him again until the next spring.

On a typical northern Wisconsin spring day, the sun is

warm with the renewed energy of a long winter's rest. The land, long frozen and blanketed with deep snow in the steep coulees and woods gives up its frost grudgingly. As the sun and ground struggle with these two forces, they produce a hard driving wind that blows from sunrise to sunset, stealing the heat from the sun. It's a difficult time to dress properly; the sun is too warm to wear a coat, the shade is too cool not to wear one. The compromise is to wear one and get used to working in a chilly sweat.

On one of these spring mornings, I was cleaning up the woodpile now reduced to a shadow of its former self in the fall. Splitting the last few large blocks down to stove size before they thawed completely. Over the winter much of the wood had been burned in the fireplace and furnace and what remained was an area littered with wood chips, separated bark scraps and splintered sticks. I was getting a good sweat on, working with the leaf rake to pile the rubbish when I heard the unmistakable sound of shod horse hooves on the still frozen road along with the odd clatter of buggy wheels. With the wind blowing, the sound was necessarily close or it would have been drowned out by its howl. Walking around the shed, I saw that the horse and buggy and its driver were already cresting the hill above the house and heading down toward me.

Turning into the yard, the horse and driver made a neat three-point turn in the driveway and came backing down the remaining twenty or so feet ending up neatly parked next to my truck less than five feet from the opened bay door of the garage/shed. It's a pretty neat trick to see performed by a well-trained horse and driver. Seated on the springed seat of the buggy, Eli smiled and nodded. Not wasting breath on any verbal greeting, he touched the brim of his wide brimmed black hat and climbed down on my side of the wagon and walked back to the small 'tailgate' and immediately began untying the ropes that secured a beautiful bent wood rocking chair tied to the buggy bed. Once it was untied he slid it back to the end of the wagon and hoisted it down before carrying it into the garage bay and setting it down.

Finally, he turned to me, "I wished you to have this," he indicated with a wave of his hand, "if you might use it."

The chair was a beautiful piece of art. The finished wood, the grain showing brightly still smelled of the glossy polyethylene sealer that had recently been applied. I was impressed by the perfect contours and craftsmanship of the piece, and I smiled back at Eli.

"Took a little while to finish, there is much to do in wintertime."

"It's beautiful Eli. Thank you very much. I can't imagine what this must cost."

"My foot is worth more."

He extended his hand and I gave it one shake as is the way of the Amish and I thanked him again. With that accomplished, he climbed back up on the buggy, coiling the tie-down rope in his hand and flipped the reins to the horse. He touched the brim of his hat again, then he and the buggy then made their way deliberately back up and over the hill.

Tarp

The area where we lived was known geologically as Wisconsin's 'driftless area.' This is the western and southwestern area of the state that was not scoured by the monstrous glacier melt during a long past age of the earth. The result was instead of the almost perfectly flat land that was the hallmark of much of the upper Midwest. The land was textured by high bluffs and deep valleys known as coulees. The slopes of these hills were much too steep to support agriculture, so was given over to forests of hardwood of varying spectacular greens in summer and greys interspersed with blue greens of evergreen in the winters. To the east where the glaciers had petered out they left high inaccessible bluffs known as drumlins the result of deposited sediments of long ago floods of glacier meltdown. The drumlins that stood above the surrounding flatness with their torpedo shapes could stretch as long as a mile and as high as seven to eight hundred feet. Where the soil gives up trying to maintain its grip on the steep slopes, ancient landslides lie piled around the feet of craggy sandstone cliff faces.

The coulees, cliffs and forested hills provide homes and refuge for countless species of flora and fauna. Deer flourish here. Bears are often seen as they move from one place of cover to the next. It is not surprising to hear of cougar sightings, coyotes, wolves, foxes, (both grey and red), along with grouse, pheasant and many raptors, including bald eagles and osprey. It would be a rare day to not see wildlife on even the most casual drive. Interspersed among the hills and valleys small farmsteads scour out a living from the rocky ground with carefully contoured fields to guard against the rush of run off when the rains fall on the hills above.

As the land flattens out to the east the ground is mostly sand, making it unsuitable for most standard farm crops such as corn, beans or wheat and oats. Here the pure groundwater is only a few feet under the ground and easily accessed for the red gold grown there. In the vast sand flats with its abundant water grows Wisconsin's money crop; cranberries. Unknown to many, Wisconsin provides the majority of cranberries grown in the United States and also contributes a large portion of its potatoes on this same ground. In spite of what those good folks in Idaho tell you.

As the winds leave the eastern slopes of the Rocky Mountains and rush across the vast plains of the Dakotas and Minnesota, the first obstacle they meet are the bluffs and coulees that line the Mississippi River. As the wind strikes this obstacle, they sweep up the slopes and create convection that results in spectacular storms and squeezes the moisture out of the clouds and their precipitation in both winter and summer. Where I live on the ridge, the snow falls almost every day, even if it is just a dusting. The first 'sticking' snow of winter usually falls in early November and is still on the ground when spring arrives in late March or early April and as a result of the almost daily snowfall it remains perpetually pure white. Snowfalls of eighteen to twenty inches are not unusual. In summer, torrential rains measured in inches instead of tenths of an inch fall with regularity creating immense and dangerous flash floods in the valleys below.

The coolness of the air on the forested hills being swept up into the hot atmosphere of summer also creates one of nature's most spectacular phenomena; lightning. Summer storms of torrential rain and continuous strobing lightning booming thunder with flashes between the thunderheads or the clouds and the ground make a fantastic display. At this elevation, the flash and the boom are simultaneous and the boys alternate their time during the light show being glued to the windows or curled on the couch in fear. One of the greatest gifts that I might have ever given to them was the gift of living in and loving all that nature offers.

When winter comes to Wisconsin, there is only one constant. That constant is that you never know what the weather will be from one day to the next. You know that it will snow—a lot—and you know that it will be cold—sort of cold, kind of cold and very cold, but the order that these things arrive in is anyone's guess. When it snows, it often snows for more than one day, and when it is cold, temperatures can drop well below zero and stay there for days or weeks. Often the temperature is so cold that the air cannot hold any moisture at all, and constant dust of frozen ice particles sprinkle down. Hot coffee will freeze in your cup before you have the chance to take your first sip. When you step out into cold, the low sunshine turns the landscape into a blinding quilt of sparkling diamonds.

Temperatures as low as forty degrees below zero are infrequent, but not rare and when that happens, schools are closed, and the people stay indoors to wait it out. However, in all of my years, I do not recall any businesses closing, or any stoppage of commerce in our hardy community. If you could not tolerate deep snow and bone-chilling cold, you simply did not live in upper Wisconsin—and if you did try to, you didn't try it for very long.

The cold brought many challenges besides just trying to

keep warm. Cattle could literally freeze to the ground when they laid down, and if you were not vigilant, they would freeze to death in short order. Livestock was in constant danger of dehydration due to their water sources freezing to the bottom of their water tanks. Wood piles froze solid and the wood had to be hammered loose before it could be carried inside. Chores that took longer than minutes became dangerous and only the most dependable of vehicles could be trusted to make any trip lest they freeze up or break down where help might be long to arrive.

It was during one of these cold snaps that the temperature dropped to forty below and stayed there for almost a week. When these episodes happened, patient traffic in our office slowed to a trickle and I would encourage my staff to stay home. There was never enough work to do that I could not handle it myself, and in fact I spent most of the time in the office reading or just staring out the window lost in thought. Often it was easier for me to go to the patient than to have the patient make the trip to town. If patients did hazard the trip to my office, they did so because their need was significant.

It was during one of these times my patience was rewarded and I spent some time with one of the other wildlife forms that lived back in the hills. They were the Markson brothers. Two very large and burly men that burst through the front door of the office and moved quickly to the counter. They were dressed in typical Wisconsin winter wear, heavy red hunting coats and hats with the ear flaps pulled down, gloves and five or six days of heavy beard growth. From the other side of the counter they gave off the distinct odor of wood smoke, kerosene, body odor and the heady aroma of whiskey.

Both were a little unsteady on their feet, their eyes bloodshot to the point where they may have been experiencing blood loss if they had kept them open much longer. They were obviously agitated. They were also very drunk, which was no surprise to me; in fact I would have been more surprised if they hadn't been, knowing them the way I did.

Everyone in town assumed they were twins, but I never knew anyone that was sure about it. They lived far back in the hills in a single wide trailer that featured a front yard with a couple of mean dogs tied to a few cannibalized pick-up trucks. A pole building three times the size of the mobile home sat at the back of the lot. The shed housed a very busy moonshine still and a productive marijuana operation. I never saw them without their cousin Olly Johansson. The three were inseparable and they had a deep affection for bar fights and trouble. Today it was just the two of them.

"Hey doc, you busy?" the giant on the right asked in a too-loud voice.

"What's up?" I never could figure out which one was which so I'd stopped trying.

"Olly's stove up again."

One or the other of them would frequently arrive in various states of severe injury.

Alcoholism and rough living were a grueling occupation. This time it was cousin Olly. "What happened this time?"

"Shovelin' the roof and he fell off."

Heavy snowfall would frequently build up on the roofs of houses and trailers. If enough accumulated before a snow melt, roof beams and rafters could crack and a roof could even collapse. Mobile homes were particularly susceptible because of their flat roofs didn't encourage runoff. The remedy for this danger was to shovel them. It could a dangerous task, especially if the snow was deep or heavy. Footing on the roof was perilous if you climbed onto it, and you risked being buried under a snow slide if it all broke loose at once. If you attempted it while intoxicated, you did so at your peril.

"How bad?"

"He can't walk, says he broke his back."

"Holy cow, we better get out there and have a look. Can you give me a minute, I'll shut down and follow you out."

"We got him out in the truck doc."

"You got him here?" I couldn't imagine trying to transport someone safely with serious spinal injury. "Can we get him in here?"

"Well we couldn't get him into the truck, so he's in the back end. Put him on a tarp and drug him into it."

"WHAT! Guys its forty below out there; you can't leave him out in that!"

"We covered him with blankets and put the dogs in with him. He's okay, but we gotta drag him in if that's okay."

"Cripes! Yeah, get him in here. But if he's as bad as you say he is, take it easy guys. Ok?"

"Yeah, we will." They both turned and reeled for the door. In what was longer than I had hoped, they eventually appeared at the glass doors dragging a large, and filthy canvas tarp weighted down by a very heavy something invisible within the folds. I hurried to the door and held it open while poor Olly arrived unceremoniously in the waiting room.

"Don't even slow down boys, drag him down the hall, first room you can pull the tarp into; they're all the same."

Once in the room, I quickly pulled back the edges of the tarp and greeted a grimacing Olly Johansson, who was starting to turn blue around the edges."Hey Olly, long time no see."

Through his gritted teeth, Olly returned the greeting. "Motherfuck doc, this hurts worse than a chimney brush up my ass."

I dropped to my knees and the boys and I began removing layers of clothing so that I could get down to the

Olly level. If Olly had been drunk, he'd sobered up considerably by now and spared no invective as we gently turned him from side to side to free up his clothes. His use of vocabulary, although colorful, lacked originality. The only addition seemed to be that he was generous enough in his distribution to graciously include me in it as well. Of the three boys, Olly was the largest, tipping the scale on the plus side of two hundred and eighty pounds and measuring well above six feet tall. His huge boots easily weighed more than five pounds apiece.

Once we could see more of Olly than blankets, I got the brothers out of the room and started a very careful examination of the giant. I was relieved when it was clear that his pelvis was apparently intact. His low back was in such a state of spasm that the muscles had splinted the entire area and there was no range of motion I could detect, which was both a good sign and a bad one. The big reveal came when I began to examine his hips. With the first orthopedic test, it became clear that his right hip had been dislocated—and still was. One of my least favorite conditions and one that required an extremely painful difficult fix, and a delicate one. In addition to the difficulty of the procedure, there was a very real possibility of disrupting the vital circulation to the hip socket, which would result in dire consequences. In this circumstance, it was also going to need to be performed with no pain medication and on a patient fully capable of hurting me if I upset him.

I ushered the two boys back into the room and explained the situation. I was surprised that in the last thirty to forty minutes, they had not sobered a bit. When I came to the point where I explained the procedure and that I would need them to restrain Olly to prevent him, and myself, from further harm, Tyler brightened up.

"Here doc, give him some of this." As he produced an

almost half-full quart bottle of clear liquid from inside his coat pocket.

"What's that?" although I was already pretty certain what it was.

"About 80-90 proof, far as we can tell."

"You make that yourself?"

"Yeah, it's safe though; we been drinkin' it all mornin'."

I took the bottle and after unscrewing the cap took a smell of it, just that whiff was almost enough to give me a buzz, but just in case I took a small sip. It was so pure that it almost disappeared in my mouth as my gums and palate absorbed it immediately. 80-90 proof and then some, Yikes.

"Okay, I'm going get some warm towels and get washed up a little. Let him have a little of it. It might help, and I don't really have anything else that I can offer him."

I was gone about five minutes. When I returned, Olly was watching me with fear in his eyes and both boys were kneeling—one on each side of him.

"Okay, were you able to give him any of that stuff?"

"Yeah doc, all of it."

"What? Seriously? All of it?"

"Yeah, he wouldn't give it back until he downed it."

"Well okay—I guess. Okay Olly, I need the boys to brace you so that the only thing that moves is your hip joint. I wish I could tell you it isn't going to hurt, but it is. It only takes a few seconds if we do it right, but if I miss or don't get it, I have to do it again. Since I know you guys won't go to the hospital for this, this is your last chance to tell me to stop."

"Just get it done doc. I don't give a shit; it already hurts like a bitch."

Kneeling down at his right knee, I slowly hefted his 'tree-trunk' of a leg, first rotating it out and began to raise it into a frog-like leg position in order to move it into position for the reduction. Immediately he stiffened and tried to sit up.

"Lean on him guys. He has to be still, there are bad things that can happen if this doesn't go well." Both of the giants dropped their collective weight down onto Olly's shoulders. He definitely wasn't going anywhere for awhile.

With that, I adjusted my grip and rotated the hip into position and made the adjustment.

The reduction of the joint was immediate and noisy with a deep satisfying crunch. Olly rearranged several of his favorite cuss words all at once, but the job was done. Surprisingly, Olly sighed with relief and sagged back onto the floor.

"You okay?"

"Oh yeah, better already."

"Okay guys, he can't be allowed to walk on this for a good while, otherwise the tendons won't knit and it will start to happen over and over. Keep him off his feet for at least a week, and if you can keep the alcohol consumption down, that would be good."

Olly was rolled back up in the tarp, and the boys exited the building the same way they had arrived, dragging the heavy tarp out through the lobby while poor Olly provided vocal encouragement. Tyler/Taylor returned in a few minutes and thumped a fifty-dollar bill onto the counter along with another pint of the clear 'shine.'

"Thanks doc, don't know what you charge, but just as soon you not say anything about this. We're not supposed to be in town these days."

"I'm not sure it works that way," Taylor/Tyler narrowed his eyes at me, "but ok I'll give it a try."

I thought that was the end of the episode, and I soon put it out of my mind as I got busy with other things.

Two days later however, my friend, the county sheriff, arrived at the counter. Jim Peters was never in a hurry, he walked slowly and talked even slower, but his mind was always way out ahead of anyone else.

He was tall and lean, with big bushy eyebrows and a long thin nose, which gave him the appearance of a friendly eagle. He was known throughout the county as just that, friendly and social. Anyone that knew him also knew that he brooked no nonsense and was a tough-minded law enforcement officer. He radiated easy manners and you absolutely trusted him within minutes of meeting him the first time. He only carried two things on his utility belt, an HK45 holstered under his left hand and his handcuffs. Most people agreed that the handcuffs were usually the second thing he reached for.

"Got a minute Emmett?"

"Sure Jim, what's up?"

"Best if we go in back."

Uh-oh.

I opened the hallway door and led him back to my office, where we both sat down. After refusing a cup of coffee, Jim leaned back and immediately stretched his long legs and put his big Wellington boots on the adjacent chair. Reaching into his shirt pocket, he pulled out a small notebook and ballpoint pen. Clicking the pen open, he immediately got down to business.

"Well Emmett, we've got a bit of a situation here and sounds like you're in the middle of

it."

"Okay Jim, but I'll need a little more information before you cuff me."

"Shit doc, naw, I need some answers that's all. So's I can close this out. I got here that the Markson boys and Olly Johansson were in to see you on Wednesday—two days ago. That right?"

"Umm, yeah Wednesday, around noon, but honest Jim, I didn't know they weren't supposed to be in town."

"That ain't it Emmett, most of the time I could give two shits what those idiots do. I don't care about that. I'm trying to get a timeline here that's all. What all were they here for?"

I took a few minutes and described the whole scene, complete with the procedure and my understanding of the cause of the accident and the general state of their alcohol consumption.

"That jibes pretty much with what they told me, so we're good there. Okay, thanks doc." He put his little spiral notebook back in his vest pocket and made ready to leave, but I couldn't contain my curiosity.

"What's going on Jim?"

"Well Olly's dead this morning, and the boys gave me this cockamamie story about how it happened. I'm just checking it out."

"What! He's dead? How did that happen?"

"Froze to death. Apparently when they got back home, the two dumb-asses forgot he was in the truck bed and just went into the house and started drinkin' again." He shrugged. "They didn't think to look for him until yesterday sometime. Spent the rest of the day tryin' to decide whether they should let anybody know. That was this morning."

A Small Town Christmas Card

Not all memories can be bad ones, and even in tragedy, perhaps there can be a small smile. Likewise, not all winter cold memories can be tragic, even when they start out that way.

One of the perks and drawbacks of having an occupation like mine is that I am also in the advice business. Each person I see in clinic is there for treatment, but also advice. Occasionally unsolicited and often unwelcomed, but at other times —requested. Over the years I have had many young people seek my advice about possible future occupations and career paths. Almost unanimously they have voiced their discomfort with the town that was too small, and the chances too few. Usually equating a change in geography as a change in personality.

I've modified my statement over the years, but it's essentially the same.

'Go follow your heart, see where it leads you, and if and when it's time, come back home to us.'

Saturdays were always busy both in our clinic and after hours were over as well. That was the day that most folks from out in the country came to town for their shopping and other business. Husbands and wives parked on Main Street and split up for various errands only to meet up later at the Coffee Cup for meatloaf and mashed potatoes, and to stroll through the restaurant tables and booths shaking hands, talking about the weather, and exchanging gossip.

Kids would take off down the street to the 5 and Dime to browse the candy and toys sections and come back for cheeseburgers and hand churned milkshakes. By three o'clock, the downtown streets would be empty. Everyone going home in time for evening chores and home repair projects. Most of them could come to town any day of the week, but Saturday was also a social day.

Over the years, I had reluctantly moved my Saturday hours earlier and earlier. When making a Saturday morning appointment, patients would invariably want the very first one of the day. They would grouse about how it would affect the rest of their morning if it wasn't early enough. As a result, what had originally been a reasonable eight o'clock opening had become a seven-thirty start, and eventually seven o'clock. I would arrive at the office fifteen minutes early to open up and find the parking lot had one or two pick-up trucks already in it. If the weather was good, people were standing around getting an early start on their gossip.

Invariably, once I got the coffee pot going and began seeing patients, the waiting room would begin to fill. This was partially due to patients arriving early for their appointments, but mostly due to the patients who had already been seen and had complained the loudest about getting an early start, who drank cup after cup of coffee and stayed to talk with the new arrivals. Even though everyone was in a hurry to get work done, no one was in a hurry until a particular subject had been thoroughly exhausted.

In our town and those like it, there was always time for a kind word and a handshake.

We didn't lose sight of the fact that we raised our children together, went to church together and walked each other to the gravesite. On a Friday afternoon in late September, businesses closed their doors for an hour so that employees could go outside and watch the high school Homecoming Parade march down the main street. Businesses still closed shop from noon until three on Good Friday no matter what their religious persuasion. Everyone decorated their storefronts and windows for each and every holiday and afterward, the high school kids helped clean the windows. Christmas, in particular, sparked an informal and good-natured competition for best window decoration and none were rarely better than the effort put forth by our local hardware store and Charlie Fedderson.

Charlie ruled the hardware store like a benevolent wizard. He was capable of simple magic and true wizardry. He knew where every screw, nut, bolt, and ax handle was. He knew how many of each he had sold this year and last, and he knew who he had sold them to. He knew how to fix just about anything, what you needed to do it and he could walk you through the necessary steps to achieve the repair. The store was filled with aisle upon aisle of every imaginable home necessity and tool and the old wooden floors creaked and groaned with the constant foot traffic of Saturday shoppers.

If you needed a knife, or mower blade sharpened, Charlie would disappear into the cellar and return with a blade you could shave with. If you needed a pipe for plumbing, Charlie could cut it and thread it for you in a jiffy. He could bend conduit, and roll out electrical wire, and he could do it all quickly. He could and would weld or solder your simple jobs, and he could do big jobs out in the alley. All of these traits made the hardware store an almost necessary stop when you were in town on Saturday, but there was one more thing that made it an absolute certainty.

Charlie knew everything about everyone in town, and he was an excellent conversationalist. The coffee never got cold on Saturday down at the hardware store.

During Christmas one year, I stopped at the hardware store on the way out of town to pick up a few things, and to spend some time in the audience. On this particular Saturday, I had also brought my young son to town with me to see if he might find a thing or two to give his mother for Christmas. At almost four years old, his eyes were big and bright as we strolled down Superior Avenue, our main street looking into the storefront windows but he stopped dead in his tracks when we got to the hardware store for indeed Charlie had truly outdone himself.

The window featured a wonderful real tree fully lit and decorated. Standing on one side of the tree was an electric heater that resembled an open fireplace, also available and discounted for the season. A rocking chair that somehow Charlie had motorized so that it rocked gently back and forth and in the chair sat a large plush teddy bear with a ribbon and bow around its neck. Christmas Carols played out of a speaker above the window. It was quite remarkable.

Inside Sean and I browsed the housewares department for a bit and he picked out a first-class stainless steel can opener and some colorful potholders. Taking them to the counter, we arrived to find Charlie in full throat. Like everyone else he caught my attention completely and I was both entertained and enlightened. Charlie though was capable of doing two things at once, and while he regaled us with his monologue, he also rang up customers, bagged merchandise, and if necessary packaged them as well.

When my turn came, I turned to Sean for our selections only to discover that he was not there. I quick scan of the immediate area didn't help and Charlie immediately curtailed his story and mobilized the troops. Sending some out the front door, and a few out the back to check the alley. The rest were detailed to check every aisle in the store, and

Charlie and I went to the cellar. Ten minutes later all searchers had returned, but there was no sign of Sean. Some had circled the entire block; I was in full panic. It was cold outside, and he was definitely not in the store.

Charlie picked up the phone and called the sheriff, Jim Peters. He arrived quickly, with full lights and siren. We watched as he came to a sharp stop, practically standing the squad car on its nose, double parked on the street out front and bolted from his squad car and around the front, but just like everyone else, the storefront window caught his attention first. He stood there for a good ten seconds gazing at all the work Charlie had done before once again heading for the front door, that opened with the familiar jingle of the bell hanging above it.

"Holy crap Charlie, that's the best Christmas window I've ever seen!"

"Thanks Jim, but we got a problem right now."

"Yeah I know, but man that window is really something anyway."

I liked Jim Peters but I was about to have a heart attack with anxiety so I spoke up. "Listen Jim, he's got his winter coat and hat on, so I think he'll be okay for a while, but it's gonna get dark pretty quick."

"Okay," he reached into his breast pocket and pulled out a little spiral notebook and clicked open his ballpoint pen, "Let's see, four-years old, 'bout three feet tall give or take?

"Yeah Jim, that's right."

"Wearing a red plaid winter coat and a blue stocking cap, with a little ball on top?" He asked as he wrote.

"Yeah, and rubber boots with zippers, hey wait a minute…."

"I think you better come on outside—all of you idiots."

He turned and just headed out the door. By this time there were quite a few of us, a full posse, gathered but we crowded out the door behind him and to where he had stopped next to the squad car. He turned to face us all and said, "I hope I never need any of you to find something for me, turn around."

As one we turned and faced the storefront again. The lights danced on the Christmas tree and the fake fire crackled in the fake fireplace and the Christmas Carols quietly played from the speaker above the window. Rocking gently with the big teddy bear on his lap in the big wooden rocker was Sean, fast asleep. He had put the perfect finishing touch on a spectacular Christmas window.

Delivery

The occasional phone calls in the winter are less frequent than warmer months when physical activity is higher, and usually involves machinery. When the phone rings on a winter night, it is always trouble, and winter adds a complicating factor. On this night, my family, used to the occasional interruption, barely noticed when the phone rang at night or in the evenings. They knew it was for me. It was during one of the howling wind storms that the phone signaled the end of an ideal evening of Scrabble, or assembling puzzles. After a brief shared glance between my wife and I, both with our eyebrows raised, I moved into the kitchen and pulled the receiver off of the wall.

"Hello, this is the Casey's."

"Is this Doctor Casey?" The language pattern was definitely Amish.

"Yes, this is Doctor Casey."

"Yes? Well, my wife Etta, she says it is time for the baby."

"Oh, I see. Etta Yoder?"

"Yes, this is Daniel Yoder. She is early, and Esther Yoder is away. Her mother is visiting out of town. She would like to go to hospital, but the weather is not good."

To say the weather was not good was putting it mildly;

the wind was howling around the eaves and the snow pellets were rattling against all of the north windows. I knew these two kids. They had not been married very long and lived in a small house that was no more than a shack on the back of his father's property. I had gone there once not long ago with the local sawbones to tend to a case of blood poisoning when he couldn't find the place himself.

"If you need a ride into town, I can bring the truck, but the snow is pretty deep so it's going to take time to get there and I may not be able to get into your lane. Is she having contractions that are pretty close together?"

"She says it is time."

Not exactly an encyclopedia of information was Daniel Yoder.

"Okay, I'll get my bag. Look for me in about an hour but if I'm not there by then, that means I couldn't get through. Okay? She may have to walk out to the road."

"We will get ready; once I am back home."

Hanging up the receiver, I took a moment to stare at the phone on the wall considering the necessary arrangements. Tomah Hospital had recently instituted a program of hiring a weekend Emergency Room physician, a Hospitalist, to cover for the regular physicians. It was a good idea and probably saved a few marriages in the long run. The young physicians that stood in on the weekends were usually cutting their teeth on practice, and most had little understanding of the simple ways of small-town life so were not as patient with the colloquial methods of rural life. In addition, they saw no reason to afford me, a mere chiropractor, even the smallest regard. Just the same I picked up the phone and called the hospital and told them I would be bringing in a patient, probably in labor and her first. My good friend Paulette Downey, who seemed to spend more time at the hospital than she did at her home, took the call and I was confident the necessary arrangements would be made.

I went to the desk and began packing my small house call valise. My wife with a sigh rose and began making sandwiches, a thermos of coffee, and some fresh cookies. With the weather closing down the ridge, I also grabbed blankets just in case I was in for a night sleeping in the truck along the road. The dogs watched the preparations from their rugs near the fire, not even remotely interested in going outside with me. I put on my foul-weather gear, galoshes and wrapped a scarf around my face before stepping out into the mudroom. Even in that enclosed space, the wind found its way in, and a light dusting of snow was beginning to cover everything. Stepping out onto the porch, the wind hit me full force and I waded through the knee-deep drifts to the truck parked facing out of the lane.

The lane into our place would prove the crucial test for the entire trip. The old farm house had been built below the crest of the ridge, far enough down to avoid the worst of the wind that blew even harder across the ridge tops. As a result, the long-graveled driveway sloped up from the shed all the way out to the road, with the last fifteen or twenty feet rising steeply to meet the grade of the road. Once on the road, it rose sharply a quarter of a mile to the top. The lane was narrow and fell away on both sides. If the truck made the road and then the ridge top, it should be able to make the long ridge run to the young couple.

For the next ten minutes, while the truck engine warmed up, I cleaned as much snow off as I could and then shoveled enough ahead of her so she could at least get a running start before encountering the first drift. The old Chevy had proved its worth on more than one occasion. I had yet to find a task that I asked it to do that it hadn't measured up. The big V-8 engine was powerful and heavy. In the winter months, the 4-wheel drive option was more the rule than the exception. It was a climb up into the truck because it also featured high road clearance. In icy conditions I kept a set of tire chains behind the driver's seat and a log chain in the back. In short, she could go just about anywhere but that didn't mean she couldn't be challenged, and tonight was one of those nights.

Already starting to work up a sweat in my winter garb, I climbed up into the truck. I assured myself that it was in 4-wheel drive and dropped it into gear. With a final wave at the faces gathered in the windows, I took a deep breath. Winter driving is an acquired skill and with deep drifted snow it is not for the sissified. Hitting the gas, I surged forward and kept the engine at high rev as we hit the first drift of snow and felt the truck shudder as blasted snow exploded up onto the hood and windshield. As the wheels lost traction, the rear end slewed around and I continued to pour the gas into it as the wheels churned and dug for the road making its way almost sideways. The only way to make the last twenty feet out to the road was to hit it with speed and momentum, and the truck engine roared as it dug for it plowing its way. We emerged out on the road in a burst of snow. With the wheels still spinning, I yanked the wheel to the left so that the rear end spun out and arrived more or less facing uphill. Making sure not to hesitate, I kept the gas pedal pressed and she began to claw her way up and out onto the ridge crest gathering speed as we went. Once up on top, the wind had swept much of the blowing snow out into the fields and the snow on the roadway was significantly less.

What would normally be a fifteen-minute drive to the Yoder's would be longer tonight. I decided to eat a cookie and let the truck do what it did best. To attempt to hurry would only be asking for trouble, and staying on the road was going to be my primary focus. When the storms of winter come to the ridges, all landmarks disappear. The roadside ditches fill with blown snow and appear to be on the same level as the road but can be as much as five or six feet deep. There are no road signs on country roads to mark the shoulders. The only way to guide you through the winding course is to watch the telephone poles that parallel the roads. It also helps to be familiar with the road. If you hurry, it is easy to become disoriented and look for a curve where there isn't one - a disastrous mistake.

I arrived at the Yoder's without mishap and turned into the narrow dirt lane that led back to their shack. Through the snow I could barely make out the silhouette of the low building.

Once in the lane, I shifted into reverse and backed out onto the road, making ruts in the deep snow that I could use them on the way out and also to give myself room to take a good run at their lane. The big Chevy churned and slewed its way up to their house, where a kerosene lamp in the window burned lighting the way to a recently shoveled walk. I swung the truck in a full circle bringing the radiator grill facing back out of the lane before it lost momentum in the snow. Climbing out I made my way to the door where it opened while I was still several feet away.

The two young people stood at the door; Daniel dressed in his black winter coat and black brimmed hat, and little Etta in her travel bonnet and shawl. He carried a valise, and in the half light of the lantern they both looked drawn and nervous. I had met the couple on occasion at other events, but couldn't help being taken aback at how tiny she was. Etta could not have been more than four foot ten and easily tipped the scale at something less than ninety pounds. In her present condition, even under her shawl, she was almost as wide as she was tall. It was a wonder that she could carry a baby to full term as tiny as she was. She appeared pale and the fear in her eyes was reason enough for the drive to here. This would be her first child and both her mother and the trusted midwife were unavailable; she was on her own in uncharted territory. She had my sympathy.

After hurriedly loading them into the front seat of the truck, I made ready to go, first cautioning them that this was going to be a different kind of ride than they may have experienced any time before and with that we set out for town. It was just shy of fifteen miles to town from the ridge but the drive took us an hour. The squared off lines of the pick-up truck streamlined by the snow that had plastered itself to it as we made our way. We waded across the short parking lot and made our way into the Emergency Room doors, a terrified Etta Yoder in tow.

Paulette met us before we could even approach the desk and without hesitation escorted Etta and Daniel away and down the hall. Paulette wasn't going to waste time putting her on a gurney in a bay, she took her directly down to the maternity room, and then returned efficient as always.

"I'm having her gown and then we'll get her in bed. The on-call is sleeping in the chapel and I didn't want to rouse him until you guys arrived. He's kind of an ass, so no jokes please Emmett he won't take them the right way."

"I don't joke."

"Geez, Emmett it's just about the only thing that ever comes out of your mouth. Anyway, don't do it tonight, okay? What do you think, she looks kind of shook up, did you do any kind of examination?"

"No, they were at the door when I got there. It's a helluva night for a drive; I figured that could wait."

"No shit, looks like about eighteen inches before it's over. You are an idiot for coming out, but I understand. Knowing you, you probably would have done it just to see if you could."

"That's harsh."

"Just sayin'. I'll go get 'what's his name.' Do you want

to talk to him?”

“Not if he’s like what you say. It might prejudice the way he treats those kids.” I got a cup of fresh coffee, thank you Paulette, and took a seat at the nurse’s station so that Paulette and I could talk once she came back. Unfortunately, the young doctor arrived first, looking like he had slept in his clothes, which he had.

“Are you Doctor Casey?”

“Yes.”

“We won’t be needing you anymore tonight.” That was it, nothing more, just dismissed.

“The weather is a little rough outside so I’m not in any hurry right now. Besides I just poured this coffee. I might as well stay for a little while and see how things work out.”

He looked at me like he had just stepped in something the dog left on the lawn, then without another word turned on his heel and went down the hall. He was back at the nurse’s station almost before my coffee had had a chance to cool enough to drink.

“Her cervix is only partially effaced and she is dilated to three centimeters. According to her *‘husband’* she is not due for another two weeks. I am not admitting her. It’s a good thing you didn’t leave so that you can take them home.”

To Paulette who stood behind him looking distressed,

“I’m going back to the chapel.” And he left.

Just the way he had said, husband, I wanted to punch him in the mouth. I’ve lived long enough though to recognize that karma has a way of punching people in the mouth in much more subtle ways and that his learning curve was going to be a long and arduous one.

“She’s getting dressed. I’m not doing any paperwork on those kids; the last thing they need is a hospital bill for being insulted.”

“Thanks Paulette, and thanks for the coffee. I got a

couple cookies left. I'll trade you for another cup to go?"

"Keep your cookies Doc, you'll probably spend the night in the ditch somewhere. I don't want them saying you starved to death when they find you."

"You're a peach."

"At least you didn't bring your two kids in drunk like last summer.

"Gee Paulette, you're never gonna let that go, are you?"

"Never," she added with an evil grin.

Once underway, the drive out of town had a somber feel. All of us were a little embarrassed by the experience with the young doctor. Them because it had been a fiasco and me because I wanted to apologize for him but couldn't find it in myself to do it. The truck performed well and we made the turn on the ridge and headed west into the teeth of the wind, blasting through the drifts and making better time on the return trip. The tracks of our previous passing were long since obliterated.

"Oh mijn gaut!" This from Etta as she rose up in her seat, her feet braced on the hump in the center of the truck.

"Mijn vasser brak"

There was no doubt about it; I could hear the gush of liquid splashing onto the floorboards above the blast of the heater.

"De baby komt"

"What! No, really!?!"

"Ja"

I stopped the truck, we were still miles from home and almost the same distance back to town. I looked across at Daniel and his look spoke volumes. If it was true, we were in a real bind. Hitting the gas again I churned the truck into the three-point turn and stopped crossways in the road with the passenger door on the leeward side of the wind.

"Switch places with me, Daniel. I need to look and

see." He was out of the truck and around to my door before I could reach into the back and grab my bag. Climbing out I plowed around the truck through the ruts the truck had made and stood in the open door.

"Etta, you must turn in your seat and put your head in Daniel's lap. Slide yourself my way; I'm going to have to look and see."

Her groan told she was in the midst of a contraction and she waited for it to pass before starting to painfully shift her bottom in my direction. With the snow pouring down the back of my neck and with my feet in a foot of snow, I reached in and switched on the trucks cabin lights and pulled my small maglight flashlight out of my bag. Her dress was soaked through and as I raised it, there could be no doubt that indeed her water had broken. Her underpants were translucent with the moisture and I wasn't about to try and wrestle them down. I took out a pair of shears and cut through the gusset and pulled them open. There in the light of the flashlight a tiny full head of hair appeared at the opening of her vagina. The time had come and there was no stopping it now.

"Daniel step outside, we need more room, pull her to you." I realized that my voice sounded harsh in my stressed-out state, so I attempted to soften it. "Cradle her head, the baby is coming and I need her to be as comfortable as we can get her. Etta, the baby is coming, you are going to have contractions that make you want to push. Please, if you can, take deep breaths and don't push yet if you can help it. I need to get some things ready."

She did not answer, but Daniel stepped back out into the snow and pulled her by her shoulders to move her father away from me and the weather. I placed her left foot against the doorpost of the truck above the dashboard and her right one on the other.

With the flashlight in my mouth, I fished in my bag.

When I was still in school and doing my internship it had been considered hip for the other students to have home births. We were all convinced that we were very sophisticated and over the five years that I studied, I attended several and assisted a few. I still had some of the equipment from those deliveries, sentimentally unable to let that little bit of my past go. Sure enough near the bottom and still sealed in its sterile package, I had a single umbilical clamp. I pulled out my bottle of alcohol and doused it. Then set it and the small shears on the dashboard, I pulled off my gloves and struggled into the surgical ones from my bag, my fingers cold almost immediately.

I had played some sports in high school, although it was never a passion, I was a good enough athlete to make first string usually. I still remember my football coach lecturing us on the proper etiquette after scoring a touchdown.

"Always, always act like you've been there before."

It was time to act like I'd been here before.

"Alright Etta, there is no hurry. Try and relax. When the next contraction comes and if you want to push, go ahead."

From my lips to God's ears. Almost immediately she huffed and her eyes bulged and she pushed back against Daniel and bore down hard. The baby's head appeared in a rush, a perfect LAO (left anterior occiput) presentation. I watched with wonder as the tiny head slowly rotated back into a natural position. Reaching in under its chin, I ran my hand around its neck searching on the off chance that the umbilical cord might be wrapped around its neck. It wasn't, and I thanked all the gods of birth. Taking the flashlight out of my mouth:

"Okay Etta, so far so good, I have the baby's head so now we need the shoulders. When you are ready, push again."

The seconds ticked by, the snow and the wind

continued unabated. Daniel was on the windy side of the truck and his hat and shoulders were starting to turn white with accumulated snow. It also blew in the open door and I held Etta's skirt up to prevent it from falling on the baby's head. Etta closed her eyes resting, her head lolling to the side. The seconds turned into a minute as I began to lose feeling in my toes. Suddenly, her eyes popped open and she heaved up in Daniel's arms, bearing down with tremendous force as her thighs bulged from pushing against the truck's doorposts. The baby's shoulders did not just appear, instead she delivered the whole child in a wet rush. A little girl, she came out with such force that I was almost wasn't quick enough to catch her before she dropped in the snow. I quickly reached into the back and pulled one of the blankets out, wrapping the slippery little bundle. Trying carefully not to put tension on the umbilical cord, I lifted her up and laid her on her mother's belly. She hadn't drawn a breath and I hid my anxiety by trying to look busy and businesslike. The baby's color looked good in the light of the flashlight and the pulse in the umbilical cord was still strong, but my heart raced and my stomach clenched. Too much could go wrong and so far, they had been leaning that way.

We waited, standing in the snow ambivalent to the weather now one minute, two minutes. Etta caught her breath and raised to look down at the little bundle. Her hair had loosened under her bonnet and hung down on her face in wet strands. Daniel met my eyes again, knowing what we waited for. Another minute, the pulse in the cord became fainter and then stopped. The time dragged, I counted seconds in my brain, trying to slow them down, make time stand still.

Then at last a small gasp, then a wail and then a cry. Suddenly, the snow falling down the back my neck didn't seem so bad. Daniel looked over at me and smiled and I smiled right back. Afterward I had a long-awaited ride home on a glorious beautiful snowy night with a smile on my face.

Today

all things considered

The day was moving into evening. It had been one of the long days of enforced inactivity spent grinding on past wins and failures. But as I stoked the fire and added more wood, I looked for a broader perspective. The failures had always been tempered with the wins. Little victories that had changed the course of someone's life, or that I had perhaps made a difference for.

I wanted to believe that in the short time that I had had, that I had helped those few people that I could, and even the ones that I ultimately couldn't help were no worse off as a result of my influence. In that thought I drew some satisfaction, and I consciously gave thanks for the solace it provided.

Reluctant Ingenue

Summers in the Coulee region of western Wisconsin are late to arrive, but when they do, they arrive all at once. Around the first week of June the weather turns to hot. But extremely hot temperatures are rare; nights are cool, and sunshine is plentiful. Daytime temperatures are modified by gentle breezes that waft down from the ridge, cooled as they flow through the misted valleys. The buzz of insects and bird songs become a constant sleepy accompaniment through the open windows during office hours. I always opted for open window air rather than the refrigerated chill of air conditioning whenever the temperatures were not too severe. Somehow the bright sunshine and open windows of those summer months seemed to foster a more casual and relaxed atmosphere in our busy clinic.

One early summer day in the middle of June, a mother who was a patient of mine presented at the office with her teenage daughter. She was a single mother, and her daughter, Jessie, was deep into post-pubescent attitude modification. The daughter, she related, had developed a deep-seated aversion to attending school, claiming migraine headaches and insomnia as justification. In addition, she had adopted some, to her mother at least, odd make-up techniques and mode of dress, which she worried were rooted in her headache and sleep issues. Her wish was that chiropractic treatment could help relieve Jessie of the symptoms, and subsequently perhaps—help her daughter return to normal.

Migraine disorders are multiple in nature, and most of them have their origin in more than one cause at a time. Causes can range anywhere from hormonal imbalance to poor pillow selection, and there is usually an emotional component that multiplies the effect of the root causes. Stress, depression, and anxiety play an enormous part in the body's general ability to care for itself and can often bring on serious illness just by distracting the body's defenses from doing their jobs. As a result, treating migraine headache is a serious undertaking from any practitioner's perspective. Whether it is a pharmaceutical approach from a medical standpoint or a mechanical approach of chiropractic, the underlying issues are always relevant, and multidisciplinary care is usually a good idea.

Once I had the mother and daughter seated in the examining room, I related all of these points to them. The mother, obviously concerned listened intently, the daughter did her best to appear bored and inattentive. While we conversed, I took the opportunity to begin my examination by taking a good look at Jessie. She was pretty, or maybe could have been. Her oval-shaped face was delicate and her eyes were big and blue, highlighted by deep indigo eye shadow that extended well beyond the eye sockets, and a complementing eye-liner. Her hair was flat black and did not match the blonde of her eyebrows. Her face was artificially pale with make-up. She wore black denim jeans, engineer boots and a matching denim vest over a Whitesnake T-shirt. She wore several different necklace chains and rings on multiple fingers. Other than that, she was unremarkable.

Winding up the interview with Mom, I turned my

attention to Jessie. "So Jessie, can you recall when the headaches began?"

"No."

"Have you had any accidents? Any falls? You know, anything that may have brought these on."

"No, except when I have to do stupid stuff like this."

"Like this?"

"Yeah this." This accompanied by a disgusted flounce as she directed her gaze out the window.

"Seems to me that if these headaches are so bad, you'd be looking for some way to stop them."

"Whatever. Nobody's cracking my bones."

"Sometimes that's what we do, but not always. It kind of depends on what we find."

"Well you ain't finding it on me."

Her mother looked at me with a pleading look.

"Well Jessie, I'd like to try and help. Would you be willing to let me take a look?" I turned to the desk and began taking out some routine equipment, a stethoscope and a blood pressure cuff, etc.

"Not a chance."

"Listen here Jessie, you're being rude and I'm not going to have it. Knock it off! Doctor Casey won't do anything he doesn't think won't help. Isn't that right Doctor Casey?"

I turned back to speak to them in time to see Jessie disappear through the open window hitting the ground below in a full sprint. As I leaned out the window, she disappeared down the street and around the corner. I couldn't control the grin that spread across my face as I turned back to Mom and her flabbergasted look. Before she could frame an apology, I cut her off.

"That girl is going to be someone special. I *like* her! Next time you see her, ask her if she'd be interested in a summer job, would you?"

Jessie worked for me for almost ten years, and her migraine headaches disappeared shortly after she started.

Bees and Barbed Wire

Spring in the Coulee Region can change at a moment's notice. Undependable is the best way to describe it. March may bring rain, sleet, snow and ice or it may bring sun and warm weather. April, too, offers the spectrum of weather change, but by May clouds or sun, the field work must be well on its way to planting. Field corn requires a ninety to one hundred-and twenty-day growing period. If it is not in the ground by the end of May and sprouted the cold rainy weather of September will come too soon. Farmers must have a sixth sense to know when the soil will be warm enough to put seed down. Too cool and the seed will not sprout before it rots; too late and the corn will not mature before the end of the growing season.

By late April the preliminary dirt work must be almost complete. For the Amish that means turning the ground by plow, disking the turned earth until it is smooth enough and then dragging to level it and remove any stones that the frost has pushed to the surface. It is an arduous process that must be repeated every year, and it is performed behind a team of horses. Plowing is done with a four-horse team, the disking is done with a two-horse team, and the drag is done with only one. The beefy, muscled Belgian-cross horses provide all the horse power necessary.

On the first Saturday in May, I was out in the wood yard, cleaning up the mess of wood chips, shed bark and leftover end cuts after a winter's worth of heating the old farmhouse. It was hot work on a hot day that we were being blessed with. Raking the fragments and burning them, restacking the remaining wood and preparing the area for the next season of cutting the forty-odd cord of wood we would need. I had started out in a coat but by midmorning I was stripped down to a T-shirt and had worked up a good sweat when a yell from the house told me I had a phone call.

I wasn't sorry to put aside the work for a bit and after grabbing my coat and sweatshirt, I headed into the house and picked up the phone, "Hello this is Dr. Casey."

"Casey, this is Amos Borntrager. One of my boys has been hurt, can you come?" Amos was one of the community elders, and I knew him quite well. His telephone etiquette was very good for one of the Amish people, but still not quite comfortable for conversation, and I needed a little more information. Many times, I had walked into a situation not expecting the gravity that I would be faced with and this was to the peril of the injured party. If I needed to notify the hospital that I would be bringing someone in it was good for me to know while I still had a telephone handy.

"How is he hurt Amos?"

"He has hurt his leg, it is not broken, but he has pain."

"I'll come out right away then. Do you think he will need to go to the hospital?"

"I will have you decide after you see him."

It was a beautiful spring afternoon, and I had no appetite to go back to the woodpile.

Most of the time these kinds of injuries were simple sprains or muscle pulls. Occasionally, there were dislocated shoulders or kneecaps, so I checked my bag to make sure I had bandages, slings and tape along with the usual things I always carried. I let my family know I'd be gone an hour or so and headed out onto the ridge road. Amos lived less than two miles from my place as the crow flies but by the roads, it was more like five.

Winding along the crest of Middle Ridge, there was no breeze to speak of, and the dust from the fieldwork hung in the air and scudded across the hood of the truck. As I passed each farm, the smell of the freshly opened earth blew in the windows. I waved at the workers whether they sat behind the wheel of a tractor or walked behind a team of horses. All of them busy and making the best of the gorgeous day as they gambled on another growing season.

Amos's house was just off the road and the yard and driveway were immaculately tended. The large old farmhouse sported fresh paint and the flower beds were neatly turned and ready for planting the summer flowers. Strangely, there was little activity going on in the barnyard. Horses stood patiently hitched to the rail near the house. The spring weather would give way to warmth and soon the flies would descend, but now they stood patiently, tails idle.

My arrival usually fosters a lot of activity. Small children run for cover, fearful that my arrival signals an uncomfortable encounter with the strange doctor, older children straighten from their labors and offer a small smile of greeting, but today there are none of these. In the back doorway, Amos stands in his shirt sleeves, no hat on his head. I climb down from the truck and grab my bag as I turn toward the house. He opens the door and waits for my approach. His silence signaling a sense of haste. Whatever awaits inside the house, it will be serious.

Once I am inside the back mudroom I bend to untie my boots, but, still silent he waves me up and into the house, yet another change in the tone of my visit.

When we enter the too warm kitchen, several young

women stand, all meeting my gaze, all of them idle. Amos moves past me quickly and I follow around the corner to the large dining area where the men are standing gathered around the massive dining table. The chairs are pulled back and arranged along the walls. Lying on the table is a small boy and my confusion regarding everything before me is immediately clarified.

The boy is lying on his back with a pillow under his head. His face is almost white, and an older woman dabs at the sweat on his forehead. He is staring at the ceiling, his jaws working overtime clenching and unclenching. His blue cotton shirt is soaked with sweat but he is absolutely still.

"He was pulling the drag in the field when the horse was stung by a bee. The horse bolted and he was dragged."

From the waist down the boy is swathed in an unmeasurable amount of barbed wire. The tangle of wire surrounds both legs and has embedded itself through his pants legs, and the table top is wet with the blood that seeps through them.

"They ran the fence line until he could stop her."

My heart is in my throat. I felt the need to cry for this poor child; the pain must have been intense, yet he made no sound. As I approached the table, the men stepped back to give me room. But the woman warned me with a look and I understood. Care and concern would be my utmost priority, or else.

Bending over I looked at the hopeless tangle of wire. From the knees down and most especially the left leg the wire had tightened to the point where it had embedded itself into the boy's flesh. There was no obvious end in sight to the wire and unwinding it was going to be an almost impossible puzzle. To do it without causing incredible pain would be impossible. It would be an insurmountable task for these folks—and for me as well. I signaled to Amos to follow me back through the kitchen and outside.

"Amos, this is very bad."

"That is why we called you Casey."

"I can't do it, there is too much. I can't even imagine how you got him into the house, and moving him again, even to the hospital, would be incredibly cruel. It's more than I can do with what I have. I'm going to need help."

"I will do whatever you need."

"No, I'm going to have to get someone with some skills that I don't have. I'm going to need to go to town and bring someone out."

"Many people do not like our ways."

"I'm going to try and get Tom Dunbar, is that okay?"

"Dunbar is a good man; he has visited before. Yes, if he can help us, please bring him. It hurts me with the boy's pain."

The twenty odd miles to town pushed the capabilities of the truck. Keeping my speed above all safety guidelines, I hit the town limits at almost eighty miles per hour. I didn't bother to look for Tom Dunbar at the hospital but drove directly to his home. Speeding into the drive, I threw the truck into park, and jumped from the truck. Tom's long-suffering wife, Kathy, was kneeling in one of the flower beds in the front yard and jumped to her feet in shock and surprise. I went past her in a rush.

"Tom home?"

"Err, yes, he's resting his leg. What is it Emmett?"

"Thanks."

I vaulted the steps and banged on the door but didn't wait for an answer. Turning the knob, I entered the front room in a rush and turned to see Tom seated in his recliner, a surprised expression on his face and an ice pack poised in his right hand over his leg.

"What the fuck! God dammit Casey, you scared the

fuckin' shit out of me."

"Tom I got a bad one."

His expression immediately changed, all business. "Two minutes."

Tom levered himself up onto his feet and began shoving his shoes into a pair of loafers sitting next to his chair. I began filling him in on the details, his face immediately registering the gravity.

"Go into the kitchen and get Paulette (Downey) on the phone; number's on the front of the reefer. Fill her in; she'll know what I need. Novocain and Morphine for sure; lots of Novocain. Tell her to meet us in the ambulance bay at the hospital."

With a quick apology to Kathy Dunbar, we were off and soon at the hospital where an agitated Paulette Downey, already dressed in her nurse's scrubs, fidgeted in the open bay, a large black doctor satchel in one hand. Without a word she moved to the passenger side and pulled open the door and began to climb in.

"Wait a minute Paulette, we just need the supplies," I said.

She gave me her patented look of dismissal. "You two are always in over your heads; you know you're going to need another hand. I just got off after pulling a double and I didn't want to make a Jell-o mold for church tomorrow anyway." Once she had flounced herself into the seat, she added, "We're going to have some explaining to do when they do the next inventory."

To say Paulette was a big girl was a monumental understatement. With the three of us crammed into the front seat of the truck—Tom, with the satchel poised on his lap —we would not draw a full breath the whole trip back up onto the ridge. Even closing the truck door took more than one try.

In deference to my passengers I kept the speed down on

the old GMC and it was almost another half hour before we were once again parked at the hitching rail in Amos B's yard. The horses were no longer there jawing their halters at the hitching rail and the rest of the yard was still empty. If Amos was surprised to see the prodigious frame of Paulette settle out of the truck, his face did not register it as he met us halfway to the house. Taking the satchel from Tom, he gave him a solid handshake and turned and proceeded us into the house.

In the ninety minutes that I had been gone, the room where the boy lay had been cleared of all furniture and people save the woman. Sheets had been hung from lines strung at both ends of the table and offered some privacy for what was to be a difficult experience for all of us.

Paulette strode up to the table and in the blink of an eye summed up the situation and took charge of the scene. She addressed the woman.

"We need some towels and we will need hot water. Does the boy speak English?"

"Only some, I will help with that."

"This will be hard for you. He is in a lot of pain."

"This is my son. I am Sarah."

"I understand." she put her hand on the woman's arm, "We will be as careful as we can

The woman nodded, turning she addressed the sheet closest to the kitchen. "Zet het water aan de kook, bring wat handdoeken mee." And to the boy. "Deze vrouw is hier om ons te helpen."

Which apparently meant boil some water, and the woman is here to help. Almost immediately there was movement and rattling of pots and water being poured. Seconds later a pile of towels appeared around the end of the bedsheet, smelling like the spring air itself.

Paulette turned to Amos and took the medical bag. Placing it on the table below the boy's feet she opened it and began arranging its contents on a spread towel. Taking up a pair of medical scissors, she turned to look at the boy's legs again and then looked a question at me, which I understood immediately.

"Amos, we need a pair of fencing pliers and a good pair of wire cutters too. I have some in the truck if you don't have them."

Without moving from his stance behind the woman, Amos spoke and the screen door in the kitchen slammed. Although the space beyond the bedsheets remained almost silent, there was immediate response and attentiveness. Within a few short minutes, a hand appeared around the end of the hanging bed sheet with an almost brand-new pair of heavy fencing pliers and a second followed with wire cutters and a good set of side cutters as well. The side cutters were a good idea, and I was thankful for them as we would be able to cut wire that we otherwise wouldn't have been able to reach.

Tom stepped up to the boy's head and with a small penlight, checked his pupils, then addressed the woman.

"What is his name?"

"Caleb."

"Have you given him anything?"

"I gave him tea for the pain."

"How long ago did this happen?"

Amos pulled his pocket watch out and consulted it. "It is three hours and some more."

Tom spoke to Paulette and me, his manner businesslike but his voice filled with tension. "Amazingly he is not in shock, but he probably will be. That's going to be the dangerous part. We'll elevate his legs as high as we dare. Paulette you'll need to monitor his blood pressure; did you bring morphine?"

"I hope I brought enough."

"We can't give him more than some. Any more and his

blood pressure will drop and we'll definitely be in a shock situation. Get that ready. Start with point 1. Also have the Norcan ready, this kid's probably never had any meds before so we'll have to see how he reacts. Let me know when it's ready and we'll start."

Turning to Amos, "I'm going to need two or three pillows, maybe four."

Again, there was activity behind the sheet and within seconds an armload of pillows appeared along with two steaming cups. The cups proved to be coffee, freshly brewed. Amos handed one to Tom and me. Tom, muttering appreciation, took a deep swallow.

"This is terrible!" Another swallow, "God I hope there's more."

Paulette set up the blood pressure cuff and draped the stethoscope around her neck. On the table she spread towels and then turned to Amos and handed him a huge bottle of alcohol and a small bottle of Betadine. Busy beyond trying to be polite, she spoke to him.

"Scrub these with this soap two times, then pour this alcohol all over them. Bring them back and set them on the towels next to Mr. Dunbar. Touch them as little as possible."

Then she handed out surgical gloves to Tom and me.

"Not that it matters, tetanus is going to be the issue here but better safe than sorry."

Then picking up the scissors, she cut both of the sleeves off of Caleb's shirt, fixed the blood pressure cuff on his right arm and swabbed the other with alcohol. For a big girl, she moved around the table with agility. Handing the prepared morphine syringe to Tom, she looked him in the eye.

"I'm ready Tom."

Tom turned to me.

"There's going to be plenty of stitching once we get

down to the boy. I don't want my hands to cramp up so you'll have to do the cutting. I'll use the pliers to pull the wire. The morphine is only going to be effective for an hour or so. I'm starting him on a low dose for his size, but I'm also worried about reaction so I don't want to have to give him any more. We need to work fast once I push this." I looked down at the boy. His jaw still clenching and unclenching, the table under him wet with fluid leaking out of him and nodded.

"Okay Tom, and thank you. I owe you one."

"Shit, you always owe me. If these nice people weren't here, I'd tell you what I really think of you."

"Boys, let's just concentrate, shall we?" This from Paulette.

Tom flicked the syringe and made eye contact with Paulette, nodded and pushed the needle into the boy's arm. Within seconds, the tension melted out of his body, his mouth went slack and dropped open, his eyes drooped to half slits.

"Watch him now Paulette. Mrs. Borntrager we need you to talk to him, it's important that he listen to you."

She leaned over him and began to speak in a low whisper into his ear. The boy moved his head from side to side and sighed.

"Okay Emmett, let's go."

As gently as possible, we lifted his legs and propped them up with the pillows. He did not respond, but his breath hitched only once. Taking a deep breath, we began. For the next ninety minutes Tom would lift out the wire and I would cut it. Where the wire had pulled tight, it embedded in his flesh and we had to work in tiny cuts of less than an inch at a time. There were places where the wire had cut deep into the muscles and it had to be teased out in tiny segments. Through it all, the whispered conversation carried on into the boy's ear and the boy made no sound.

At one point, drops of water appeared and began to land on the area where we were working. I looked up to see the source. Tears streamed down Tom's face as he worked. I didn't have to wonder; I felt the same way. From then on, Sarah using the cotton diaper that she had been periodically wiping the boy's forehead with, also dried the tears that continued from Tom.

Once the wire was fully removed, we cut off Caleb's pants. Working with tweezers, I plucked the remaining loose threads out of the wounds while Tom prepared the sutures and Novocain. Amazingly, between the massive supplies that Paulette had packed and those in my own bag, we had enough suture to do the job; but only barely, as we lost count of the number of stitches. For every one that I tied, Tom tied three. If we had run out of silk, we would have had to use horse hair. Two hours later we were outside in the warm spring evening. Tom sat on the truck seat in the open door. We stretched our backs and looked out across the fields as the dew began to fall. I leaned against the fender while Tom languidly smoked and drank another cup of coffee. Taking another swallow of the terrible coffee, Tom sighed, "Well that was something different."

Amos B. stepped out of the back door and approaching us handed us each a bundle. By its weight and feel I could tell it was fresh meat.

"I thank you Doctor, you will give us a bill for this."

"I'm not a doctor Mr. B."

"Then you are like Casey?"

"No thank god, I would never want to be like Casey, but I'm not a doctor either."

"What you do is what you are. What you are called does not matter."

Amen to that.

What You Do is What You Are

I had remembered those words for the rest of my life. It seemed that no matter what station in life people assumed, their actions told the tale of their person, not their title or the level of their education. I had met people with stunning academic credentials who almost literally couldn't find their ass with a flashlight. Conversely, I met people with no formal education to speak of who displayed a nobility of character far exceeding those around them.

At the end of the day, people were still just people. Subject to their instincts and emotions dependent upon each other. Each one capable of spectacular ignorance or brilliant insight. But all of us in this together and demonstrating our distinct personalities as we walk through this life.

Rain Storms and Doctors

Near our office in Tomah the sprawl of the Veteran's Hospital occupied a massive expanse of acreage. The facility was originally built to house the retired veterans of previous wars. The facility itself offered all of the amenities of a hospital and a retirement community in one and even featured a beautiful nine-hole golf course. Over the years after the Vietnam conflict, it had grown into a facility that treated the influx of veterans who also served at nearby Fort McCoy. It also specialized in the treatment of those veterans with mental and psychological disorders that grew out of the conflict resulting in trauma they had encountered in and after their service. This was long before the term PTSD was common. We were often blessed to offer our services to some of these veterans, which we performed free of charge and to the dedicated people who worked to assist them in their struggles.

One such person was a young psychiatrist, Doctor B. She was young, enthusiastic and a dedicated long-distance runner. During her exercise regimen, she had developed a nagging hip discomfort that worsened when she would run. After trying the available medical and physical therapy avenues of relief, she was desperate enough to give chiropractic a try. Although she remained skeptical, her constituents had encouraged her enough and so she presented at our office.

Doctor B. was completely versed in complications of her injury, and related in detail all of the interventions she had already undergone. She related that her condition had evolved into the 'what have you got to lose category' so that she was willing to give us a try. She refused x- rays, and basically informed me what she needed and how I should proceed in my treatment, all of which I took into account.

After a brief examination, I was able to rule out any hip dysfunction. The hip was obviously inflamed though however, the root cause of the ensuing bursitis was not joint related. It appeared that she was more likely suffering from a sacro-iliac condition which caused her to alter her gait when running and bring too much weight too bear onto the right hip when she ran. I asked her if she ran on a track or on the road surface and she confessed that she ran on country roads, and I immediately understood the problem.

Country roads are 'crowned' in order to provide maximum drainage during rain and snow storms. Walking or running on the side of the road produces the effect of running on the side of a hill, with one leg lower than the other, and bringing much more weight to bear on the downhill leg. If you do it enough, the body will eventually attempt to correct the mechanical difficulty and compensate by shortening muscle and tendon to prevent injury. This in turn produced mechanical issues when she walked on level surfaces and so she had trouble with the hip whether she was running or not. The correction for the problem is a simple chiropractic adjust that should be repeated a few times until the problem and the body's attempt at compensation are overcome, and the runner needs to start running on flat surfaces.

In a matter of minutes, the first treatment was

accomplished, and over the course of a week her problem had resolved completely. As a result, she immediately discontinued her care and it was several months before I saw her again, this time with a completely different clinical presentation. She presented this time with a series of severe headaches that began at the back of her head and worked their way over her head, eventually lodging behind her right eye. What we chiropractors would call an occipital migraine. She had no incident or trauma that she could recall, and although skeptical once again, she had exhausted her medical options.

Again, after a brief examination, she had significant muscle tightness on one side of her neck, and the range of motion when she turned her head one way was much less than when she turned it the other. Briefly pressing on the muscles revealed soreness and reproduced the symptoms of pain at the base of her skull. In her own words, she wanted her neck 'cracked,' what a chiropractor would call a cervical adjustment.

I explained the procedure to her. I said that we would lie her on our table face down, and first adjust her upper shoulder muscles, and then turn her over and adjust her upper neck. This would in effect relieve the muscle tension and as a result, relieve her headaches which were most likely caused by a circulation problem brought on by the tight muscles. She was agreeable and we began the procedure. Unfortunately, as they say, 'That's where the trouble started.'

It was spring, and a late afternoon thunderstorm had rolled in from the west. We could hear the rain pounding on the roof above our heads, the crack and vibration of the thunder could be heard and felt as the skies gave up their demonstration of power. During these times, our new computer system and the x-ray equipment were always shut down to avoid any damage from lightning or stray voltage strikes, but otherwise we proceeded with business as usual. In the midst of Doctor B.'s first cervical adjust, lightning struck the radio antenna that connected our little medical facility with the hospital and emergency services in town and the lights immediately went out.

Without windows in the room, we were immediately plunged into pitch blackness. The young doctor, face down on the table, had no way of knowing that the lights were out, but there was no mistaking the blast of the thunder that followed on the heels of the lightning. She bolted up off the table in a reflex reaction and immediately discovered that she was blind.

"Oh my God! I'm blind! Oh my God!' she screamed at the top of her lungs and immediately sprinted into the nearest wall. Bouncing off she changed direction and threw herself into another. "I'm blind! I'm blind!'

Although I knew where she was, she proved hard to catch, like a bird trapped in a room when you've accidentally left the window open. The door of the room burst open and my assistant alerted by sounds of struggle entered from the equally dark hallway.

"What's going on?!"

"Help me catch her Viki."

"I'm blind, I'm blind, oh my God, I'm blind!" Blam! another wall, this time clearing most of the equipment off of shelves, and the accompanying sound of glass breakage.

With the two of us working together we were able to corner her with some effort. Taking control of her we each took an elbow and headed down the windowless hallway ricocheting from one side to the other as she wailed her predicament and struggled to get free. Finally, at the end of the hallway we collided with the door at the end that we could not see either owing to the pitch blackness and opening it, exited into the large waiting room. A waiting room that was filled with patients, all of them staring wide eyed our way. The waiting room had been designed with a large bay window that faced west. Even in the midst of the raging storm that threw rain at it, the room was bright with the late afternoon light in spite of there being no internal lighting. Yanking herself free from us at last Doctor B., stood in complete shock, staring at and out of the window as the tears streaked down her cheeks.

"Oh my god. Oh Geez. Oh dear, I'm so embarrassed."

And with that she bolted for the door and left leaving behind her jacket and umbrella, never to return.

The Sprained Back

After a decade and more of practice, there is a tendency to think that you've seen just about everything that will walk into your office. From serious traumatic events like car accidents and other whiplash injuries, to the smallest micro-trauma, such as stressful lives or poor family relationships. The cause of the injuries may be different, our bodies only have so many ways to alert us to trouble after all, but the resulting complaint is usually something that you have treated in previous years.

Over the years I had not hesitated to take on the tough cases, and I had never stopped advocating and mediating for my patients. As a result, I had gone toe-to-toe with many physicians, navigating patients through the maze of specialty care and arguing for more personalized treatment. Perhaps as a result of my approach, I had continued to see more and more interesting conditions and even more interesting cases. It was never dull in my office, and my staff never hesitated to remind me of it.

During the winter months, even when the temperature moved far below zero, the patient traffic in our office did not slow. People who lived in Monroe County were hardy and used to it; they knew how to handle it. In the winter months the office always added another coat rack in the waiting room to handle the additional layers of coats and hats that people needed to wear when they ventured out.

My wife was a native and her level of preparedness never ceased to impress me. I had grown up mostly in northern Illinois and southern Wisconsin, which my wife laughingly referred to as the **sun belt**. I had not developed the necessary skill set required to function in the extreme weather conditions that were frequent during the winter months. By her example, I had learned how to handle the weather and the cold. But house calls in mid-winter took on a whole new challenge when the thermometer went south.

"Hello. This is the Doctor Casey."

"Hey Doc, this is Becca Townsend, you know, down by the bridge at Potter's Marsh."

"Oh sure, I know your place."

Although I had never been there, Bob Townsend had been a patient of mine for many years. I knew where their farm was because it was on the way to one of my favorite fishing holes and I passed by it often as a result.

"Bob done his back again. He can't move the pain is so bad."

"Oh, that's not good. Can you get him to the office this morning?"

"I can't get him moved, there's no way I could get him in the car Doc."

Well damn, it was really cold this morning and my early office schedule was jam-packed. "Well okay Becca, I can probably get out there about noon or a little after."

"Doc, he can't move, and he's outside. He'll freeze to death by noon Doc." Well that added a layer of 'Oh shit' to the situation.

"Becca, you might need to have the fire department boys come and get him."

"Can't do that either Doc, he's up in the silo. They won't be able to get him down the chute."

"He's up in the silo!?!

"Yeah, the 'unloader' jammed and he went up to clear it. I was milkin' so I didn't miss him for a while. When I hollered up the chute, I found out he was hurt. I had to shut off the unloader and climb up myself. He's draped over the unloader shield but I can't budge him and he said he hurts so bad that he'd kill me if I tried."

Silo design is universally the same. They are cylindrical structures, made that way to distribute the weight and subsequent pressure resulting from being filled with tens of thousands of cubic yards of livestock feed. The one difference in them is how tall each of them might be. Some are a mere thirty feet and many can be sixty to a whopping eighty feet tall.

During the summer growing season crops such as alfalfa, corn or a combination of hay and oats, referred to as oatlage or silage are cut, chopped into fine pieces and then loaded into these silos to be used as livestock feed during the cold months. The solid structure silos are filled from the top using a massive blower to blow the feed up a long tube. Then it simply pours the product into the inside, much the same as filling a glass by pouring water in from the faucet.

To unload the silo an 'unloader' is installed on top of the feed pile after the silo is filled.

The unloader is not a technological phenomenon, it simply consists of a long eight- or ten-inch diameter screw, called an auger that hangs by a cable from the roof and can be lowered from the ground by a hand crank as the level in the silo goes down. The auger is long enough to reach from the center of the silo to its inside wall. The unloader is electric, and when activated the screw auger will begin to rotate and literally 'screw' the feed into a tube that then dumps the feed through a hole in the side of the silo and into a metal chute attached to the outside of the silo where gravity takes over and the feed arrives at ground level. At the end of the auger is a gear box that rotates with the auger and turns a large wheel set at the inside wall of the silo. While the auger is unloading feed into the chute, the wheel slowly turns pulling the auger in a circle around the inside. This way the silo is emptied evenly all season long.

In winter, the top layers of the 'silage' will freeze, which is no problem for the powerful auger, but can be a problem for the wheel. The silage along the outside wall will always freeze harder than the stuff further toward the center. As a result, the outside foot or so of frozen sileage can become hard enough so that instead of digging in, the wheel will ride up over the frozen collection. After a few revolutions, the wheel will become much higher than the level elsewhere and lift the auger up out of the silage. The unloader is a dumb machine and will continue to run whether it is expelling product or not.

When that happens, the feed stops coming down the chute and it requires someone to climb the ladder inside the feed chute to the top, through the window and into the silo itself. Once inside, they go back down to the silage and auger below to clear it. The frozen silage along the inside has to be broken down and moved closer to center, lowering the wheel and the auger back into the feed.

It sounds simple and would be except for the fact that during the operation the auger has to be left running. This is necessary to ensure that the unloader is working properly before undertaking the laborious task of climbing all the way back out of the silo only to discover that it is still jammed up. Once the auger was cleared and blowing the massive amounts of feed back into the chute while properly making its circuit around and around, the person would then have to follow the dangerous auger around the inside until it passed the exit ladder, so that he could escape. Even that sounds simple, until you remember that now you have to climb down the sixty foot chute while the unloader is pouring dozens of pounds of frozen silage on top of you at a high rate. You arrive at the bottom of the chute with your shirt, face, mouth and nose packed with it. I had myself performed this operation, and can honestly say that it isn't my favorite farm chore.

Bob Townsend was stranded at the top of a sixty-foot silo in below zero weather, and had been for what was probably a couple of hours. Even if she had called the rescue squad, I couldn't imagine how they would have managed getting him down. The silage chute was only as wide as a big man's shoulders might be, there would be no way to get a stretcher or even a 'back-board' up to him. I could only imagine how long he been walking behind the auger before Becca Townsend had finally turned it off. "Geez Becca, I'll be on my way in a few minutes. I'm gonna call Tom Dunbar and see if he can come along, is that okay?"

"Doc, I'd piss on a spark plug if I thought it would help. Yeah, bring him too."

It had been too cold to ask the staff to come into the office, so I was answering the phones myself. Once I hung up, I walked across the parking lot to the medical clinic in our complex and asked for Tom at the counter. They took me back to his little alcove office, and he arrived shortly thereafter. I gave him the entire story in less than a minute. He was quick with his decision.

"No can do my man."

"Oh…why not?"

"Dipshit, I can hardly walk down a hallway, how do you expect me to climb a sixty-foot ladder?"

"Oh, um, yeah. I'm sorry Tom, I wasn't thinking."

"Nobody has come to expect that you think dumbass." Then he smiled, "This is a job for the Doc anyway. I'll be right back."

Three minutes later he was back, with him was Jim

Kearney already dressed in his coat and pulling on his gloves.

"Tom'll take my patient load until I get back, we'll take my car. You guys always have the best stories to tell. This one should be a doozy."

Fifteen or twenty minutes later we swung Jim Kearney's sedan into the barnyard at the Townsend's. As soon as she heard us pull in, Becca Townsend exited the barn with a quizzical look on her face, not recognizing the car, but once she sighted who it was, her smile of relief was almost tangible.

"Wow! Dr. Kearney! Thank you, thank you so much!" Turning to me, "I pulled some extra horse blankets up to him and tried to make him comfortable. He was taking a nap, so I didn't wake him up, just covered him up. I just got down, just now."

"What Becca? He was taking a nap?" Jim looked over her head at me, the concern on his face speaking volumes. We both were immediately alerted to the possibility that Bob was going into hypothermia.

"We've got to get up there right away." Jim no longer appeared to be enjoying his adventure. "Mrs. Townsend, please go to the phone and call the rescue department. We will need them to warm him up once we get him down here."

"I'll just take him in the house and put him in a hot bath."

"I insist, Mrs. Townsend. Right away." What followed was one of the first stern looks I'd ever seen on Jim Kearney's face. "Doctor Casey will find the way up into the silo for us you need to make that phone call now."

Cowed, Becca Townsend headed toward the farmhouse and we entered the barn.

In winter the milk cows were kept inside the barn, and this one was no exception. Two rows of cow butts began just inside the doorway and extended down both sides of the center aisle. Just the presence of this many nine hundred-pound animals raised the temperature in the barn by at least ten degrees.

I stepped past the first cow on the right and walked up into the manger that ran along the outside wall of the barn and created an aisle between the whitewashed stone wall on the right and the roughly three dozen cow faces on my left. Halfway down this narrow 'hallway' a small pile of silage marked the location of the silo chute and the beginning of the ladder we would have to climb.

Turning to Jim, "You should put everything you think you'll need in your coat pockets Jim. You can't carry that bag up there, you're gonna need both hands. Anything that doesn't fit give to me and I'll put it in my pockets. Keep your gloves on, the rungs are cold steel." Jim began filling his pockets with packets of syringes, and vials. Once he was ready I gave him a nod, "Okay Jim, it's tight and straight up. The steps might be slippery so be careful, don't hurry and go first. That way if you fall you'll land on top of me and we'll get stuck in the chute so we shouldn't be able to fall all the way to the bottom."

He looked at me with shock on his face. "I'm kidding Jim, just be careful."

I got a weak smile, reality was setting in for him; this was not just a mission of mercy; it was about to get personally and challengingly physical. With a nod he turned to the ladder and started up. He stopped twice, taking breaths and stared at the outside of the concrete silo inches from his face.

"I'm a little claustrophobic, it's really tight in here."

Staring up at the heels of his shoes above me, I couldn't resist saying it, but I thought he needed to be pragmatic.

"It's gonna be a lot tighter if we have to carry Bob down with us. He's a big guy."

Finally arriving at the open chute window, we wedged our way into the silo. Almost directly across from us, the giant auger rested silently. Draped over the safety shield lay Bob, face down, a mountain of horse blankets on top of him. Both of us were winded from the climb and the squeeze through the window and the cloud of our breaths hung in the air.

"Hey Bob! You awake? Cavalry's here! Bob!"

"Mmmm…"

"Bob! C'mon Bob, you need to wake up."

"Help me get him turned over Emmett, pull those blankets off of him." One of the advantages of having Bob only semi-conscious was that he didn't put up any fuss when he turned him over and laid him flat on his back on the cold silage.

"Let's get his coat off, and you too Emmett."

I looked at him like he was nuts.

"Lay down next to him as close as you can. I'll cover you with your coats and the rest of these blankets."

I had started to shiver even before Jim buried me underneath the pile of fabric. I could hear him working but couldn't see what he was doing. Pretty soon, he appeared again.

"Hand me his arm."

Lifting his arm, I reached it across my body. Jim took the arm and bracing it against my chest used surgical scissors to cut the shirt sleeve from his wrist to his mid-bicep. Then he reached into the inside of his coat and shirt lifting out a full bag of saline solution. He fitted the IV apparatus and then spent some time locating a vein in Bob's ice-cold arm. Once he had it going, he handed it to me.

"I've got it turned up as fast as I can and it's pretty close to body temperature. Hang on to it Emmett, keep it as warm as you can. He won't get all of it, but it will warm him some. I've got to keep an eye on his vitals. Be ready to spell me on CPR if I need it."

Jim Kearney had always impressed me, but now I was just 'wowed.' "Where'd you get that saline?"

"I was an Eagle Scout. Be Prepared." he smiled at me and then dropped the blankets over my face.

"Somebody order a pizza!?!" The distant voice boomed up from below, echoing up the hay chute. The rescue squad had arrived. "Hey you guys, glad you made it. What've you got for us." Kearney hollered back down.

I could hear the sound of someone climbing the chute ladder, and then struggling through the narrow window.

"Got some warm blankets, but not for long, and hot chocolate. What have you got for us, that's a big pile of blankets, gotta be a pretty big guy from the look of it. Oh, my aching back."

"Half of it is Doctor Casey, the other half's Bob Townsend."

"Well shit! I'd like to see what a Doc Casey popsicle looks like."

"Me too, take a long time to freeze all his bullshit though." Apparently, the whole squad had made the climb.

"Well at least we'll all get adjusted while we're up here in this ice box."

"You guys are the best, but don't even think about it," I yelled from under the blankets. "Yeah, yeah, yeah, you guys can all kiss and hug once we get this guy outta here." Big Joe

Dempsey had also made the climb.

"You doin' okay Doc, throw them blankets back and take these warm ones. We're gonna start gettin' rigged up and ready."

"Mr. Townsend is in at least the beginnings of acute hypothermia. He's only semi-consciouss, so I don't dare give him anything for pain or to relax his muscle spasms for fear that his vitals will crash. Hopefully, you guys can be tender in your approach."

"Hey Doc, we're gonna be makin' some of this up as we go along, but we've trained in rock climbing rescue, and we're gonna try some of that. Half of us will be at the bottom and the rest of us up here will rig him up and lower him down, but while he's in the chute we won't be able to keep him bundled up much and we don't dare hurry."

"I understand, but hurrying is what we need to be doing here Joe."

"Well, I guess we could do a practice run and use Doc Casey."

"Screw you guys, and the horse you rode in on!" I yelled from under the blankets.

"How about that, a talking space heater! Don't worry Doc, we're only goin' to try this

once."

The three firemen talked in low whispers accompanied by the snap and clink of clasps and carabineers. Covered in blankets and snuggled up to Bob the Ice Cube, I couldn't see what they were doing, so I listened and did my part trying to transmit as much of my body heat to keep Bob alive, while I slowly froze to death myself.

Once they got moving, they moved quickly and efficiently and thirty minutes later, Bob lay on a stretcher in the back of the ambulance while they continued to work on his vitals. I sat on an old and cracked truck seat leaning against the side of the barn, wrapped in two hot blankets and drinking hot chocolate, watching from a distance while my body shivered uncontrollably.

I have always appreciated it, but right then and there I decided that quiet and efficient competence was probably my favorite thing to watch as I thought about how lucky it is to live in a community where everyone plays a part in everyone else's welfare.

Today

nighttime, at last

Struggling up out of the wing chair and wincing the first couple of steps to the front room closet, I pull out a scoop of cat food and fill the dish near the kitchen stove and well out of reach from the dogs. Armed with a large scoop of dog food, I quickly open the back door of the mudroom and dump it into the dish on the back stoop, struggling to not pour it onto the heads of the 'overly enthusiastic' dogs. Once I have finished with these few menial chores, I reheat the coffee in the percolator, my mind now geared toward the past immediately turns back to memory.

I realize that there are many memories that I am both proud and perhaps a little ashamed of simultaneously and both emotions evoke an inward wry smile. I'm old enough now that the past has softened the memories because after all, 'you can't win them all.'

Donna

Not everything that you do as a health care provider has anything to do with your particular technique or approach. Sometimes chiropractic or allopathic medicine takes a back seat to just encompassing the patient and trying to be a good person.

I first met Donna when she applied for a job opening that we had at our office. She was sunny and bright, but overqualified for the position. She had previously worked as a CPA for one of the accounting firms in town. She left that position because, in her words, she felt it was too stressful. Since that job, she had worked at different occupations and was currently managing a small supper club located just outside of town. She was smart and well-informed, and I enjoyed our exchange during the interview, extending it well past the necessary time to determine if she would be a good fit.

As a result of the openness of our discussion, she confided that she was bi-polar and given to periods of extreme mood swings. She frankly discussed her periods of agitated anxiety and bottomless despair, expressing the hope that by working in our office, she might find some peace. It was unfortunate that she was not a good fit for the position, because I enjoyed her wit, and at least in this particular instance, her energy.

I expressed this sentiment, taking a cue from her own frankness, but also that I felt a great appreciation for her honesty. In exchange, she asked to become a patient and was curious if a more holistic approach to her condition might prove more effective than the medication route she was now pursuing. I agreed that we might be able to help, but only with the understanding that she would continue to undergo the standard treatment with her personal physician. She agreed and I began to see Donna on a regular basis as a patient.

Donna tolerated the care well, and when she was in a calm state remained delightfully droll and perky. She enjoyed just being at the office and often stopped by with fresh donuts or coffee thus befriending the entire staff, and even occasionally offering to run errands and do small tasks around the office. In a short time, she became a fixture at the office; even my children looked forward to seeing her when the occasion arose that they were at the office simultaneously.

The honeymoon did not last, however. As the low light of late fall and early winter encroached, Donna's moods became ever more capricious. She would appear as high as a kite on one day and in a deep funk the very next. As the cloudy weather of winter and the shorter days deepened it became increasingly hard for her to cope with her moods. Her manic periods became ever more agitated with nervous energy seeping out of her every pore. In order to remain functional, she would go for long walks. Often as much as twenty miles at a time, and many times in the middle of the night. When the nervous anxiety would dissipate, she was left with no energy at all. Empty of motivation or emotion.

She would arrive in our office after walking to town, a distance of almost ten miles, sometimes with a vacant stare and at other times with an almost electric light flashing in her eyes. At either of these times, she would beg me to help her, to find some way out of the inescapable tunnel that was her life and robbed her of all but fleeting happiness. I placed numerous calls to her doctors, trying in some way to help her. They were always sympathetic, and usually offered an adjustment in medication, but Donna had been having her medications adjusted for most of her adult life and had no more patience for another change.

The physicians would ask her to come in for an office visit, which Donna dreaded. The closest one was sixty miles and she did not drive. She had surrendered her driver's license years ago when her medications made it dangerous for her to operate a motor vehicle. Instead, she depended on friends for rides, but her friends were slowly abandoning her. In the end, I had taken her for the last few sessions myself. Her doctors spoke to both of us and recommended that she be admitted for psychiatric treatment. Donna refused. Instead she became suicidal.

Finally, my concern for her heightened when I did not hear from her for several days, and she did not answer her phone. I took it seriously and drove to her home. Where her car that she could no longer drove, but wouldn't part with, sat in the driveway. Smoke drifted out of the chimney, which gave me some comfort, but the yard and the little house seemed quiet and empty of any hominess. After I had knocked on the door several times without an answer, I tried the knob and it turned in my hand. Opening it while calling her name, I got no response.

Walking down the narrow hallway, I stepped into the living room to find Donna sitting on the end of her couch staring at nothing, oblivious even to my presence. She was naked except for a shawl draped across her shoulder. Her hair was matted on one side. She and the room smelled of body odor and urine. The wood stove was smoldering, but the house was cold.

"Donna?"

She roused but slowly, like coming out of a deep sleep. "Oh hey…Doc."

"Donna, what's up? You haven't been answering the phone."

"Ah, what's the use. Nobody I want to talk to."

"Donna, I want you to go for a ride with me."

"Nah Doc, I gotta clean up around here, gotta get busy."

"I bet you'd feel a lot better if we just get out in the fresh air for a little while. Honestly dear, you look like hell. I think we should go in and have the doctor take a look at you. What do ya' say?"

"They'll just give me more medicine. I hate taking that shit. Makes me stupid, like I can't function."

She got to her feet and started moving around the room in an aimless frenzy. Picking up dirty socks and then dropping them somewhere else.

"Sides I went in last week, and they sent me to LaCrosse. Those bastards wanted me to get admitted. I know what that means, the psych ward, locked in, no way out, nope not for me, been there, done that already."

"Well Donna, no offense, but you're kinda' not functioning now. C'mon what'dya say, couldn't hurt could it?"

"I'm not going to LaCrosse again. I wanna go to Mayo, they oughta be able to help me.

They're the best, right?"

LaCrosse hospitals were sixty miles away. Mayo Clinic in Rochester was twice that.

"They're supposed to be pretty good."

"Okay, then that's where I want to go."

"Well sweetie, okay but I can't take you all the way to Rochester, I've gotta get back to the office. Anybody else that we can ask to drive you?"

"I need you to take me Doc. I trust you."

She did another circuit of the little room and ended up back where she started but with a dirty glass in her hand. I took the glass from her and she sat back down on the end of the couch again, dropping her hands in her lap and disappearing into another vacant stare.

"I'm sorry sweetie, I just can't do it right now. How about if I send Jessie with you?"

Jessie was a young lady who had started working for me while she was in high school. Now in her early twenties, she was both capable and friendly and the linchpin of our day to day activities. She had taken night classes in accounting and the new computer technology and handled all of our billing. Because of her, I had 'bitten the bullet' and invested in an office computer and she had even begun teaching me how to do more than play solitaire on it. Without exception, the patients gravitated to her and she returned their trust with a smile and unequivocal competence and emotional enfoldment.

She had worked for me for almost ten years. She ran my office, knew my patients and understood what the real mission of a health care clinic meant. Jessie was one of the foundations that anchored my professional life.

"Jessie? Jessie'd be okay. She's a nice kid."

"Not a kid anymore, getting married in about a month."

"No shit? Maybe I'll get her a shower gift—nah, fuck it."

I crossed to the phone on the kitchen counter and called the office. Donna had a gift for making people nervous around her when she was in her manic phase but after a brief conversation with Jessie, she reluctantly agreed and I gave her the directions to Donna's house. Once she arrived, I gave her the keys to my truck and enough cash to cover any expenses for the trip. I took her keys in exchange. Then, under the pretense of showing her how to operate the truck, we went outside to talk.

"Thanks for doing this Jess. You'll need to be careful though, she's a little rough right now, so watch what topics you choose to talk about. It's a long way to Rochester. My guess is they'll probably admit her, so call me when you leave so I'll know you're on your way back. The weather's supposed to be good so no worries there anyway. I'll meet you when you get home, okay?"

"Okay boss, Donna and me are tight. We'll be fine."

Once dressed and with a piece of toast in her hand, Donna shuffled out of the house and we boosted her up into the truck—her reluctance showed in every step—but she climbed into the passenger seat nonetheless, and they were soon on their way and I headed back to the office.

The rest of the day passed in a normal routine, and although concerned about them, I allowed thoughts of Donna and Jessie to slide to the back of my mind. I went home to eat dinner and wrestle with the boys. When the phone rang later that night, I had almost forgotten the whole episode.

"Good evening, this is the Casey's."

"Doc? Oh shit, oh shit…**oh shit!"**

"Jessie? What is it Jess?"

"She's dead Doc!"

"Who's dead? Donna?"

"Yeah, oh shit, yeah Donna."

"What happened honey? Wait…are you okay? Just try and take it easy, tell me."

"No Doc! I'm not okay. They wouldn't treat her without admitting her, she said they'd lock her up and she got a little crazy, she wanted medicine but then she said she didn't want medicine. So then they said they wouldn't just give her any. Then she got mad and said she wouldn't stay either. She was crazed Doc."

"Well that's not a good thing, but what happened?"

"She started yelling about how no one would help her

and throwing anything she could get her hands on. Then she took off running down the hall. Nobody could catch her. Then we lost her. Oh God, Doc! Oh God."

"You lost her? Where?'

I was trying to get us ready to leave, you know, her coat and stuff when she took off. We tried to catch up to her but she ran up the stairs. Then we saw her at the top of that big atrium thing that's in the middle of the hospital; you know where all the plants and stuff are? Oh God, oh Jesus!"

There was a long pause while she gathered herself, but I already suspected what was to come next.

"She climbed over the railing!:" She paused to sniffle and take a deep breath. "She just jumped off. She's dead, she died right there, oh shit Doc, she jumped and died. I saw her do it. Oh Jesus!"

"Jessie, do not leave where you are. I'm on my way, do not drive back. I'm coming to get

you."

I had known it before but this was my hardest lesson that not all endings are happy ones.

Today

falling snow and time for more wood

I got up from the chair and paced the room. Absent mindedly moving things randomly, agitated at the memory of Donna and the guilt it triggered in me. Somehow believing that the outcome might have been avoided if it had been me with her instead of poor Jessie. Part of the guilt being my shame in precipitating what must have been the most traumatic event in young Jessie's life and never being able to apologize enough for it.

Once I had walked off the anxiety, I returned to my chair. Staring at nothing, still lost in failure. Knowing that there were other better memories and struggling to find them.

The Boy with the Glasses

When I first began my practice, I was filled with the exuberance of a fire and brimstone evangelical. I took every opportunity, in almost any setting, to expound upon the wonders chiropractic could bring to a world in need. As in all things, time and experience are much better teachers than classroom lectures and mental hyperbole, but in the beginning, I had not gotten there yet. I was a convert that couldn't wait to convert everyone else.

One such opportunity presented itself shortly after my arrival in town when I visited the local bank to open an account, so I would have a place for the mountains of cash I was sure to make. While I filled out the necessary forms, I engaged the bank teller in conversation and was more than happy to tell her who I was, what I did and where I did it. To my tremendous delight, she appeared interested, and began to ask questions involving certain conditions and how they were treated. Our banking business was soon completed, but being a small town, there was no one waiting behind me and we continued our conversation for a few minutes more.

She asked whether chiropractic was good for headaches, which I didn't hesitate to expound on how terrific they were for headaches. She asked me if they helped with seizures, to which I replied that there were cases where chiropractic had been successfully employed to control or limit seizure activity. She asked me if I treated children, to which I replied that I loved to treat children. Then she asked me to treat her son, to which I readily agreed, and an appointment time was soon agreed upon.

She arrived punctually shortly after the bank closed with her young son in tow. He was a handsome fellow, with a shock of dark hair that hung over his forehead and featured a permanent cow-lick at the back of his head. His round, expressive face was mostly obscured by a pair of black-framed eyeglasses that were so thick that they magnified his eyes, giving him a look a goggle-eyed surprise. The rest of his appearance was otherwise normal right down to his well- worn sneakers. His name was Tommy.

Tommy was now eight years old and had been plagued by severe migraine headaches ever since he was a small boy. The headaches were so bad that he occasionally would suffer from seizure-like fits that the doctors were reluctant to label as epilepsy. He was heavily medicated in order to prevent them and to help control the headaches, but as a result, he was often lethargic and was not progressing well in his school activities. The young mother was desperate to help the poor fellow, and as such, more than willing to grasp at chiropractic as a possibility.

Tommy was an otherwise healthy boy in most respects, although he did not participate in most outdoor activities, and avoided sports activity at school, often being picked last for team events. His balance, reflexes, and muscle tone all seemed normal, and with the exception of his amazing eyeglasses, his ear, nose, and throat examination were completely normal.

Questioning his mother further, I inquired as to whether he had any accidents as a baby or small child. These could be as innocent as rolling off of the bed during a diaper change, or falls at home. She related that he had been treated in the hospital after an accident when he was two years old. The accident, it seemed, occurred when he ran out of the house to greet his father as he returned home from work. He had arrived at the car door at the precise moment that his father opened the door and had run headlong into the open door, striking his head and knocking him somewhat senseless to the ground. The hospital had examined Tommy, even taking x-rays to ensure that nothing had been damaged and released him, but the mother believed that most of Tommy's problems had begun shortly after that episode.

Two years old is sometimes the age that children will begin to show signs of autism, but I was unaware of this age, heralding the onset of seizure disorders. After a few more questions, I believed that the collision with the car door might be suspect, and asked the mother to sign a release so that I could get copies of Tommy's x-rays. Once I had these, I thought we would be in a position to see whether we could work with his condition.

In a day or two, the x-rays arrived and I had to agree that there appeared to be no sign of fracture or other critical injuries to the skull, although a good-sized lump had formed on the forehead where the blow had occurred that was actually visible on the film. However, with further examination and looking at it with a more chiropractic eye, it was apparent that the upper vertebra in the neck were fairly mispositioned. Vertebral malposition is often quite subtle, but in this case, it was very obvious and would have been hard to miss. I contacted the family and both of the parents returned with the boy. Both were anxious, having had no previous experience with chiropractic treatment, and the father was more than a little skeptical.

I showed them what I had found on the x-rays and

asked permission to take another more abbreviated set to see if any repositioning had taken place over the last six years, which they agreed to. The subsequent films showed the exact same malposition, and I showed them the result. They could clearly see the difference between a picture of a normally positioned vertebra and the ones in Tommy's neck and agreed to proceed with a series of adjustments.

I explained to both them and Tommy how we would go about the treatment, and that it would involve gently coaxing the two bones back to where they should be. I explained that we would try not to do it all at once but over a short period of time to allow the body to adjust to the difference. They were agreeable and we began by lying Tommy on his back on the chiropractic table and first palpating the area, which according to Tommy was quite tender. I then set up on the spot and gave a slight adjustment. The vertebra moved immediately, loudly, and much further than I expected it too.

Tommy immediately began to have a seizure. Both parents were immediately on their feet as I struggled to contain my anxiety and continue to focus on the patient.

Recalling my early training as a criminal, 'act like you've been there before,' I stabilized him so that he wouldn't fall off of the table and attempted to reassure the parents in the best professional demeanor I could muster that this kind of thing could happen in cases like this. In truth, my antiperspirant was no match for the amount of sweat my armpits were producing.

Within minutes the seizure subsided and Tommy resurfaced. Exhausted and disoriented, he was helped off the table and his father picked him up and carried him out of the room. The mother turned to me with tears in her eyes, but thinking better of it said nothing and left the office. For my part, I sweat bullets for the next twenty-four hours, wondering what I could have done differently.

At the end of next business day, I was totally amazed when the family returned for the appointment they had previously set up but that I had never expected them to keep. Tommy had slept through the night and when he woke the next day, he had no headache. They had kept him home from school and for the first time they could remember, Tommy had a headache free day. They were all smiles, and they thanked me and shook my hand.

Over the next three months I saw Tommy on a regular basis. He occasionally still had headaches but sporadically, and in a moment of inspiration, I suggested that they have his eyes checked, which they did only to discover that his eyeglass prescription was now far too strong. With the new eyeglasses, his headaches disappeared entirely, and after one year, Tommy went out for the soccer team at the park district.

Score one point for enthusiasm, take one point away for lack of experience.

Tonight

I am roused from my reverie by a spasm of coughing. The room has gone cold and the fireplace is steeped in ash from the long day of burning. Early darkness has reduced the room to shadows and only glowing ashes remain of the fire. The cough is deep and productive and I gasp for breath between the spasms. Bringing up a bit of phlegm, I spit it into my handkerchief. I am not surprised when I see it is dark in color against the twilight of the room. The coughing continues and I become dizzy as spots dance in front of my eyes. I bend forward and wheeze as the spell finally passes, except for the occasional brief hack and I sag back into the chair to catch my breath.

Finally over, I challenge my balance and I push myself up onto my feet, my knees screaming protest and shuffle to the door to open it and usher in the dogs. They rush in bringing in the biting cold attached to their fur, pulling it in with them through the door. The cats pause at the door, peering around the doorjamb out into the frigid darkness. I stand on my aching knees while they try my patience with their indecision. Eventually they both turn away, tails held high and tiptoe back to the hearth where they judgmentally gaze at me, waiting for me to rebuild the fire and return to my seat. Instead, I stand in the open doorway, looking out at the riot of tracks in the snow from the dogs' daily activity and the immense expanse of winter stars bright in the sky. The air is so cold that it smells clean and thin. I take a deep breath in through my nose. The air catches in my throat and immediately another fit of coughing racks my chest. I almost lose my balance before I can grab the doorframe. For a full minute, the cough takes control as stars swim in my eyes and the edges of my vision darken. With each fit another gout of fluid rises and I spit bloody splotches onto the porch floor, getting ready for the next spasm.

The cough subsides, finally leaving my knees weak and unsteady. Rather than make it back to the chair in the house, I step outside instead, pulling the door shut behind me. Sitting on the woodpile next to the door, I lean back against the side of the house. The air is so clean that there is no twinkle to the starlight. I don't feel the cold. Instead, I feel the quiet peace of deep winter, and vastness of the pristine star fields. Reaching into the pocket of my sweater, I pull out the crumpled pack of cigarettes and a book of matches. Taking the last one out of the pack I light it and feel the calm peace spread through my body. Time is short now, a smoke and the stars should be enough. I tilt my head back against the outside wall of the house and close my eyes. That should be enough for any man, and then perhaps tonight—I will finally sleep.

Tomorrow would have been Thursday.

Epilogue

Only the occasional cough broke the stillness in the small church. Incense that had been burned during the funeral mass still hung above the heads of those gathered in the pews, the cloying scent still heavy in the air. Around the perimeter those who could not be seated stood leaning against the walls and gathered at the back, spilling out into the entry alcove. On the right side in the front row, two men sat shoulder to shoulder, heads bowed their young families spread out in either direction. Across the aisle on the left, a young woman, her husband and small brood filled the pew, the youngest blanket wrapped sleeping in her arms. The hymns had been sung and the prayers had been said.

In the third row a phalanx of somber black coated men sat stoically, their stark black wide brimmed hats firmly in place on the right-hand side. Directly opposite on the left, sat a row of women similarly garbed, their black Amish travel bonnets firmly in place. Many in the gathering gazed at the coffin at the foot of the altar, some surprised at the covering of the American Flag, and honor guard of uniformed soldiers that stood at its feet, politely at rest.

At last the old priest stirred from his seat behind the pulpit. Rising he carefully arranged his vestments before he shuffled to the microphone. Arriving, he cleared his throat and took a long moment to gaze up at the choir loft as he organized his thoughts.

"It has been my honor to officiate at this service for a man that we all knew and whom I knew to be a man who lived in the service of his fellow man and his community. I am proud to say that he was also my friend. In each person in this gathering there is a story that we could tell that would bear out our mutual respect for this man and our sense of loss at his passing. As in life, Robert Emmett Casey left it on his own terms, unable to be anything other than his own unique self. Emmett once told me that when someone dies that it was like having a library in town burn to the ground. In his case, I couldn't agree more to that statement.

Many of you knew R. E. Casey as a family physician. Many of you knew him for many years, and almost all of you knew him for a good story, a clever quip or turn of the phrase. He was the kind of person that you looked forward to spending time with, and I spent far too little. Everyone in this congregation today, could stand and offer an amusing and illustrative story about the gift that Doctor Casey was to our community, but I believe that there is far too little time in this day for all of them because I am sure that no two of them would be exactly alike.

As you can see, the United States Army has also seen it appropriate to express its appreciation for this man. They represent a chapter in his life that very few of you are aware of. It was only in his final days that Emmett shared some of the details of this chapter with me, and I would be remiss if I attempted to share it with you, because I could not do it justice, and it would be quite a long narrative indeed." He paused for a moment and smiled again at the memory.

"However, after a good deal of hard searching, I believe that we have someone here who might shed some light on this subject and in doing so, perhaps deepen our understanding of this very amusing but incredibly complex man. I have asked this someone here to speak with you, and I think you might appreciate it. I can guarantee that his presence will come as a complete surprise to all gathered and it is only *with* the permission of Emmett's family that he is here today.

Sir, if you would be so kind may we have your words?"

At the back of the room an elderly gentleman rose from the last pew and stepped out into the center aisle. He appeared ancient yet unbent, tall and stately, impeccably attired. His posture was ramrod straight as he walked toward the front with the aid of an elegant ebony cane, the tip of which thumped the carpeted aisle with each step. His face was alert, with a straight nose apparently once broken, and a square jaw that gave him an austere appearance. Looking neither right nor left, he made his way up the aisle with a measured pace as many turned and craned their necks in an attempt to see this unexpected interruption.

Eventually arriving at the dais of the altar, he turned, and after a pause where he took in the throng, he spoke, eschewing the microphone. His voice matched his appearance, strong and deep, sonorous.

"I have been asked to speak to you today by the good father. I do so only because the man behind me can no longer speak for himself. I knew R. E. Casey as a much younger man. Over the course of his young life I had the opportunity to get to know him, and at times work with him. Like most of you, I was impressed by this man who, even at the young age I knew him, was unique. For most of you, there are things about Emmett Casey that you could not know and still feel the same way about him in this time. As a result, he kept it to himself; as well he should have and you will decide for yourselves about the wisdom of that decision. As you all know, he could often present a challenge to work with."

He paused as smiles were exchanged and many nodded to each other.

"At the time that I first met R. E. Casey, he was a Private First Class in the Army and I was employed by the Criminal Investigation Department of the Department of Defense. Later I worked for and retired from the Federal Bureau of Investigation. In both of these capacities, Doctor Casey played an important role in the direction of my career, and as such, I was in a unique position to know him. I am also uniquely qualified to share his secret with you. My name is Lieutenant Colonel Walter Dunn, and I would like to tell you a story."